--- ★ ---

Sanderson opened the glove box and more water spilled out. She peered over his shoulder as he pulled out a soggy plastic sleeve, the kind insurance companies handed out for insurance and registration papers. He pulled open the folded plastic and peered at the papers.

"Made out to a Judy Hollingsworth. From BC."

Kate nodded. They had examined everything in the car.

That left the trunk.

This was Brandon, Manitoba. Not Toronto, or Montreal. There wouldn't be a body in the trunk.

There wouldn't be.

Sanderson tucked the plastic sleeve into an evidence bag that he stashed in his breast pocket before turning to the tow-truck operator, who stood by the trunk, waiting. The smirk was gone, replaced by a grim look. He had a crowbar in hand. Sanderson took a deep breath.

"Open her up, Smitty."

Kate held her breath while Smitty slipped the end of the bar between the trunk lid and the car. With a quick jerk, the trunk popped open and they all leaned forward to peer inside.

A spare tire. A plastic container of engine oil floating in a foot of water.

No body.

No suitcases.

Kate didn't know if she was disappointed or relieved.

--- ★ ---

THE
SHOELESS
KID
MARCELLE DUBÉ

WORLDWIDE

TORONTO • NEW YORK • LONDON
AMSTERDAM • PARIS • SYDNEY • HAMBURG
STOCKHOLM • ATHENS • TOKYO • MILAN
MADRID • WARSAW • BUDAPEST • AUCKLAND

This story is dedicated to my parents,
Claude and Jean Dubé, my first and best fans.

Recycling programs
for this product may
not exist in your area.

THE SHOELESS KID

A Worldwide Mystery/February 2012

ISBN-13: 978-0-373-26788-0

Copyright © 2011 by Marcelle Dubé

Printed in U.S.A.

Acknowledgments

I would like to thank Brigitte Parker for her patience in answering my endless questions about police procedures. Any mistakes that may have slipped in rest at my feet, not hers. And my deepest gratitude goes to Karen Abrahamson, Barbara Dunlop and Claire Eamer—good friends, fabulous writers and World's Best Critiquers.

ONE

THE SHOE APPEARED on her desk, gently deposited on top of the pile of occurrence reports from the last week.

It was a kid's high-top—left foot—and it was red and grubby, but not worn.

Kate automatically picked it up, more to keep it from dirtying her paperwork than out of curiosity. It was damp. On the inside of the tongue, in red marker, was written "Josh H." She flipped the shoe over to look at the underside. A size four. It would fit a…what? A four- or five-year-old?

Bobby MacAllister's age.

She slowly looked up. Marco Trepalli, youngest and newest member of the Mendenhall police force—and too handsome for his own good—smiled down at her. The morning sun gilded his tanned cheek and added a twinkle to his eye. Kate stifled a sigh. Marco had the makings of a good cop, if he ever learned to get over himself.

Whatever he'd been planning to say, he obviously thought better of it when he saw her raised eyebrow. The smile left his face. "Guy just brought this in," he said seriously. "Wants to talk to you."

"Where is Deputy Chief McKell?" She was surprised Trepalli hadn't taken it to the DC first. In the two months since becoming chief of police for Mendenhall, she'd learned that nobody passed wind in this station without checking with McKell first.

"He had a meeting with his lawyer at ten o'clock."

Ah, yes. Divorce number three for the good DC.

"Constable Trepalli," said Kate, sitting back in her ergonomically designed chair, the one she had brought from home to save her aching back. "I'm sure there's a good reason you put a wet shoe on my nice clean desk, although it can't be because you don't know how to take a statement. I know for a fact they covered witness statements at the academy."

Trepalli blushed and Kate suddenly felt like a turd. He was so young. Still, he had to learn to deal with the incidents that crossed the duty desk. This was Mendenhall, Manitoba, population 16,334, most of whom were farmers or connected to farming. It wasn't east-side Vancouver. If he couldn't handle the run-of-the-mill stuff that came in on a Thursday morning, what would he do on a Saturday night shift?

Use some judgment, for Pete's sake.

"Yes, Chief." He turned away and Kate went back to her to-do list.

Work had piled up alarmingly in the four days she'd been in Vancouver for the Policing in Rural Communities conference. And McKell, true to form, hadn't done any of it, even though he was in charge during her absence.

She realized she was still holding the shoe.

Bobby MacAllister had been just shy of his sixth birthday. He would have been thirty-three, if he'd lived.

"Trepalli."

He stopped just outside the door and turned to look at her.

"The shoe."

With a nod, he walked back to her littered desk and took the shoe from her.

Dirty but not worn. The kid who belonged in that shoe hadn't been in it long enough to wear it out.

"What's so special about the guy with the shoe?" she asked past the sudden tightness in her throat.

Trepalli tried to hide his relief but it was there in the sudden gush of words. "Dunno, really, but there's something about him, you know?" At her expectant look, he spread his hands to express the size of his frustration. "Okay—he's probably nuts. He comes in with the shoe. Says he saw a monster on a white horse grab a kid on the highway and that this is the kid's shoe."

"A monster on a horse?" Come on.

He shrugged, his color high. She tried to remember his personnel file but could only bring up that he was the youngest of five kids. She wondered if they were all as good-looking as him.

"I know. It sounds crazy." He looked discouraged suddenly. "But there's something about him…and he does have the shoe…"

Kate examined Trepalli's face. He wore his thick black hair combed straight back, a style that showed off his high cheekbones and piercing blue eyes. He was embarrassed. He knew exactly how flimsy this was.

And yet, he felt strongly enough about it to risk ridicule.

She glanced at her list and pursed her lips. She had to inspect the sites for the Southern Manitoba Cop Games one last time, speak to Daisy about the banquet preparation for Sunday night and make sure the medals had arrived.

None of which had anything to do with real police work.

Besides, the uncomfortable look on Trepalli's face told her something was bothering him, something he probably wasn't able to put into words.

If she had listened to her gut feeling back when she was a rookie, Bobby MacAllister would still be alive.

What the hell. She could work late tonight. It wasn't as if she had anyone to go home to. With a sigh, she pushed back her chair and stood up.

"All right," she said. "Let's go talk to the guy."

The man's body odor hit her the minute she opened the door to the duty room. At the duty desk, Charlotte looked up, and her carefully controlled expression told Kate that she'd had quite enough of his smell, thank you very much. Behind her, Kate could see Boychuk working on a report, hunting and pecking on the keyboard. His hair needed trimming again and his uniform looked as if he had slept in it. Johansen and Tremblay were on patrol, not due back for another hour, as were Fallon and Annett.

Charlotte nodded toward the row of chairs against the wall in the hallway, where a man in a ragged overcoat too heavy for the September morning sat. A green garbage bag, half-full, sat nestled on the floor between his feet and he cradled a mug of coffee between big, grimy hands. He sat on the farthest chair, the one closest to the doorway. His face was turned away, as if he didn't dare take his eyes off the door.

"I got the old guy a coffee," said Charlotte in a low voice. "He looked like he could use it." The headset she wore pushed her glossy brown curls away from her forehead and made her look even younger than her twenty-five years.

Kate nodded and headed toward the man.

From the little she could see of his face, the guy was older than her, maybe sixty, though it was hard to tell with these homeless ones. The road was a hard place. It aged a man fast.

He had thick hair, gray and greasy, long enough that it was held back in a low ponytail, and a scruffy beard to match. As she got closer, she could smell the rank sweat on him competing with the smell of furniture polish and the stink of old clothes needing a good wash. Or last rites. His hiking boots had seen a lot of miles, judging by the duct tape keeping some parts together.

At her approach, the man sprang to his feet and whirled to face her, an expression of alarm on his face.

Kate's placating smile froze on her face as she met his gaze. He had haunted eyes in a familiar face, though she couldn't place him.

"Chief Williams," said Trepalli formally, "this is Mr. Boiseman." His gaze slid over to Kate in sly acknowledgment that the name "Boiseman" was awfully close to "Boisevain," a small farming community to the south. Either Mr. "Boiseman" was remarkably unimaginative or he didn't care that they knew he was lying about his name.

Kate couldn't stop staring. The shock of his gray gaze was like a jolt of electricity through her system. Where had she seen those eyes before?

"The boy?" said Mr. Boiseman, clutching the garbage bag in one hand and the mug in the other. He was so tense he practically vibrated. His eyes looked feverish even as he nodded to the shoe in Trepalli's hand. "Have you found him?"

Kate's heartbeat slowed, slowed, slowed, until there was nothing left but the awareness of sluggish blood trying to pump through her arteries.

Stop it. But she couldn't. It was always like this when she had to deal with missing kids.

She took a deep breath and forced herself to sound normal. "Why don't you tell me what happened?"

Like an elastic pulled too tight, the old man snapped.

"It was a monster!" He swept a hand in the direction of the highway, sloshing coffee over the freshly waxed hallway floor. "He rode a white horse!" His eyes glittered with fervor. "He left the shoe to taunt me!"

Right. Monsters in Mendenhall, here to taunt Mr. Boiseman.

She still couldn't shake the feeling that she knew him, but she couldn't place him, probably because he looked like every other homeless man she had seen over the years.

Mr. Boiseman—or whoever he was—obviously lived in a nightmare world of his own devising. There was no reason to join him there.

"Thank you, Mr. Boiseman," she said formally. "We'll look

into it." She turned to Trepalli. "Constable, why don't you give Mr. Boiseman a ride to the Sally Ann? I think today is spaghetti day." She would have Charlotte call ahead to the Salvation Army and make sure someone was watching for Boiseman.

"Don't patronize me."

The voice was so rational that everyone swiveled toward Boiseman. Even Boychuk looked up from the keyboard. Then a look of confusion replaced the intelligence in Boiseman's eyes. "Don't let the monster get her!" he entreated. His eyes filled with tears. "My little Ellie!"

Kate's heart squeezed and a chill ran through her, as if someone had stepped on her grave. She gave herself a shake.

First he'd said a boy was taken by a monster on a white horse. Now he said it was a girl named Ellie. Whatever monsters chased Mr. Boiseman, they lived in his head.

"Thank you for your help," she said automatically, turning away from the accusing memories that reached out of her past to stab at her. "Constable." She gave Trepalli a look and he came over to stand next to her.

"Get him to show you where his monster was. Take a quick look."

"Yes, ma'am."

You never know, she thought. *Maybe he'll find hoofprints.*

McKELL RETURNED TO the station half an hour later. Through her half-open door, Kate heard him ask Charlotte where Trepalli was. Moments later, the DC stood in her doorway, his face carefully neutral. As always. For everyone else in the station, he was pleasant and cheerful. For her, he was Mr. Don't-Give-Anything-Away.

"You sent Trepalli out?" Only the tightness in his jaw betrayed his annoyance.

Kate set the log book down and sat back, swallowing a sigh.

She was never going to get through it today. Everywhere else she'd worked, the DC handled the paperwork when the chief was away. She had assumed it would be the same here. Silly her.

McKell was a big guy, almost six feet tall, with the strength and solidity some men got with maturity. He kept his graying brown hair cropped close to his skull, which emphasized the strong lines of his jaw and cheekbones. He kept fit by running and working out with weights—she saw him occasionally at the gym, when their schedules coincided, which was rarely, thank goodness.

Yes, indeed, Deputy Chief Rob McKell would be an attractive man, if he wasn't such a pain in the ass.

"I asked him to drive someone to the Sally Ann," she said calmly. "Is there a problem?"

McKell stepped into the office uninvited and closed the door. Kate tried to keep her own annoyance from showing. *Be patient,* she told herself. *He'll get used to not being in charge.*

"Ma'am," he said carefully, "you asked me to train him in our procedures. It's kind of hard to do that if you keep pulling him off the desk."

Kate's eyebrows rose in spite of her best intentions. "DC McKell, I hardly think I keep pulling him off the desk. He came to me because you were away." Again.

McKell nodded thoughtfully. "See, in that case, I would have let him deal with the transient on his own. He needs to learn to handle these situations."

Kate bit her tongue. She couldn't argue with the man, much as she wanted to. After all, she had been thinking along those lines, too. And she didn't want to tell him that she had wanted Trepalli to check out the location of the supposed abduction.

How did McKell always manage to put her on the defensive?

Maybe it was the way he strolled along the edge of

insolence—never going far enough to be insubordinate, but always far enough to put her teeth on edge.

Or maybe it was because she didn't have as much experience leading a police department as he did. Oh, she had acted as chief in Toronto and in Vancouver—once for a month—but never the day-in, day-out, month-after-month experience that McKell had gained over almost a year when the old chief was dying and before she was hired.

But the mayor had hired *her,* not McKell.

"That's a good point, DC McKell," she said calmly. She could afford to be generous.

"And I don't approve of civilians on the duty desk," he added.

Civilians? Did he mean Charlotte? The girl knew as much about running the duty desk as any officer. Kate opened her mouth to say so, but McKell beat her to it.

"Of course, if you don't like the way I'm handling training and personnel matters…"

Kate closed her mouth at the not-so-subtle hint.

Damn the man. She had asked him to retain responsibility for personnel, hoping it would prove she had confidence in him. She hadn't wanted to create too many changes too soon. And frankly, she hated working out shift schedules.

Now she wondered if that had been a mistake, if instead of making the station hers, she had divided staff loyalties. If instead of showing her flexibility, she had made herself an interloper in her own station.

McKell looked at her expectantly.

"No," she finally said. "You're doing a good job."

He nodded smartly and left, but not before she saw the hint of a smirk on his face.

Jerk.

TWO

FIFTEEN MINUTES LATER, Kate pulled the Explorer out of the station parking lot and headed for the firing range. She had too much work to do to waste time fretting about McKell. She wouldn't have time to check out all the venues for the cop games—Daisy was doing that—but this one she wanted to check out personally. Twenty years ago, she'd competed in the L.A. Cop Games and a bystander had been grazed by a ricochet off a badly placed target.

That wasn't going to happen at *her* games.

She drove past the fire hall where three firefighters washed the fire engine, which they seemed to do every other day. They waved at her and she waved back.

She drove with her window down, enjoying the feel of the warm prairie wind on her face. So far, September in Manitoba was a whole lot like September in Ontario. Evenings were cooler, of course, and there was a hint—but just a hint—of yellow in the maple leaves, but all in all, she could live with this.

By now in Toronto, they'd be digging out their heavier raincoats as the fall grew colder and wetter. She glanced at her hands on the steering wheel and sighed. Of course, there were advantages to a moist climate. In Toronto, she never had dry skin. Here, she slathered on moisturizers morning and night and still looked like the Incredible Lizard Woman.

Main Street hummed with low-key activity as merchants walked to either the Toronto Dominion Bank or the Royal Bank, kitty-corner to each other.

At the Tim Hortons donut shop, customers were already lining up for late coffee break or early lunch. More likely coffee break, since it wasn't even eleven yet.

There were only two honest-to-God coffee shops in town and Tim Hortons catered mostly to farmers and business people. The Java Jive, on the other hand, was at the other end of Main Street and the other end of the spectrum, customer-wise. Its clientele consisted of what passed for hippies in Mendenhall: teenage girls with pierced lips and eyebrows, Johnny Depp wannabes with tattoos of Chinese ideograms on their forearms, and middle-aged men with ponytails and laptop computers.

As near as she could tell, the coffee tasted pretty much the same in both shops.

Five minutes later, she turned onto the Trans-Canada Highway and rolled the window partway up to preserve her hair in its bun as she picked up speed. The sun warmed her shoulder and arm.

The firing range was a few miles south of town, in an abandoned gravel quarry. The local gun club had bought the land and built a little clubhouse.

Manitoba sunlight had a peculiar quality she'd never experienced elsewhere. She couldn't quite put her finger on what the difference was. Maybe it was because the enormous sky lorded it over mile after mile of canola, wheat and sunflowers. Maybe there was more room here for the light to spread. Or maybe the air was so clean and crisp there was nothing to come between her and the light.

She gave up trying to put it into words. It was something she had come to appreciate about the prairies. She hadn't expected that she would love the open space as much as she did.

She hadn't known what to expect, really.

She'd known that Mendenhall was small. Well, small compared to the bigger centers in which she'd worked. Not so small when compared to the really tiny communities nearby, like Winkler or Virden.

She had thought she would be smack-dab in the middle of the province. But Mendenhall was in southern Manitoba, almost halfway between Winnipeg and Brandon on the Trans-Canada, and so close to the North Dakota border that—if there were a road—she could reach the border in twenty minutes.

The sun glinted off a tractor in a sunflower field on her right. The farmers had been pulling in their crops for the last ten days, praying for the weather to hold. Every local newscast carried the haying forecast for the next few days.

This was such a foreign world to her. She was used to working in big cities, dealing with traffic pile-ups, drive-by shootings, smog and water restrictions. She had been a beat cop in Vancouver and a detective in Toronto, investigating fraud and murder. In Mendenhall, the closest she had come to rush hour was a five-minute slowdown after everyone got out of work at four-thirty in the afternoon. Heck, she'd seen people turn away when they saw a five-person line-up at the bank.

The worst crime she'd encountered so far was the regular Saturday brawl in the parking lot of the Ruggles Sports Bar. The last and only murder in Mendenhall occurred in 1954.

She had told herself she was tired of big cities. Tired of the constant noise, the crime, the politics of policing in a big city. The job as chief of police in Mendenhall had seemed perfect— a not-too-challenging new job in a quiet community where there'd be no cutthroat politics in the police station.

Naive, that's what she was.

She sighed. Lately, she'd noticed herself sighing a lot. Maybe it was time to admit she wasn't cut out to be chief. In the few months she'd been in Mendenhall, she had completely failed to make the police force hers.

McKell, along with the rest of the staff, had expected that he would automatically get the job after the old chief died. A logical assumption, as he'd been acting chief for a year. But City Council had decided to advertise across the country instead. It was a slap in the face for McKell and he couldn't seem to get past it. She was surprised he hadn't quit.

She should have wrested control of the station from him the minute she arrived, but ruthlessness was never her style. She didn't want a rigid hierarchy. She wanted a police force that worked as a team. So she allowed McKell to hang on to part of his power. That had been her first mistake.

Her second was allowing the mayor to volunteer Mendenhall as the next host city for the Southern Manitoba Cop Games.

She hadn't been on the job two weeks when Mayor Dabbs blithely informed her that Mendenhall would step in for Brandon, the scheduled host city. Brandon had suffered a damaging flood and was in no shape to receive hundreds of police officers from all over the southern half of the province. Winnipeg had hosted the last time, so it had only seemed fair that Mendenhall, as the third largest town in Manitoba, take on the games this year.

What was he thinking?

Daisy Washburn, the mayor's secretary, had been—oh, what was the right word?—*horrified* when she found out. With a population under 16,500, Mendenhall was too small to afford it, too small to accommodate all the competitors. She knew that. Kate knew that. Apparently the mayor didn't know that.

Kate smelled a political agenda at work. She suspected the mayor planned to run in the next provincial election and wanted to make a splash. He'd overridden all of her objections and offered up city hall staff to help her.

The planning had taken up almost all of Kate's time for the past six weeks, except for the few days she'd spent at the conference in Vancouver, which she was now paying for.

At least it would all be over after this weekend. Maybe

then she could get back to building a solid police force. Or trying to.

The firing range was run by a retired army colonel who had settled in Mendenhall after serving in the military at Canadian Forces Base Shilo, next door to Brandon. He assured her that he had received his new targets and that his volunteers—most of them young privates from CFB Shilo, with lots of weapons and range experience—were lined up to help when the competition began on Saturday morning. He tried to shoo her away but she insisted on a walk-through.

She left half an hour later, reassured that the colonel ran as tight a firing range as she had ever seen.

Next she drove to the Joe Langley Arena. The motorcycle competition was scheduled for Saturday afternoon and the only place big enough to host it was the arena parking lot. Which meant less parking for onlookers, who would then park on the shoulders of the road. Which meant that she'd need to assign someone to traffic duty.

And wouldn't that make her Miss Popularity around the station.

IT WAS LUNCHTIME when she got back. Trepalli tracked her down in the lunchroom, where she'd gone to catch up on the logbook while she ate her tomato sandwich.

"Chief?" He stood in the doorway, tall and trim, still in his short-sleeved summer uniform, his cap held loosely in one hand. She had seen Charlotte eyeing him a few times as he walked by and hoped they wouldn't develop a romance. These office romances never worked out, as she had learned the hard way. Twice.

Surely a good-looking guy like that already had a girlfriend back in Toronto.

"What is it, Trepalli?" she asked as she stirred sugar into her coffee. Sunshine poured through the lunchroom window, filtering through the leaves of the oak tree growing in front of it. She sipped. Perfect.

"I had Boiseman show me where he found the shoe," said Trepalli.

She turned to look at him, coffee cup poised halfway to her lips.

"And…?"

He glanced at her then away. "There's a ditch there with six inches of water in the bottom."

Meaning that a kid could have run through the ditch and ended up with wet shoes. So what? That didn't mean a monster on a white horse had abducted him. Or her.

Kate sighed and put her cup down on the table.

"I take it there were no hoofprints?"

Trepalli shook his head. "No, ma'am. But there were tire marks on the shoulder where someone had pulled over."

"Happens all the time," she said firmly. "Someone pulled over to rearrange luggage and a shoe fell out or somehow got left behind. How many times have you seen a boot or a shoe left on the shoulder? Besides," she added with a smile, "monsters don't ride horses." Young Josh H., whoever he was, would have a heck of a time explaining to Mom or Dad where his shoe was.

Trepalli shrugged, but there was a mulish cast to his expression. "Yes, ma'am. But what if what he saw got jumbled up in his head somehow?"

She'd had enough of this conversation. It was turning the coffee to acid in her stomach. Trepalli wouldn't have had this conversation with McKell because McKell would have cut it short long before now. "The man's a brick shy of a full load, Constable. He thinks monsters are kidnapping kids. First the kid was a boy, then it was a girl." She swallowed against the sudden taste of bile in her mouth. "It's his imagination."

Trepalli nodded again. His eyes looked troubled as he stared at Kate. "But what if he really saw something?"

Kate crossed her arms over her chest to hide her trembling hands. "Did you check for missing children?"

"Yes, ma'am," he said promptly. "Nothing for Manitoba or Saskatchewan. Or the north. Three missing in Alberta, but they're teenagers and they disappeared together. Charlotte is checking on B.C. and the east."

Bobby MacAllister might have been a husband and father today, if only Kate had listened to that quiet little voice.

"You have a feeling, Constable Trepalli?" she asked softly.

He looked at her uncertainly, then nodded. "I don't know if it's a feeling," he said slowly. "But my grandmother always said that the crazy ones are God's chosen." He shrugged, obviously embarrassed. "It's a slow day, Chief. What can it hurt to check it out?"

Kate looked up at the young, too-handsome constable and pursed her lips. A slow day for him, maybe. McKell would get his knickers in a twist if he thought she was interfering again. Then she shrugged. What the hell. She was the chief, not McKell.

"All right, Trepalli. Let's go check it out."

THE SPOT TREPALLI pointed out looked like any other spot on the Trans-Canada: a four-lane highway, bordered by a wide, shallow ditch on either side, beyond which fields of wheat, canola and mustard disappeared over the horizon.

They parked the patrol car on the shoulder and got out.

"There." He pointed to an area about five yards behind the squad car.

It had rained recently, so that the soft shoulder beyond the pavement retained tire impressions. But aside from noting that the tires were wide, probably from a truck or SUV, there wasn't much Kate could tell from just looking at it.

The whole world smelled green, dusty and dry.

She kept walking along the shoulder, while Trepalli crossed the highway to search the ditch on the other side. A semi passed by, heading for Winnipeg. The wind of its passage flapped her jacket behind her and she held her breath until the stink of exhaust had dissipated.

This was ridiculous. She had work to do back at the station. So what if a kid had run through the ditch? Maybe the driver had pulled over so the kid could have a pee. The kid probably crossed the ditch to get to the privacy of the wheat field.

Besides, why would a hypothetical kidnapper have stopped here? There was nothing around but miles of fields. To her right, a skeletal watering contraption loomed over the fields, waiting for the command that would send water spraying over the crops. Maybe that, not the little bit of rain they'd had last week, accounted for the water in the ditch.

Two cars passed by in quick succession, one heading east, the other west. Subaru and Honda, she noted absently. Newer models.

She climbed down the ditch, avoiding the water in the bottom, and back up the other side into the wheat field. She stood there listening for a full minute. Across the highway, Trepalli made his way along the shoulder, his boots thumping a dull beat as he walked head down, scanning. The wind sighed through the tall stalks of wheat, bending them toward the west. From the fields all around rose the soft whirring of grasshoppers in the heat of the day. Or maybe cicadas. She wasn't so good with insects.

So peaceful. No sign of monsters anywhere.

Next to the wheat field was a dirt road and on the other side, a field of mustard. She headed for the road, following the edge of the field. The ground rose slightly so that by the time she reached the road, she had a better vantage point.

And that's when she saw the school. Or rather, its roof,

peeking over the horizon at the far end of the road. At once perspective reasserted itself and she realized exactly where they were.

Henrietta Blum Elementary School didn't sit at the end of the dirt road, despite the optical illusion. It sat below the ridge at which the dirt road ended.

Anyone could park on the highway shoulder, walk down the farmer's road and down the slope to the school yard. There was a fence, of course, but she'd bet a cold cup of coffee that some enterprising kid had dug a hole beneath the chain-link fence to skip school without being seen.

She glanced over her shoulder to see Trepalli working his way back toward the squad car. He caught her eye and shrugged.

"I got nothing here, Chief," he called. "What about you?"

She pointed at the dirt road. "I'm going to walk to the end. Follow me in the squad car, but don't crowd me."

If there were tracks, she didn't want him messing them up before she could see them.

She walked down the center of the road, her boots kicking up puffs of dust with every step, and looked for anything that didn't belong. The squad car engine started up and Trepalli pulled out onto the highway, then onto the dirt road.

The sun was warm on her face and she opened her jacket to let the breeze cool her down. The smell of warm earth and growing things filled her up with each breath. If it wasn't for the squad car following her like a chastened puppy, she could be out on a stroll in the countryside.

What a pointless little exercise this was.

Where the highway shoulder was soft and retained an imprint, the dirt road was hard-packed after a summer of rain and heat. Any tracks could be old ones. But she kept walking. About halfway down, she spotted a flattened area in the wheat edging the road and headed for it.

The flattened area turned into a trail, which led to a small circle of flattened wheat, like a deer bed. Or what she imagined a deer bed would look like. She catalogued the loot lying on top: a couple of full cans of a store-brand cola, an empty can of Coors beer, a Mars bar wrapper and a plastic bag like the ones the grocery stores used to bag groceries, tied shut. She picked up the bag and pried open the knot, already suspecting what she'd find. Inside the white plastic bag were a *Playboy Magazine* and a well-thumbed copy of *Hustler,* plus a small sandwich bag with a couple of cigarettes and a lighter in it.

A car door slammed shut and moments later Trepalli came up behind her.

"What's this?" He glanced at the magazines in her hand and his face flamed. "Do you want me to bag it all?"

Kate tried not to smile. "And ruin a perfectly good hide-out?" She tied the bag back up and dropped it where she found it. "Anyway, its days are numbered," she pointed out. Any day now, the farmer would bring along a combine and when it was all over, there'd be nothing left of this field but stubble.

She turned and shooed Trepalli ahead of her. What a waste of time. And while they were traipsing through the woods, Trepalli wasn't on the duty desk.

Speaking of which, why hadn't Trepalli waited for McKell? Was it because he felt she was an easier touch? *Was* she an easy touch? Maybe she should cut this short and get back to the station.

Even as she told herself to be reasonable, she got back on the dirt road and turned toward the school. If she didn't check it out now, it would bug her until she did.

She would pay for crossing McKell, of course. He always found a way to make her pay.

She hated that she felt this way about her second-in-command. She kept waiting for his resentment to pass, but McKell had staying power. He always found something to criticize in the way she ran the station. Last week, it was the computers. McKell insisted they needed to update their antiquated computers and frankly, she agreed. In fact, she had been horrified to learn that there were no laptops in any of the squad cars. The constables were still calling in licenses for whoever was on duty desk to check, for Pete's sake.

However. She had a tight budget and one of the squad cars would need to be replaced this year. The computers, old as they were, still worked.

He knew that. But he still managed to imply to the staff that she was too tight-fisted to replace the old computers.

If it was so important, why hadn't he replaced them when he was acting chief?

She was nearly at the end of the road before she finally found something. Another path, this one not so well beaten, led to a tamped-down area near the edge of the wheat field. Beyond it was a strip of long grass that grew right up to and past the chain-link fence of the school.

Kate searched the spot but saw nothing save for trampled wheat. No cigarette butts or empty cans. She walked over and stood on the spot. From here she could see the school yard with its monkey bars, swings and hopscotch pads. A Manitoba maple, its leaves already starting to turn, grew inside the fence, far enough away that nimble young bodies couldn't leap from a branch to land on the other side of the fence. Closer to the fence, long grasses grew among a stand of young ash trees surrounded by black currant bushes and wild rosebushes heavy with rose hips.

If she were a kid, that's where she'd climb the fence.

"Find something?"

Kate jumped. Next to her, Trepalli stepped back, startled at her reaction.

"Sorry, Chief," he said. "I thought you heard me coming."

Kate shook her head and pushed through the last of the

wheat into the grassy verge next to the fence. She led the way along the fence to where the trees grew on the other side. And there she found what she was looking for. The fence was pulled up from the bottom and the ground below it was dug out, leaving a space big enough for a ten- or twelve-year-old to crawl through. Something red was caught on the bottom of the fence. She yanked and it came free—a ragged, three-inch-long by almost inch-wide strip of red fabric. She rubbed it between her finger and thumb, trying to figure out what it had been torn from. It was a thick fabric, coated. Rough, like canvas or vinyl.

Like a backpack.

She stood up suddenly and her knees popped.

"Chief…"

She looked around at Trepalli but he was staring at something in the bushes just beyond the fence. Following his gaze, she spotted a running shoe. It was a kid's red high-top.

One shoe in a ditch a quarter mile away and its mate in a school yard, next to a hole in the fence.

Trepalli grasped the chain-link fence in both hands and in one smooth move vaulted over it and into the school yard. He bent to retrieve the shoe.

"Trepalli—"

The school bell rang and Trepalli dropped the shoe. The back door to the school sprang open and a horde of kids burst through into the yard. For a split second, Kate was grateful there was a fence between her and them. Even Trepalli looked a little panicked. Before she could warn him, he picked up the shoe and tossed it over the fence before scrambling over the fence like a thief running from dogs.

Kate almost rolled her eyes. Honestly, these rookies. "Constable Trepalli," she said gently, "there might be evidence on that shoe."

He looked at her, his expression stricken, then his face flamed with mortification. "Ma'am…"

Kids swarmed over the swings, the monkey bar and a big contraption with swinging bridges and ladders that looked like a cross between a pirate ship and oil rig. They shrieked with laughter or shouted with outrage or to catch each other's attention.

Kate blinked. Time to get out of here.

"Don't worry about it," she said briskly. "Do you have a plastic bag?" Surely McKell had drummed that into him?

"Yes, ma'am." He reached for his chest pocket. After a moment of fruitless patting, he looked at her in dismay. "In my jacket, in the squad car."

Brother. Without a word, she pulled a large-format self-sealing bag out of her pocket and handed it to him.

"Are you a policeman?"

She turned to see a little girl, maybe eight years old, standing on the other side of the fence. Her brown hair was in braids that were mostly undone and she had a smattering of freckles on her nose and cheeks. She was staring up at Trepalli as though he was some kind of comic-book hero.

So much for a quick getaway.

"Yes, I am," said Trepalli, stepping up to the fence. "I'm Constable Trepalli and this is Chief of Police Williams. What's your name?"

"Lucy," said the girl. She had a soccer ball tucked between her ribs and the crook of her elbow. She wore shorts and a grubby T-shirt that said Mendenhall Soccer Club in small letters on her chest.

"Lucy," repeated Trepalli. He nodded at the ball under her arm. "Are you any good?"

Her sharp little chin pointed up. "I'm the best soccer player in my division."

Kate hid a smile. Must be nice to have that kind of self-confidence. She glanced around the school yard. A couple of kids were looking their way. A woman was at the swing set, dealing with a crying child. A man holding a whistle to his mouth was at the other end of the playground, supervising a game of capture the flag.

Trepalli gave her a look and she nodded at him. He was doing fine so far. Certainly better than she'd do.

"Lucy, do you know whose shoe this is?" asked Trepalli, showing the girl the shoe he'd found in the bushes. He'd slipped it into the plastic bag.

Kate held her breath but after a cursory glance, the girl shook her head. She glanced over her shoulder at her friends, already bored with police business.

"Then do you know a kid called Josh?" asked Trepalli, reclaiming her attention. Josh H., according to the name on shoe they had left back at the station.

Lucy frowned. "I know three Joshes."

"Well, this one is five or six years old," said Trepalli, discreetly tucking the plastic bag under his arm. "So you probably don't know him."

She shrugged again. Six-year-olds were obviously beneath her notice. Then she frowned. "Does he play soccer?"

Ah.

"You tell me," said Trepalli easily. "His last name starts with an *H*."

She thought for a moment. "Josh Hollister. He's in the bantam division. He's a good player. For his size," she added grudgingly.

"Lucy Arnot!"

Kate looked up to see the woman who had been at the swings charging toward them.

"Gotta go," said Lucy, glancing over her shoulder. "We're not supposed to play near the fence." And with that she dropped the ball and kicked it toward the center of the yard.

She took off after it, leaving Kate and Trepalli to wait for the woman.

The woman watched Lucy run toward her friends then turned to Trepalli. She was a short little thing, with wavy brown hair pulled back in a ponytail and hazel eyes that skewered Trepalli to the spot.

"Officer, if you want to talk to one of our students, go through the main office," she snapped.

"I—"

"We discourage the children from talking to strangers, even in uniform," continued the woman. There was a bloom of red high on her cheeks. If not for the fence, Kate had no doubt the woman would have been inches from Trepalli, shaking a finger under his chin.

Trepalli glanced at Kate, a panicky look in his eye.

A bubble of laughter threatened to burst out of Kate but she swallowed it back down. She didn't want that little spitfire turning against her next.

Still, she was the boss. She had to protect her subordinates.

She stepped toward the woman whose eyes snapped toward her, as if she hadn't noticed Kate before then.

"Ma'am," said Kate mildly. "I apologize for disrupting your day." Out of the corner of her eye, she saw Lucy and her pals clumped together, watching from a safe distance. The ball once more was tucked under Lucy's arm. The woman opened her mouth but Kate continued before she could get a word out. "Is there a Josh Hollister at this school?"

The anger in the woman's eyes faded, to be replaced by concern. "He's in my class, in grade one. I'm Miss Plaskett— Annie Plaskett. Did something happen to Josh?"

"Not that we're aware of," said Kate. "He's not in class today?"

Annie Plaskett shook her head. "No. And there was no answer when we called his home."

"Can we talk to some of his classmates?"

"They were only here this morning," replied the teacher. "It's half days for them the first couple of weeks." She looked from Kate to Trepalli. "If nothing happened to him, why are you here?"

Trepalli couldn't seem to find his voice, so Kate plucked the shoe from him and showed it to the teacher. "Is this Josh's shoe?"

The woman's hand flew to her mouth and she nodded. "They're his gym shoes. He loves those shoes."

Something cold and unpleasant settled in the bottom of Kate's stomach.

"Can you describe him, please?" Kate gave Trepalli a look and he hastily fished out his notebook and a pen from his breast pocket.

"He's small for his age," said the teacher. "He's got thick blond hair that's growing out of a buzz cut. Big brown eyes. Skinny. He has a birth mark on his right temple." Her eyes filled with tears. "Oh, no. You found his body, haven't you?"

Good grief. People watched way too much television.

Kate shook her head. "No," she said firmly. "There are no bodies, and as far as we know, no missing children. For all we know, he's home sick with the flu."

"Then why didn't you check there first?" she asked, obviously wanting to believe her.

Trepalli looked up from his notebook. "Ma'am, until Lucy told us his full name, we didn't know whose shoe it was. And it *is* just a shoe," he added gently. "More than likely, he took them off to put on his inside shoes and forgot the gym shoes."

Kate's eyebrow rose and she glanced at Trepalli but he kept his gaze on the teacher, whose face cleared of fear, leaving behind a frown. "But why are you asking about him, then?" She turned to Kate, who shrugged.

"It's our job." She smiled, reassuringly she thought, but the young teacher's frown only deepened. Stifling a sigh, Kate continued, "What else can you tell us about the boy?"

The schoolteacher shrugged. "Not much, I'm afraid. He just moved here with his mother and this is only the second week of school." She studied the shoe in Kate's hand for a moment. "He comes to school every day with his backpack so full that his gym shoes won't fit." She nodded at the shoe in Kate's hand. "He has to tie them to the outside of the backpack."

If the kid had tried crawling under the fence, his pack would have gotten caught on the metal. Maybe one of the shoes came off at the same time.

"What's in his backpack?" asked Trepalli.

Annie Plaskett smiled and frowned at the same time, a peculiar look that managed to look charming on her.

"His treasures," said Annie. "His collection of baseball cards, a baseball, comic books, stones, a pillow…" She looked at Trepalli and spread her hands out. "Stuff. Treasures."

Kate looked down at the grass spreading beneath the fence and the hole that patient little hands had worn in the ground. Treasures. The kinds of things a kid wouldn't want to leave behind if he had to move fast. She fingered the red cloth she had plucked from the fence.

"What color is his backpack?" she asked softly, her voice barely audible above the shouts and cries of the kids playing in the school yard.

"It's red," said Annie Plaskett after a moment. "Why?"

Kate exchanged a glance with Trepalli. Red.

It didn't mean anything. The kid could have torn his backpack last week. Heck, he could have lost his *shoes* last week. Boiseman could have found the shoe by the ditch and his broken brain conjured up a monster stealing a child. Just because he found the shoe today didn't mean anything.

It didn't mean anything.

THREE

KATE DROVE ON the way back while Trepalli sat next to her, staring out the passenger window. She needed something to do to keep the thoughts running through her head from wearing out a rut.

Was she allowing her past to affect her judgment? Every time a kid went missing… She couldn't tell if she was overreacting or not. She'd certainly been accused of it in Toronto.

Mom would say she was overthinking again. But Mom didn't understand how it felt to be responsible for a child's death. In her thirty years as a professor of English Literature at McGill University, Mom had never lost a student. Dad had been a cop, too. He had understood.

But in a way, Mom was right.

All she had to go on was a pair of running shoes and a kid who wasn't in class.

"Chief?"

After leaving the playground, they had returned to the squad car parked on the dirt road and driven around to the school. Annie Plaskett had met them at the office, Josh Hollister's address in hand—614 Dieppe Road. Miss Plaskett had spoken to a couple of kids who took the same bus as Josh and they confirmed he'd been on the bus that morning. Maybe he decided to go back home after the bus dropped him off. He hadn't been present during attendance first thing that morning. So, somewhere between the bus dropping him off and the start of school, Josh Hollister had decided to skip school.

At six years old? What would motivate a kid that young to skip school?

"Chief?"

Kate looked at Trepalli. "What is it, Constable?"

"Are we going to check out his house?"

Kate stopped at the red light on Main Street, one of the half dozen in Mendenhall. The sidewalks were full of pedestrians and shoppers. She glanced at the clock on the dashboard—2:03. McKell would be furious, but from the radio traffic, nothing much was happening in the way of a crime spree. What the heck. McKell would just have to deal with it.

The light turned green and she pulled into the intersection. "Yes, Constable. We are going to check out his house."

No one had reported the kid missing and this wasn't a police state, where citizens had to account for all their actions. But there were enough questions niggling at her that she wanted answers.

"Oh, good." Trepalli's blue eyes glittered with excitement. "I don't know if I could live with myself if something happened to a little kid and I did nothing to stop it."

All the blood in Kate's veins turned to ice and her hands clenched on the steering wheel. But Trepalli had no idea what he had just said. How could he? It had all happened before he was born.

Bobby McAllister had been five years old and living with his parents in Halifax when he was abducted by Samuel J. Boynton. Boynton had drugged the boy and driven him to Montreal. Along the way, he'd been stopped by a highway patrol in New Brunswick because his taillight was out. Kate had been a rookie with less than six months on the job. She had flashed a light around the inside of the car while Boynton got out his registration and insurance papers. The kid was asleep in the backseat with a man's coat over him as a blanket. She couldn't even tell if it was a girl or a boy. Something had niggled at her about the scene but the driver was relaxed and obviously unworried, so she shrugged off the niggling voice. They exchanged pleasantries about children's ability to sleep anywhere while Kate wrote him a warning ticket for the taillight and sent him on his way.

They found Bobby six days later in a field near the Quebec border.

His battered, abused little body was barely recognizable, but Kate had recognized him. She looked at his picture taken in a Montreal morgue and tried to come to grips with the fact that she'd had the monster in her sights and had let him go. Ironically, it was her warning ticket that had led the investigators to Boynton—it placed him on the road in New Brunswick, when his alibi would have had him still in Halifax and far from the boy's body.

Ever since, she had tried to avoid cases involving kids. Heck, she avoided kids, period. They always brought back memories of Bobby MacAllister and her failure to save him.

But Trepalli didn't know any of that. Nothing had ever appeared in her record and the newspapers had never named her. No one had ever blamed her—until twenty-five years later, in Toronto. That's when all the ugly rumors started. She was a good cop and she knew it, but it had taken a long time to let go of the guilt. She had done well, until she applied for the position of deputy chief of the Toronto Police Department.

She sighed. Trepalli and his "feeling" would be the death of her yet.

KATE LET TREPALLI interview the mother. It seemed only fair, as this was his investigation—if that's what it was. Besides, he needed the experience. And, from what she'd seen, he was better with people than she was.

Dieppe Road was one of the older streets in Mendenhall, built in the mid-fifties when the Canadian Air Force had a training base just outside of town. A lot of the duplexes on the street dated from that period, but they were well kept, their small front lawns dotted with flowers and trees.

While Trepalli went to number 614, Kate wandered down the sidewalk, studying the neighborhood. A couple of kids, no more than four or five years old, played with a puppy partway up the block, their laughter high and clear in the late afternoon air. She could hear more children playing in nearby backyards.

This, too, was different from most big cities where she'd worked. In the middle of the school day in most residential areas of a big city, even in the suburbs, you would rarely see kids playing. If they were too young for school, then they were in day care while Mom and Dad worked to make ends meet.

Kate's stomach rumbled and she told it to be patient. Two doors down from Josh Hollister's house, she found what she was looking for.

An old man dressed in a short-sleeved, plaid cotton shirt and casual gray slacks was watering his flower beds in front of the house. She could feel the weight of his curious gaze from under the shade of his straw hat.

"Afternoon," she greeted him as she got closer.

He tipped his hat and nodded. "Officer." The spray from his hose danced in the sunlight and refracted into a rainbow. He kept watering, placidly waiting for her to say her piece.

Kate turned a little, ostensibly to admire his flower beds but also giving him a good view of her shoulder patch with the title Chief of Police stitched in gold beneath the badge. Sometimes these older guys needed a little help accepting women in authority.

"Lovely place," she said. And it was. The board-and-batten siding glowed with a fresh coat of pale green paint with darker green trim. The windows gleamed from a recent scrubbing. The lawn was newly mown. "You keep it up well."

His gaze slid over to her and he smiled slightly, his expression telling her that she wasn't fooling him. Oh yes, this old man with his sharp eye would know everything about his neighborhood.

"Thank you," he said. "My sons help out." He turned the spray off and began coiling the hose. "Now, how can I help you?"

In other words, thought Kate, stop beating around the bush. She smiled at his back when he turned to hang the coiled hose neatly on a holder fastened to the side of the house.

"Do you know the Hollisters, a couple of doors down?" she asked.

That surprised the old man. He turned, brushing his palms against each other to wipe off the dirt. "I see them around." His eyes were a light brown and deep lines surrounded them, as if he had spent a lifetime squinting into the sun.

"Have you seen the boy today?"

The movement of the old man's hands stilled as he considered. "I saw him this morning," he finally said. "His mother walks him to the bus stop every day before she leaves. She has a job in Winnipeg, I think."

Kate nodded. Many farm families around Mendenhall supplemented their income with wage work. Usually the wife commuted to work in Winnipeg or Brandon, leaving the husband behind to work the land.

"Is she from a farming family?"

He shook his head. "I don't think so. She moved here from away a few months ago." He cocked his head at her. "Why?"

Kate shrugged. "Routine questions, sir, connected to an investigation. Did you notice anything out of the ordinary this morning? Maybe when Mrs. Hollister took the boy to the bus?"

The old man shook his head. "Nothing," he said. "The boy left on the bus at the same time as usual. She left a few minutes later."

"No father in the picture?" More often than not, a child abduction was related to a custody battle.

But the old man shook his head again. "None that I ever saw. She keeps to herself, mostly. But her boy plays with Emmie and Isabelle, the West twins." He nodded toward a house across the street. "The place with the cinquefoil bushes lining the driveway."

Kate knew next to nothing about shrubs and flowers, but the house in question was the only one with bushes lining the driveway.

"Thank you for your time, sir." She nodded and headed for the West home. Trepalli had disappeared inside the Hollister house while she was talking to the old man. Maybe he was talking to Josh right now.

Mrs. West was a tall, leggy woman in pedal pushers and a tank top. She opened the door and smiled in surprise.

"Hello, Chief Williams," she said. "What a pleasant surprise."

It took a moment, but Kate finally recognized her as one of the women on the town's public safety committee. What was her name? Melanie? Maddie?

"Good afternoon, Mrs. West," she said politely. "I wonder if you could answer a few questions."

The woman nodded and stepped back, waving Kate inside. From the front hallway she could see right into the kitchen and the eating area, separated from each other by a long counter. There were toys scattered in the hallway and in the living room, which opened off to her right.

Seated at the table were two little blonde girls, about five or six, dressed in shorts and T-shirts, their feet bare. They each had a glass of milk and a muffin in front of them. A toddler sat in a high chair, making a mess of something mushy in a bowl in front of him. Or her.

Kate became aware that she was the focus of intense scrutiny on the part of the little girls. She looked away from them.

"Sorry to interrupt your day," said Kate, turning her attention back to Mrs. West.

"Would you like to sit down?" asked the woman, indicating the living room. She pushed back the blond wavy hair that kept falling into her eyes.

"No thank you, ma'am," said Kate. "I don't think this will take very long."

"It's Madeline, please," said the woman absently. "In that case, what can I do for you?"

Kate glanced at the twins, then back at Madeline West. "Half days this week?"

Madeline West's warm smile became uncertain. "That's right. They're in grade one."

Kate nodded at the confirmation. So Josh might well be at home. "Do you know the Hollisters, ma'a...Madeline?"

Madeline West looked blank for a moment. Then she frowned. "Do you mean Judy Hollister and her boy?"

Kate nodded and waited.

"Not well," said Madeline. She stuck her hands in her pockets and frowned up at the ceiling. Although her skin was pale, there was a dusting of faint freckles across her cheekbones. The woman probably wore a hat everywhere she went.

"They live across the street," she continued. "Judy Hollister keeps to herself. They just moved here. Her little boy plays with the girls sometimes." She nodded over at the twins, who were eyeing Kate with interest. She paused and looked directly at Kate. "Why? Did something happen?"

Kate's skin itched under the twins' curious stares. "Have you seen him today?"

The expression on Madeline West's face turned slowly from interest to dismay as the implications of Kate's question registered.

"No. He goes to school with the girls. I can ask them... Has something happened to Josh?" She glanced over at the table where the twins had finally lost interest in Kate and were attacking their muffins as if they hadn't eaten in days.

"Not that we know of." Kate smiled reassuringly. "Could I talk to the girls?" Her mouth went dry and she swallowed. She was *so* not good at talking to kids.

Madeline nodded jerkily. "Girls?" she called. They looked up at her. "Come here, please."

Emmie and Isabelle obediently jumped off their chairs and ran to either side of their mother. One had a ponytail and the other had braids. As far as Kate could tell, that was the only difference between them.

"Girls," said Madeline gently, "this is Chief Williams. She's the police chief. Answer her questions, all right?"

They nodded in unison and turned big blue eyes on Kate, whose mind suddenly went blank. The girls' heads tilted questioningly, again in unison, and Kate's palms were damp.

"Go ahead, Chief," said Madeline encouragingly.

They won't bite, Kate assured herself. She tried a smile. The girls' heads jerked back in alarm. Kate sighed and abandoned the smile.

"Hello, girls," she said. "I'm looking for Josh Hollister. Have you seen him today?"

The girls glanced up uncertainly at their mother, who nodded at them. One of them, the one with the braids, answered.

"He was on the bus this morning."

"He wasn't on the bus at lunchtime." That was the one with the ponytail.

"Is he in your class?" asked Kate.

The one with the braids gave her a look of exasperation. "Yes."

"Did he get off the bus with you at school?"

They both nodded.

"Did you see where he went after he got off the bus?"

They glanced at each other then shook their heads in unison. "We didn't see him all day."

"Okay. Thank you."

Madeline shooed the girls back to the dinner table and turned back to Kate.

"What's going on?" she asked softly.

"We're just following up on another investigation. Thank you for your time, Madeline. I'll let you get back to your day."

She left Madeline West looking uncertain and followed the walk back to the sidewalk. This was ridiculous. No crime had been reported and yet here she was, disturbing a family and causing concern.

Trepalli wasn't at the squad car, so she headed for the Hollister house. While it was neat and uncluttered, the flower beds beneath the window needed weeding and the lawn could use some water.

The door to number 614 opened just as she climbed the two steps to the stoop. Trepalli emerged into the sunshine, blinking in surprise as he came face-to-face with Kate. He carried his hat in one hand and the red high-top he had found in the school yard in the other. He turned to the woman who had followed him out.

"Mrs. Hollister," he said formally, "this is Chief Williams."

The woman stepped out onto the stoop, shading her eyes with her hand.

"Hello, Chief," she said warmly. "I was just telling Sergeant Trepalli that Josh is fine."

Trepalli placed his hat on his head and smiled politely. "That would be Constable, ma'am."

Judy Hollister was tall and willowy. Her thick auburn hair was cut in curls that framed her heart-shaped face and brought out the green of her eyes. She wore short shorts that displayed her long, shapely legs and a T-shirt that barely covered her belly button. The scent of oranges wafted out the door with her.

Kate glanced at Trepalli, taking in his stiff shoulders and clenched jaw. He did *not* like Judy Hollister.

Well, well, well.

"I'm glad to hear it, ma'am," said Kate with a friendly grin. "So that's not Josh's shoe?" She nodded to the bagged shoe in Trepalli's hand.

Judy Hollister shook her head. "No, it isn't." Her smile became even wider. "Is all this really about a *shoe?*"

Was that a hint of condescension in her voice?

"We're following up on a possible child abduction," said Kate impulsively, watching the other woman carefully.

The smile froze momentarily on Judy Hollister's face. "Abduction?" She glanced uncertainly at Trepalli. Kate had instructed the constable to say only that someone had reported a boy missing and not to mention anything about Boiseman's story.

"Yes, ma'am," continued Kate. "We have a report of a child matching your son's description possibly abducted near the school." Trepalli glanced at her but she ignored him. "Is your son home?"

Judy Hollister's face was white. "That's horrible! Do you know who it was?"

"Who was kidnapped, or who did the kidnapping?"

"Both. Either."

"No, ma'am," said Kate, studying the woman's face. "Is Josh home?"

Judy Hollister took a deep breath, visibly trying to calm herself. "No, he's not. As I was telling Sergea—Constable Trepalli, I took him to his grandmother's this morning on my way to work."

Kate smiled. "But he was on the bus to school."

Judy Hollister's face flamed, then she grinned shamefacedly. "Mornings aren't my best time," she admitted. "I'd already put him on the bus when I remembered he was supposed to come in with me." She shrugged. "I just picked him up at school on my way in." She sighed and looked away. "I've been overtired lately. I need a few days to myself. And Mom loves having Josh over."

"Josh's teacher identified the shoe as his," said Trepalli.

Judy Hollister looked at Trepalli then back at Kate.

"Josh's shoes are with him at my mother's. I bought a pair exactly like those—" she nodded at the shoe in Trepalli's hand "—for him in Winnipeg about a month ago. They were on sale. I'm sure there are many like them in the area."

"They wouldn't all have the name Josh H. in them, would they?" said Kate.

The woman's face suddenly grew hard.

"Chief Williams, I appreciate that you're only doing your job. But I don't know how many more ways I can say this. Josh is fine. He's at my mother's. There are red shoes exactly like his all over Manitoba and I'm sure some of those shoes belong to other little boys named Josh." She was breathing a little fast and her mouth looked pinched.

Kate nodded slowly. "Of course." She paused for a moment, as if considering. "Would you mind if we took a look around the house?"

"As a matter of fact, I *would* mind!" Judy Hollister no longer looked attractive.

Trepalli shifted slightly, as if he were uncomfortable at the turn of events, but Kate only smiled. "Thank you for your time, Mrs. Hollister."

The woman nodded stiffly and Kate turned to go down the two steps to the walk. Trepalli followed closely and almost stumbled into her when she stopped abruptly and turned around.

"You wouldn't mind giving us your mother's address, would you?" she asked casually. "Just for our files."

The woman had been closing the door. Now she glared at

Kate and for a moment, Kate thought she would refuse. Then Judy Hollister sighed. "Just a moment, I'll write it down." She turned and disappeared inside. Before Trepalli could say anything, Kate put up a hand to silence him. They could talk in the privacy of the squad car.

Judy Hollister returned a moment later with a scrap of paper with a scribbled name, address and phone number.

"I'd appreciate it if you didn't alarm my mother for nothing," she said stiffly.

"Of course not." Kate took the scrap from Judy Hollister and stuck it in her pocket. "Thank you," she said, turning away. Then she turned back to look at the woman. "You're home early," she said with a smile.

Judy Hollister didn't smile. "As I mentioned," she said, "I need some time off. I only worked this morning."

"And where do you work, Mrs. Hollister?"

"In Winnipeg."

Judy Hollister slammed the door in their faces.

Kate grinned and turned to walk down the path to the sidewalk. She listened for the sound of Trepalli following. Finally she heard the scrape of his boot on the sidewalk.

She slid into the passenger seat and opened the window to let in the breeze. The car smelled faintly of coffee, vomit from the time Arnie Cullen threw up in the back, and the Armor All that Boychuk used obsessively on the dashboard.

Trepalli opened the door and folded himself into the driver's seat. He tucked the shoe under the armrest between them then removed his cap and placed it on the dashboard.

"Wow." He turned slowly to look at her.

"What?" She had pulled out her notebook and was busy transcribing the grandmother's address and phone number. She always liked to take notes as soon as possible after an interview.

"That was…"

When he didn't finish, she looked up at him. There was a look in his eye, something like horrified admiration. For a moment, her mind was blank. Then she realized he was reacting to her interrogation of the Hollister woman. She felt herself blushing.

She hated blushing.

"You will find, Constable Trepalli," she said brusquely, "that you often get more information if you rattle the cage. Now. Did you learn anything more?"

He finally looked away and started the engine. "She says she decided to take the boy in to see his grandmother because it's half days at school this week." He did a quick shoulder check and pulled out into the road. "There was a soccer ball and a pair of kids' soccer shoes in the entryway. A radio was on in the kitchen, but she didn't invite me past the entryway. No sign of pets. No sign of a man, either." He paused. "She was vacuuming when I rang the bell. It took a few tries before she heard it."

Kate nodded, jotting the information down in her notebook.

The sun was low in the sky, chasing long shadows east. This was her favorite time of the day, when the heat ebbed and the light softened. She loved to drive down the highway at this time of day, just to go by the fields of sunflowers with their faces all turned toward the sun, streaming shadows behind them.

Trepalli turned onto Sixth Avenue, leaving the residential area behind. His shoulders twitched. "She said she'd just spoken to him on the phone and he was fine." He was frowning at nothing in particular, driving almost on autopilot.

A Super A Foods grocery store stood off to the right, its parking lot filled with last-minute shoppers picking up dinner makings. Across the avenue, a small strip mall housed a Kentucky Fried Chicken, a video store and a dry cleaner. The smell of the fried chicken wafted through the car, reminding her that she hadn't eaten much all day. *Be quiet,* she told her rumbling stomach. *You know that stuff puts you off.*

"You don't believe her," she stated.

Trepalli shrugged again, but it was more as if he was trying to get rid of something clinging to his back. "I dunno, Chief. She had an answer for everything and it all made sense. But there was something about the look on her face when I showed her the shoe."

Kate sighed. She felt the same way. Something was off with that woman.

"If she was telling us the truth, why wouldn't she have told the teacher she was taking her kid out of school?" Trepalli asked.

Kate shrugged and decided to play devil's advocate. "She was running late when she picked him up. Maybe she planned to call the school when she got to work, but forgot all about it."

He slowed to a stop at a red light and glanced at her. "I suppose that could be right. But her face when I showed her that shoe… She just looked…I dunno. Funny." He smiled lamely and pulled into the intersection when the light turned green.

Funny. Kate's shoulders twitched, as if the monkey on Trepalli's back had suddenly jumped onto hers.

FOUR

THAT EVENING, while Neil Young sang about harvest moons in the background, Kate opened a bottle of Stella Artois, grilled herself some halibut with slivered almonds and made a spinach salad. The early fall breeze blew the kitchen curtains open, bringing the scent of fresh-cut grass and a hint of coming rain into the room. She hummed along with Neil, even though she could never find the right pitch. Lily, her sister, was the only one of the three siblings who had inherited Dad's singing ability.

She glanced at the clock on the stove. It was too late to call Montreal and check in on Mom and Lily, and way too late to call her brother, Charlie, in St. John's. Lily had mentioned the possibility of coming for a visit before the snow flew. Kate hoped it would work out. She hadn't seen her sister in two years.

She wanted to sit out on the deck, beneath the sky and the stars and listen to Neil croon about undying love, but she was too fidgety.

The Hollister kid kept creeping back into her mind, even though there was nothing more she could do tonight.

Trepalli had called the Winnipeg number Judy Hollister had given them but there was no answer, and no voice mail. It was a cell phone number and so didn't appear in the reverse directory. She had tried finding the street on a Winnipeg map, but it was in a newer subdivision that hadn't made its way onto the maps yet, according to the dispatch clerk at the Winnipeg Police Service. The clerk promised to send a patrol car out tonight and check on the address, although she said she would have to talk to her boss about knocking on the door to find out if Josh Hollister was actually with his grandmother.

Kate wanted to push but didn't. As far as she knew, no crime had been committed. There were no Amber Alerts anywhere in the Prairie provinces and no BOLO reports mentioning young males. She had even checked with Jerry Wolsynuk, her RCMP pal in Winnipeg, and his sources reported nothing.

She had considered the possibility that the kid had been kidnapped, but that theory felt all wrong. Judy Hollister did not behave like a woman worried sick about her kidnapped child.

Sighing in frustration, Kate flipped the fish and tried to settle her thoughts. There was nothing she could do until she heard back from Winnipeg. Until then, she had phone calls to make.

The games started in two days and the damned medals still hadn't arrived. She needed to confirm with the high-school principal that the repairs on the racing oval were complete. At least she didn't have to worry about the dozens of volunteers who would time the races, set up the motorcycle obstacle course and feed the participants. Daisy Washburn, the mayor's assistant, was handling all that. Thank God for Daisy. That woman could organize Armageddon and make it look easy.

The games had to be a success. Not only did Mendenhall's reputation depend on it, so did hers. It didn't matter that it wasn't her decision to hold them in Mendenhall. If the games were a flop, she'd be the laughing stock of the Canadian policing community. And McKell would have one more weapon against her.

The town had pulled together, more to support Daisy than Kate, she suspected. But there hadn't been enough time to do things properly. She'd been in regional cop games before and they were *events*. In spite of Daisy's formidable organizing skills and the volunteers she'd persuaded to help, this wasn't going to be an event.

It didn't matter. Mendenhall had stepped up to keep the games going when Brandon had to beg off. That's what people would remember, not the glitches.

And with a bit of luck, the glitches wouldn't turn into disasters.

When the fish was cooked, she brought it over to the dining room table where the salad bowl and the one bottle of Stella Artois she allowed herself waited.

While the kitchen gleamed with silver pulls, a polished granite countertop and brushed aluminum refrigerator and stove, the dining room was an oasis of wood and upholstered chairs. The French doors led off the dining room onto her deck. She might still go out there later and finish her beer while watching the stars.

She pushed up the sleeves of her henley tee and sat down.

Decades ago, she had set herself a few rules when she found herself slipping into the kind of habits she associated with older, single cops. One of these rules was to change out of uniform as soon as she was off duty and store her weapon away. Another was never to eat in front of the television.

She saw nothing wrong with reading while she ate, however, and pulled the book she was reading—Diane Ackerman's *Deep Play*—closer.

She had just taken a bite of the fish when the phone rang. She finished chewing and took a sip of beer as the phone rang a second time. Finally, she pushed back from the table and took her time walking over to the wall phone. She glared at it as it rang a fifth time, then picked it up.

"Hello?"

"Why haven't any of your men signed up for the competitions?"

Kate pulled the receiver away from her ear and stared at it, then brought it back to her ear.

"Daisy?"

"Of course it's Daisy," said the mayor's assistant impatiently. "I'm compiling the event lists and checking them against registration forms. No one from Mendenhall signed up!"

Kate leaned her forehead against the wall and stifled a sigh. So. This was how they were going to punish her for taking McKell's job. By boycotting the competition and making her look like a fool.

"Kate?" Daisy's voice was sharp. "We'll be the laughingstock of the games if no one competes. I know we can't compete in the motorcycle technical competition, but we've always had someone in the races and in the martial arts competition. And Rob McKell always takes home a medal for sharpshooting."

"When's the deadline?"

"Tomorrow at four," said Daisy. Then, after a pause, she added, "I know all these fellows, Kate. I can call and shake them up."

Kate straightened and shook her head. "No." She took a deep breath. She was *not* going to guilt anyone into participating. "Sign me up for the hand-to-hand and the 1600-meter race." She might not be fast, but she had endurance, thanks to her daily runs. There was no way she would win against the younger ones, but she stood a chance in the senior category. And at least Mendenhall would be represented.

Why would her men cheat themselves out of their chance at the national competition? Did they hate her that much?

Daisy didn't say anything for a long time. When she finally spoke, there was anger in her voice. "Chiefs don't compete."

Daisy left unspoken what Kate knew she was thinking. Chiefs didn't compete because they didn't have to. They gave pretty speeches and handed out the medals and shook the hands of the winners.

"Well, this one does," said Kate.

Daisy sighed at the other end of the line. "Fine. We're still meeting tomorrow at one, right?" Kate agreed and Daisy continued, "I'll have the forms there for your signature." And then she hung up.

Kate looked back at her meal. With a sigh, she cleared the table and put the fish away in a plastic container. Maybe she could have it tomorrow night.

She brought the beer and the salad to the kitchen counter and began to make her phone calls, taking bites of the salad in between calls.

Half an hour later, she'd done everything she could for the night, including the dishes, and decided that a cup of decaf on the back deck would be in order. Then she'd run the mile to the station, check in with Martins on the duty desk to make sure everything was all right and run back. Surely Winnipeg would have called by then.

The house sat on an escarpment overlooking Mendenhall. There were other houses around, but they were below hers and their lights didn't interfere with her view of the stars or the town. She sank into her favorite Adirondack chair—painted bright red in a moment of whimsy she had yet to regret—and let the warm evening breeze play over her loose hair as she sipped. There was a hint of freshness in the air, a promise of the cool nights to come.

Then she heard a sound that didn't belong and held her breath to listen more carefully. The sound came again, the whisper of a shoe on wood chips.

She levitated out of the chair and turned to face the path that led from her driveway to the back of the house.

"Nice view," said Boiseman, less than ten feet away. Then, "That coffee smells really good."

She gripped the cup tighter, ready to bash it against the man's skull.

"I did knock." He was nothing but a dark shape against the

tall cedar hedge while she knew she was outlined against the spill of light from the kitchen. "You should install a doorbell."

"Hate 'em," she said, forcing herself to relax. She squinted into the darkness but he remained invisible. "What do you take in your coffee?"

"Just black. Thank you." There was a note of relief in his voice, as if her reaction reassured him.

"Have a seat," she said. "I'll be right back." She used the kitchen door rather than the French doors and stepped into the brightly lit kitchen. As she pulled out a mug from the cupboard, she thought about calling the station and getting Martins to send someone, but she knew she wouldn't.

It would be admitting fear or, at best, weakness. It would convince them all that she was the wrong choice.

And wouldn't McKell love that?

Besides, Boiseman hadn't done anything threatening and was keeping his distance. He even sounded rational. It wasn't against the law to visit the chief of police at home, even if he wasn't invited.

And frankly, she was curious about the man.

As an afterthought, she pulled out a box of tea biscuits and placed some on a plate. Then she set both cup and plate on the silver tray from Mom's collection and opened the door to the deck.

Boiseman was now on the deck, hovering near the table, as though hesitant to sit down yet. She flicked on the deck light with her elbow before stepping onto the deck. Boiseman turned and came toward her, and she stopped in surprise.

He had changed his clothes. They were still old and shabby, but they were clean and they fit. And he had shaved.

Boiseman stopped a few feet away and waited. His hair was still in a ponytail but it had been washed. He glanced at the tray in her hands.

"May I?" When she nodded, he took the tray from her and

carried it to the table where he set it down with a rattle on the glass top. Then he pulled out one of the wrought-iron chairs for her and waited for her to sit down.

A gentleman tramp? Hadn't they gone the way of the silent movie?

He sat down and took the cup from the tray, wrapping his big hands around it as if they were cold. While he sipped and watched the lights below, she studied him.

Probably Fred at the Sally Ann had found clothes to fit him. Or maybe they'd been in his bag all along. But that would imply that he kept a clean change of clothes, which in turn implied that he found a way to clean his clothes regularly. Maybe he wasn't as lost as she'd thought.

"Help yourself to the cookies," she told him.

He nodded gravely and picked up the plate to give her first choice.

"No, thanks," she said.

He dunked the tea biscuits into the coffee and swooped them into his mouth with the focus of a man who needed to pay attention to his food. He didn't stop until he had finished the plate.

His shoulders were wide under the long-sleeved work shirt, but with the angularity of a man who should have a lot more flesh on his bones. And while his jeans were the right length, they would fall off him if not for the worn belt keeping them up.

The muscles in his jaw worked as he ate. He had a plain face, with thick eyebrows and a big nose. Deep lines scored his cheeks and between his brows. She couldn't tell exactly what color his eyes were in this light but she had noticed them at the station. Gray. Everything about the man was gray, as if he'd been leached of color.

He still looked familiar but he didn't look as old to her as he had that morning.

Finally he finished the last of the coffee and set it on the plate, on her mother's silver tray.

"Thank you." He looked at her and there was clarity and intelligence in his gaze. His eyes glittered. He was thanking her for much more than the cookies.

This hardly seemed like the same man who stood in her station ranting about monsters abducting young children.

He turned away from her and concentrated on the stars.

"You didn't find the boy, did you?"

Kate took a deep breath and blew it out on a silent sigh. "No. The only child who matches your description and whose shoe that might be is with his grandmother." *I hope.*

He nodded. "Maybe the boy isn't from here at all," he said softly.

Kate swallowed hard and gripped her hands together. Her heart pounded against her chest wall as if it wanted to escape.

"I checked," she said evenly. "No one's reported a missing child by that description."

Boiseman's eyes squeezed shut and he hung his head. "The monster gets another one," he whispered.

Kate took a deep breath. *Here goes nothing.*

"What do you mean by a monster?"

He opened his eyes to look at her. "What would you call a man who steals children?"

A shiver coursed its way down her scalp. "You said a monster on a white horse."

"A horse?" He blinked slowly. Then he nodded. "Sometimes my mind plays tricks on me," he admitted. "It wasn't a horse. It was a white TrailBlazer. Four doors. British Columbia plates."

Holy… Her mouth was suddenly dry. Had he actually *seen* an abduction?

"Mr. Boiseman—" she began, but he stood up abruptly and looked down at her. The movement startled her so that she stood up, too, glad there was a table between them.

"Thank you for your hospitality," he said formally. "I'll be leaving now."

She wasn't finished asking him questions, but apparently he was done talking. Before she could stop herself, she said, "Would you like a ride back to the Sally Ann?"

He shook his head. "Thank you, no. I'm used to walking." And with that, he went down the stairs to the path, bent down to pick something up and disappeared around the house. It was only after the fact that she realized he had swung his bag over his shoulder.

She stared at nothing for a long time, trying to decide what to do. First he claimed a boy was abducted, then a girl, then a boy again. And first it had been a monster on a white horse but now it was a man in a white SUV with B.C. plates. If she talked to him tomorrow, would the abductor be an alien in a white spaceship?

She shook her head and picked up the tray before going into the kitchen. She turned the deck light off and locked the door behind her. Then she rummaged around her drawers until she found a clean paper bag. Using tongs, she picked up the cup Boiseman had been using and emptied the dregs into the sink. Then she placed the cup in the bag.

She took the bag with her when she drove to the station. According to Charlotte, the new scanner could send digital images, including fingerprints, to CPIC. She had no idea how long it would take for CPIC to get to Boiseman's prints, but it was worth a try. Maybe he was in the system, somewhere.

MARTINS NODDED COOLLY when she walked in later that night.

"Any calls for me?"

"No, ma'am."

She nodded and took the bag containing the cup to the Ident room, where she dusted it for prints and sealed the prints in an evidence envelope. She recorded the time and date in the register. Boychuk was the only one trained on the new scanner; she would get him to send the prints in to CPIC tomorrow morning. Then she took the log book into the lunchroom and went through all the entries from the four days she was away.

Nothing about a white SUV, suspicious or otherwise. If Mr. Boiseman's boogeyman existed, he hadn't done anything to attract the attention of Mendenhall's police.

FIVE

"I'M TELLING YOU, she's not in the system!"

Kate stopped just shy of the half-open door to the lunchroom. That was Charlotte's voice. She was obviously trying to be quiet but the frustration was clear in her loud whisper.

"You tried the regular databases?" came Trepalli's low voice.

"And Motor Vehicles and Vital Stats. There is no Judy Hollister registered in the province. At least, not one that's alive."

Kate closed the file she had been reading and leaned her back against the cool plaster wall.

"What do you mean, 'not alive'?" asked Trepalli.

That rookie was like a terrier.

"There was an Anne Judith Hollister born in 1982, but she died in 1983."

"Really?" In his interest, Trepalli forgot all about whispering.

Kate rolled her eyes. Now he was going to invent a conspiracy involving identity theft.

Apparently Charlotte thought so, too. "All it means, Marco, is that she's not registered in Manitoba. She probably moved here from somewhere else." Her voice sounded strained. Trepalli had that effect on people.

"Not necess—"

Charlotte interrupted. "Instead of worrying about a woman who hasn't done anything wrong and a kid who isn't missing," she said deliberately, "why don't you figure out how to help the chief with these games?"

There was a pause. "How do you mean?" asked Trepalli cautiously.

Charlotte's voice dropped to a furious whisper. "You know darned well what I mean, Marco Trepalli. She's your chief and you should be supporting her instead of letting the other guys bully you into shunning her!"

Trepalli's voice dropped back to a whisper, too. "I'm not shunning her!"

"Just because Rob McKell's in a tizzy doesn't mean you have to follow his example," said Charlotte. "He's soured everyone against her and it's not right. Yes, he should have gotten the job, but it's not her fault he didn't and he knows it. You should all be ashamed of yourselves."

Enough.

Kate took a few steps back and then deliberately dropped the file folder on the hallway floor. She stooped to pick it up and wasn't surprised to see Trepalli peering out the lunchroom door when she straightened.

"Oh. Hi, Chief." His cheeks were pink.

"Constable." She walked in and dropped the folder on the table. "Good morning, Charlotte. How are you?"

"Fine, Chief," said Charlotte. She gave Kate a small smile. "Well, better get back to work." She sailed past Trepalli without looking at him and Kate could almost hear the whoosh of displaced air.

She helped herself to coffee and added sugar before turning to the constable, who eyed her warily. She sat down at the table and pulled the file toward her. "You can help drive competitors to their venues tomorrow. We've borrowed the high school's mini bus. Swimming is the first event, starting at ten o'clock. The athletes are meeting here at nine."

Trepalli's mouth opened as if to say something and she looked at him above her reading glasses.

"Unless you're competing, too?"

He hesitated then shook his head.

"No, ma'am," he said and left.

Jesus *Murphy*.

After the first flush of anger receded, she had to resist the urge to bury her head in her arms and hide.

Even Trepalli? He was brand new, even newer than she was to the station—he had no history with McKell at all prior to coming to Mendenhall. Which meant that she had managed to alienate him all on her own.

If they weren't willing to stand behind her in something as fun as the cop games, how could she expect to lead them when things got really tough and she needed them to obey without question?

Maybe it was time to quit. At fifty-three, she had enough time in to retire comfortably. If she wanted.

With a sigh, she opened the file and read Constable Albertson's arrest report. Mendenhall's local thief, Hugh Schornick, had graduated from break-and-enters to stealing hay. He'd stolen a truck to haul the huge round bales and talked two buddies into helping him. He got caught by the RCMP near the Saskatchewan border because he hadn't bothered to change the plates on the stolen truck.

While most criminals weren't very smart, Hugh was dimmer than most.

But at least he was entertaining.

She took a sip then set the cup down. The coffee tasted burnt. She got up and poured the cup out in the sink. Then she made a fresh pot and wandered to the window while it brewed.

She stared out the window and through the branches of the oak tree at the blue morning sky. The leaves were already starting to fade. Pretty soon they'd be turning red.

Winnipeg had finally phoned last night, just before she left the station. The patrol officer told her that he had driven to the address Judy Hollister had given to find it was a condo development geared to seniors. There was a security fence around the perimeter and a speaker phone by the main gate but the officer didn't know the grandmother's condo number so he didn't pursue. Judy Hollister had not mentioned that her mother lived in a condo—Kate had assumed it was a house. Stupid of her.

But at least now she knew the grandmother existed. Probably.

Kate had asked the duty officer to keep trying the phone number. Someone was bound to answer, eventually.

The sound of a lawnmower droning in the distance came through the open window, and somewhere in the room a fly was buzzing.

Charlotte was right. The most logical reason for Judy Hollister's absence from the Motor Vehicles database was that she had moved from out of province and hadn't switched her driver's license over yet. The West woman had said that Hollister had moved to Dieppe Road a few months ago. And the old man a few houses down had mentioned that she was from away.

Kate tried to remember a car parked in front of the Hollister house but whatever the woman drove, it was probably parked in the back. The older sections of Mendenhall, the ones that had formed the military base before it was decommissioned, had a lane bisecting each block of houses. Local residents got to their parking spots—or more rarely, a garage—from the lane and the garbage trucks used them for access to trash cans.

If she wanted to see Judy Hollister's car, she'd have to drive down the lane.

And she did want to see the car. And the car's plates. Boiseman had said the white SUV had British Columbia plates.

Wouldn't it be just so coincidental if Mrs. Hollister's plates were also from B.C.?

Or if she drove a white TrailBlazer?

As the coffee began to drip fragrantly into the pot, she took off her glasses and slipped them into her shirt pocket, then picked up the file from the table and headed out of the lunch-room.

Charlotte looked up from her computer screen when Kate walked into the duty room. The duty desk was empty. At the back of the room, Boychuk had his hands buried in the photo-copier's entrails. There was a streak of dry ink on his cheek and a grim expression on his face.

She'd never met anyone who had as much trouble with ma-chines as Boychuk did.

"I'm going out for a bit," Kate told Charlotte. "I've got the cell phone if you need me."

"Yes, ma'am," said Charlotte. She gave Kate a genuine smile. "Don't forget you have a one o'clock with Daisy Wash-burn."

"I'll be back in time," promised Kate.

As she walked out of the station, she wondered if Charlotte had really meant it when she told Trepalli that McKell should have gotten the job.

SHE TOOK HER Explorer since a squad car in the same neigh-borhood two days in a row would be too noticeable. She drove with the window down even though the wind was pulling hairs out of her bun and whipping them at her face. It was warm out now but the forecast called for a chilly night.

Out of nowhere, a picture came to her fully formed from her too-fertile imagination: Boiseman sleeping in a damp ditch, shivering the night away.

She still couldn't place him. And now that she thought on it, she didn't actually think she had recognized him. Maybe he reminded her of another vagrant she had seen around. *Something* about him was familiar. Names she needed help with, but faces—faces she never forgot. Hopefully she'd know more when the results on his prints came back.

Not that it mattered. He was probably long gone, on his way to who knew where. Mendenhall got its share of wanderers, especially during the summer, but they were usually kids looking for adventure before college started in the fall.

The ones underage she shipped to Social Services in Winnipeg but the old ones, the ones past all hope of normal life, there wasn't much she could do for them except make sure they got a hot meal and a dry bed before they went on their way. They never stuck around long. The pickings were much better in the bigger centers, like Winnipeg or Edmonton.

Maybe she'd stop by and visit Fred Bellows at the Sally Ann on her way back. Check out Mr. Boiseman.

She drove past Dieppe Road. It looked pretty much the same as it had the day before. Little kids played in their yards or driveways. The older kids were all in school.

She turned up the lane behind the Hollister house and counted houses until she came to the right one. No garage and no car parked in the tidy space next to the garbage cans on their little platform.

What the heck. She was here, she might as well snoop. Kate turned off the engine and got out of the Explorer. A fence separated the lane and its utilitarian space from the backyard proper and, not being tall, she had to stand on her tiptoes to peer over the top. The lawn had been mowed recently and there were flower boxes filled with pansies and nasturtiums hanging off the deck railing. There was a small brown metal shed, the kind you bought at Canadian Tire or Sears, in the corner of the yard. A kid's two-wheeler, still with its training wheels on, leaned against the back of the house.

"Can I help you?"

Kate startled and dropped to her heels. Her teeth snapped shut painfully, barely missing her tongue. She turned to find a tall, straight-backed old woman staring at her disapprovingly from across the lane. She held a white kitchen garbage bag in her hand and had obviously been headed for the trash can when she saw Kate.

Kate studied the old woman.

"Good afternoon, ma'am," she said politely. The woman had to be eighty, at least, but her eyes were bright with intelligence and curiosity. She wore one of those cotton print smocks that fluttered around her bony frame like a tent flapping around a pole.

"Is there something of interest in Mrs. Hollister's backyard?"

Heat crept up Kate's cheeks. For the first time in many decades, she felt like a little girl caught doing something wrong.

I'll bet you used to be a schoolteacher.

"Do you live here, ma'am?" she asked the old woman.

"I do, indeed," replied the woman. Her hair was bone-white and up in a bun that the wind kept trying to pull out. She constantly smoothed wispy bits away from her face.

"Then would you happen to know where Mrs. Hollister is?"

"And why would you need to know that?" asked the old woman with a frown.

For the first time in years, Kate floundered for something to say. Did the woman really expect her to explain herself? She crossed the lane so they wouldn't have to shout and provide entertainment for the neighbors.

As Kate approached, the woman's gaze swept up and down Kate's uniform and a faint tinge of red colored her cheeks. It occurred to Kate that maybe the woman couldn't see as clearly as all that.

"My name is Kate Williams," she said as politely as she could. "I'm the chief of police in Mendenhall."

"How do you do," said the woman stiffly. "My name is Eugenia Weissner."

"Mrs. Weissner, do you know where Mrs. Hollister is?"

"There's no need to shout," said Eugenia Weissner in irritation. "There's nothing wrong with my ears."

Eugenia Weissner bent that ramrod back of hers enough to lift the lid of the trash can and drop the bag in. Now that Kate thought about it, the bag was suspiciously light. The old woman had probably grabbed the half-full bag the moment she realized someone was in the alley, as an excuse to come outside.

And suddenly, Kate felt like a hypocrite. This woman was looking out for her neighbors, even if there was a little bit of nosiness in her altruism. If more people were like her, Kate's job would be a heck of a lot easier.

"No, I don't," said Mrs. Weissner finally. She brushed imaginary dirt off her hands.

"Do you happen to know where she works?"

The old woman shook her head. "No. But I don't think she went to work today. She left yesterday afternoon. I saw suitcases in her trunk so she must be gone for the weekend."

Kate nodded. Hollister had mentioned she needed time off. Maybe she was meeting a lover for a romantic weekend and that's why Grandma had the kid in Winnipeg.

"Thank you, ma'am," she said finally.

Eugenia Weissner nodded stiffly.

Kate opened the door to her vehicle, then paused. "Ma'am?"

Mrs. Weissner turned back to her. "Yes?"

"Was anyone with her?"

Mrs. Weissner shook her head. "No. She was alone."

All right. Confirmation.

"In fact," continued Mrs. Weissner, "I can't imagine what she did with her son."

"He's with his grandmother in Winnipeg." The sun warmed

the top of her head and shoulders while the breeze, still morning-fresh, carried the sound of playing children from the street.

"He doesn't have a grandmother."

Kate stared at the old woman. The breeze suddenly felt colder.

"I'm sorry?"

Mrs. Weissner came closer. "Judy told me that Josh has no grandparents and that his father is dead. Poor child."

Kate's stomach tightened with unease. The woman could easily be mistaken. Or confused.

"Are you sure, ma'am?"

Some of the acerbity returned. "I'm old, young woman, not stupid. Of course I'm sure."

Kate hadn't been called a young woman in many years, and being called one by Mrs. Weissner now inclined her to be charitable.

So she wouldn't worry the woman.

"Then I must have misunderstood," she said. "Thank you again for your help."

Under Mrs. Weissner's watchful eye, she slid into the Explorer then buckled her seat belt before starting the engine. Just before pulling away, she remembered why she had come in the first place and peered out the window.

"Mrs. Weissner, do you happen to know what kind of car Mrs. Hollister drives?"

"It's a blue sedan," said the old woman. "A Honda, I think."

Kate smiled. "And the plates?"

"I hope you don't expect me to remember the number," said the old woman sharply.

"No, ma'am," said Kate. "Were they Manitoba plates?"

"No. They were from British Columbia."

"Thank you, Mrs. Weissner. You've been a great help."

The smile faded as she drove away. Either Judy Hollister had lied to Mrs. Weissner, or she had lied to Kate.

And now she was gone.

WHILE THERE WERE a few real-estate agents in Mendenhall, Kate only knew two personally: Tom Hubbard and his wife, Sally Thompson. They operated out of their home on Tenth Avenue and acted as the unofficial Land Titles office when Kate didn't want to deal with Winnipeg bureaucracy.

Sally came to the screen door, still wiping her hands on a rag that smelled of turpentine. Her face crinkled up in a smile when she saw Kate.

"Kate Williams! It's about time you dropped by for a visit!" She pushed open the screen door and held it open while Kate stepped in.

"Hello, Sally." Kate grinned. Every time she saw Sally, she felt like laughing.

Sally's oil paintings hung in some of the richest homes in the country and Kate knew of at least three art gallery owners in Winnipeg who were always after Sally to move to the city and concentrate on her art, but Sally wasn't interested. She loved her life in Mendenhall, loved working beside her husband in the real-estate office part-time and painting whenever she felt like it. She even taught at the high school and gave evening classes—which was where Kate had met her when she first moved to Mendenhall.

For some lunatic reason, Kate had thought it was time to explore the creative side of her personality and she'd thought painting would be a good place to start. It took four weeks for her and Sally to reach the sorry conclusion that Kate might have many talents, but painting wasn't one of them.

They'd become friends, even though Sally was a good fifteen years younger.

"What are you working on now?" she asked Sally.

"Come see," said Sally and she led the way down the hallway to the stairs. Sally and Tom had taken all the walls out on the second floor and added a few windows, so that the space was flooded with light. They'd also added a door at the top of the stairs to control the smell of solvents that could easily ruin supper.

The door was already open and a breeze flowed out, carrying the smell of the turpentine Sally used to clean her brushes. Kate walked in behind her. She'd only been up here twice before but her impression was still the same—a jumble of tables and shelves stacked with cans, pads of paper, jars of pencils, canvases. An easel stood at the north end of the room, by the windows. More canvases leaned against walls. Old cups of coffee rested on just about every flat surface in the room.

Sally led the way around chairs, tables and canvases to the easel. Kate stopped in front of it and examined the painting. A dozen or so boulders, in different shapes and sizes, were strewn around a lake. The painting was clearly not finished but Kate was pretty sure she wouldn't get the meaning of the boulders even when it was.

"It's for my parents' fortieth wedding anniversary," explained Sally. "Each boulder represents a member of my family."

Kate slid a sideways glance at her and Sally laughed. "No, really! See? That's George." She pointed at a boulder that seemed about to topple over. "He always looks like he's going to lose it, but somehow he always manages to save himself." She pointed at a round boulder that seemed to be bulging. "That's Allison. She's pregnant."

Kate nodded at each of the descriptions. Finally Sally stopped and looked at her. "You didn't really come for a visit, did you?"

"A visit *and* information." Kate smiled.

"What kind of information?"

"I want to know who owns a certain house."

Sally's eyebrows rose. She dropped the rag onto the stool in front of the easel. "In that case, we'd better go to the office."

They went back downstairs and to the kitchen, where a door led into their real-estate office. Tom looked up from the bulletin board where he was posting a picture of a house. The room was dominated by an antique oak desk with a laptop perched incongruously on it.

"Hello, Chief," he said with a smile. "How's it going?"

"Just fine, Tom, thanks. Things are good with you?"

He waved at the wall of house listings. "Market's booming, even in Mendenhall." He glanced at his wife.

"Kate wants some information on a house," explained Sally. Her husband moved toward the computer and she turned to Kate.

"What's the address?"

"614 Dieppe."

Tom looked up in surprise. "That's a rental. I just rented it out five months ago for the owner."

Kate smiled. Where she never forgot a face, Tom never forgot a house. "Who did you rent it to?"

"Hang on," said Tom, punching a few keys. "Ah—here we are. A Judy Hollister."

"What do you know about her?" asked Kate, moving toward the computer. All it showed was a picture of the house in the top left-hand corner and a form that was mostly blank.

Tom nodded at the screen. "Not much. The owner must know her because he waived the last-month payment and the damage deposit."

It was Kate's turn to raise her eyebrows. "Who's the owner?"

"George Yawkichuk. He's a dentist in Winnipeg. Nice guy."

"You got a business name or an address for him?"

Tom sat back in his old-fashioned, wooden roller chair. "What's going on, Chief?"

Tom had never warmed to her the way Sally had, but Kate still liked him. He was obviously in an uncomfortable position, but she wasn't asking him to violate any real-estate code of conduct or ethics. This was public information that she could get from the city clerk. Eventually.

"It's part of an investigation, Tom," she said evenly.

They stared at each other for a few seconds.

"Tom," said Sally, "it's not exactly a national secret."

Tom blinked, then grinned sheepishly.

KATE STAYED FOR an early lunch and then headed back to the station after solemnly promising Sally that she would come for dinner the following week. She made it back to the station with plenty of time to spare.

Charlotte looked up from the duty desk and grinned when she walked in. "Quarter to one. Want me to get one of the patrol cars to pick you up?"

Kate shook her head and glanced around the empty room. McKell would be ticked off if he saw Charlotte on the duty desk, but frankly, it made sense to have her answering phones and dealing with visitors, especially when they were short-staffed. "It's a nice day. I could use the walk. Things quiet here?"

"A couple of calls from a member in Dauphin and one in Killarney," she replied. "One to cancel and one to ask if it's too late to register. I gave them both Daisy's number." She glanced at the computer screen. "Nothing else so far." Charlotte had her hair up in a ponytail today and a yellow pencil was stuck just above the elastic. She managed to look efficient and charming at the same time.

"And DC McKell?"

"Lunch," said Charlotte. "Noon to one, rain or shine. He's not one for making his own lunch."

Kate nodded and headed for her office. Good. She wasn't in

the mood for McKell's passive aggression today. She grabbed the games file from her desk and headed back out. "I have the cell phone if you need me," she called over her shoulder.

"Okay," came Charlotte's voice from behind her.

City hall was only five blocks from the station. A few clouds had moved in from the east and the wind had picked up. Change in the weather, thought Kate. Storm by tonight, maybe.

Daisy was waiting for her in the city hall boardroom. She had a file folder open in front of her, a blank, lined paper pad to the right and an open laptop to the left. She looked up as Kate entered and waved her to the seat next to her.

Daisy was from Mendenhall, born and raised, and had come back to live after taking a two-year business administration course at Red River Community College, in Winnipeg. She was smart and good-looking in a no-nonsense way and the most capable woman Kate had ever met.

Daisy married Frank Washburn three years ago, the week after graduating from Red River. Frank was the manager of the Royal Bank and was doing well for himself, but Kate fully expected Daisy Pitcairn-Washburn to be mayor of Mendenhall one day.

Kate sat down on Daisy's left. The leather chair gave off a whiff of mustiness as her bottom settled. The room itself was paneled in a dark wood and it was small, at least compared to most boardrooms she'd seen. The chairs were oversize, giving a crowded effect.

"Sign here," said Daisy, placing a sheet of paper in front of her. Kate glanced at it and almost groaned. She had forgotten that she was competing in two events. She signed the registration form, the indemnification clause the city's lawyer had insisted on and ticked off the two events. Then she sent a little prayer to anyone listening that she would survive the weekend.

"Okay," said Daisy, tucking the registration form away at

the bottom of her file folder. "Let's compare our lists and see what needs to be done."

As they worked through their various lists, Kate had to admit that, all things considered, organizing the games had been much less painful than she had expected. She and Daisy worked well together and Kate had come to trust that whatever Daisy committed to doing would get done. And Daisy had come to know that Kate did whatever it was she said she was going to do. With the two of them following up on details, the jobs got done fast.

But now that the games were here, they needed help.

Kate had given her staff notice a month ago that they would be pulled in as needed, as would the emergency medical staff and the fire crews. She had the mayor's backing and everyone had cheerfully volunteered their efforts.

Except for her staff. Not only had they not registered for the games, save for Charlotte not one of them had stepped forward to volunteer. McKell had made sure of that. But this was one area Kate refused to compromise. The games would be disruptive and she needed officers to make sure everything remained safe. If they wouldn't volunteer, she would assign them overtime duty.

And if that put Rob McKell's nose out of joint, so be it. She was putting *him* on traffic duty.

When the meeting finally broke up an hour later, she was stiff from sitting so long.

"Okay," said Daisy with satisfaction. "I think we're good. You have your men lined up for traffic and parking duty?"

"Yes," said Kate, without elaborating.

"Good." Daisy closed the laptop and gathered her papers before standing up.

"Daisy…" Kate stopped, unsure how to continue.

"Yes?" Daisy prompted, looking down at her.

"Nothing," said Kate. She had been about to ask Daisy why

McKell hadn't gotten the job of chief. She'd seen his personnel file—it was exemplary. She could see no reason why the man hadn't gotten the job, which meant the reason wasn't in the file.

But it would be unprofessional to ask Daisy. And it would put the woman in an awkward position.

Daisy waited a moment, then smiled. "All right. See you tomorrow."

"Tomorrow." Kate stood up and began putting her papers in order. It was still early enough to drive to Winnipeg, interview Dr. Yawkichuk and get back in time for dinner with Jerry, who was driving in from Winnipeg for the games. She should really give John Stendel a courtesy call, let him know she'd be in his jurisdiction. But the guy's smugness irritated the heck out of her.

Every time she saw the Winnipeg chief of police, he had a different woman on his arm, usually a Sweet Young Thing in high heels and expensive perfume.

She could never understand what it was young gorgeous women saw in older men when they could have any guy they wanted. And it never ceased to amaze her that older men were willing to be naked in front of these young women. Didn't they have any pride? Or mirrors?

Although she had to admit that John Stendel didn't seem to have anything to be embarrassed about in that department. He looked pretty fit. And he was handsome enough, if you liked that smug look.

Still, he was old enough to be their father, for Pete's sake.

She stood in front of city hall, enjoying the warm sun on her face for a few minutes before she headed back to the station.

She'd ask Charlotte to call Chief Stendel, once she'd left.

But first, she needed to talk to Fred.

SIX

"FIRST HE TOOK a shower, then he ate enough for three men. After that he washed his clothes and then slept for about eight hours. Then he left and I haven't seen him since."

Kate watched the top of Fred Bellows's head as he picked carrots from the raised garden bed behind the Salvation Army shelter.

"What time was that?" she asked. Clarissa Bellows peered out the kitchen window, gave Kate a cheery wave and went back to cooking for the dozen or so men who habitually ended up at the shelter for the night. In winter, it was more.

Fred straightened with a groan and rested a foot against the wood frame of the raised bed. "Let me think." He looked up at the sky as if asking for help with his memory. His balding head was sunburnt, as was the tip of his nose. He and Clarissa had run the Sally Ann for at least ten years. They never lost their compassion for the poor souls who came under their roof, no matter how often they saw them. "Your young constable dropped him off around ten in the morning…" He did a mental calculation and then looked back down at Kate. "I'd say he was out of here by eight or nine o'clock last night. Why? Did he get in trouble?"

Kate shook her head. "No. Just following up." Boiseman had shown up at her place at around ten last night, just as she was thinking of jogging to the station. He must have walked pretty fast to make it to her place on foot by that time.

"Poor guy," said Fred, shaking his head.

"What do you mean?"

Fred shrugged. "Nightmares. Most of the guys who end up here are down on their luck. They're either addicts or drunks or have trouble coping with the world. But this guy…" He shook his head again and looked at Kate with a frown. "He cried in his sleep, cried like a baby. Kept calling out a name. I touched his pillow after he left—it was soaking wet."

A shiver ran up Kate's back. Someone was walking over her grave again.

"What name did he call out?"

Fred looked up again for inspiration. "Can't rightly remember. Something like Ellie, or maybe Nellie."

Ellie. That was the name Boiseman had used yesterday. *My little Ellie.* Who was Ellie? His wife? Sister?

His daughter?

This was getting her nowhere and she still wanted to drive to Winnipeg.

"Okay, thanks, Fred." She took her leave and headed back to the station. Boychuk was eating in the lunchroom.

"Everything okay?" she asked as she walked by the doorway.

He finished chewing his wife's leftover lasagna and swallowed. As usual, his uniform shirt had worked its way out of his baggy trousers and he looked as though he'd forgotten to comb his hair that morning. But Kate had discovered a keen, alert mind behind the bags under his eyes and the sleepy expression.

"Tremblay and Johansen are on patrol. Tourmeline went home for lunch. He's got the pager on. Trepalli is finishing up paperwork on the accident today."

"What accident?"

"Corner of Fourth and Main," said Boychuk. "Guy with an iPod stepped out between two cars just in time to get clipped by a passing motorbike. Driver was transferred to the Grace in Winnipeg."

"Seriously hurt?"

"Don't think so," said Boychuk around another mouthful. "That's where he's from."

"Pedestrian?"

"Shook up but fine."

Kate liked Boychuk's terseness, though it drove Charlotte crazy and she could just imagine how Boychuk's wife liked it. But he always got to the point in the fewest words possible. That was something to admire.

"Where's McKell?" she asked.

Boychuk shrugged. "Lawyer's."

Kate resisted an urge to sigh. Instead she nodded and headed for the duty room, where Charlotte was just packing up for the day. Her day started at seven in the morning, but unlike the officers on day duty, she didn't work a twelve-hour shift and finished at three in the afternoon.

Behind her, Trepalli sat at one of the common desks, staring intently at the computer screen as he typed in information.

Kate stopped Charlotte as she was about to walk away from the duty desk. "Do you have any contacts with Motor Vehicles in B.C.?" Out of the corner of her eye, she caught Trepalli's sudden stillness as he stopped typing to listen.

Charlotte shook her head. "Nope." Then she grinned wickedly, her green eyes dancing with laughter. "But I do have a pretty good contact with Motor Vehicles in Winnipeg. And *he* knows someone in B.C."

Kate shook her head in admiration. "Charlotte, you are full of wonders."

"That's what all the boys tell me," replied Charlotte cheekily. She replaced her handbag in the drawer and pulled her notepad out of its slot. "What do you need?"

"Check Judy Hollister's name against B.C. registrations. Then run her name through CPIC."

Charlotte swallowed and kept her gaze on the paper on

which she was writing. Trepalli started typing furiously. "Right," said Charlotte. "Do you need this tonight?"

"The CPIC info should come up right away, if there is any." She glanced at her watch. It was two hours earlier in B.C., still plenty of time to get the request in. "You can ask your friend today," she said. "No need to stick around for the answer, though. He can call the station if anything comes up. And, Charlotte, can your friend be discreet? This isn't exactly an official investigation."

Charlotte nodded and picked up the phone.

"Oh," Kate suddenly remembered. "Could you also call Winnipeg and let them know I'll be interviewing a witness there?"

"Yes, ma'am," said Charlotte, jotting the info down on the pad.

Kate turned her attention to Trepalli. Despite having been on duty since seven, he still looked neat and fresh, whereas she could feel the shirt sticking to her sweaty back.

"Constable."

"Chief." He reluctantly raised his gaze from the screen.

"How would you like to go for a ride?"

He remained silent for a split second while searching her expression for clues. Then he said, "To Winnipeg?" He hesitated. "I need a statement from a motorcyclist who hit a pedestrian. He's at Grace Hospital."

She nodded. "I know. You can do that while I interview my own witness. Unless you've got something better to do?"

He immediately shook his head and stood up. "No, ma'am." He plucked his cap from the top of a pile of file folders and placed it on his head.

"Save it," said Kate.

He stared at her uncertainly.

"Your file." She pointed at the monitor. "Save it before you lose it."

SHE DECIDED to let Trepalli wear his uniform, but she changed into the spare set of civilian clothes she kept at the office. The uniform would be useful to extract statements from witnesses to an accident, but interviewing the dentist might require some finesse. She didn't think showing up at his door wearing a police uniform from another jurisdiction would qualify as finesse.

They took her Explorer. She didn't want to ruffle John Stendel's feathers any more than she had to. She was less likely to have her movements reported back to him if she wasn't driving around his turf in a Mendenhall patrol car.

"Want to drive?" she asked Trepalli. His eyes widened at the cherry-red Ford Explorer and he nodded.

"Yes, ma'am!"

"Don't get excited." She handed him the keys. "You still have to go the speed limit."

She'd long ago stopped caring about the little power game of who drove. She'd always liked riding shotgun. It gave her the opportunity to see a lot more than the driver did. Real patrolling should be done on bicycle, she sometimes thought. You missed too much whizzing by in a car.

They left Mendenhall behind and headed east on the Trans-Canada Highway. The sun sank behind them, chasing velvet shadows across the fields. The farther they got out of town, the more fields they passed, many still with crops bobbing high. Cylindrical haystacks packed in white sleeves already lay like giant sausages on the horizon.

"About Mrs. Hollister," said Trepalli abruptly, not looking at her. "Why B.C.?"

She kept her gaze on the passing scenery, unwilling to give up her peace so soon.

"I asked Charlotte to run a search on her," he continued, "but she didn't find anything in Manitoba." He glanced at her sideways. "I know you said the case was closed, Chief, but…" He trailed off.

She glanced at him. His mouth was set in a stubborn line. Then she looked more closely. He had shaved while she changed into her civvies. She didn't know whether to approve or roll her eyes. Or both.

"What is it about the…" she hesitated, reluctant to call it a case "…the old man's story that's got you so bothered?"

He drove in silence for a few minutes, considering. Finally he shrugged. "Dunno. Not one thing in particular. Everything can be explained logically, I know." He glanced at her. "But… it's an accumulation of little things that just don't add up."

The kid had potential.

"She's gone."

He looked at her. "Mrs. Hollister?"

She nodded. "She left yesterday, after we interviewed her. Packed her suitcases and left, according to her neighbor."

"The neighbor," he said. Then he guessed, "She's the one who told you about Mrs. Hollister having B.C. plates." He nodded as if that solved one mystery, then leaned back against the seat. "So where did she go?"

"Good question."

"Maybe she joined her son in Winnipeg, at the grand-mother's place." He didn't sound convinced.

Kate shook her head. "The neighbor says there is no grand-mother."

He frowned. "Why would Mrs. Hollister lie? Where's her kid?"

Kate looked at the vast prairie rolling out beyond the pas-senger window.

"I don't know, Constable."

THE FIRST THING they did when they got to Winnipeg was hunt down the address Judy Hollister had given them. The condo development was to the north of town, almost to the city limits. A tall fence surrounded what appeared to be one street looping around on itself. The condo units were in shades of green and blue. They rang the caretaker's buzzer and soon a chatty little man with a faint British accent came to let them in.

"We have twenty-two units," said the caretaker, Sean. "For people sixty and over." His brown eyes twinkled as he looked Kate up and down. "I'm afraid you have a bit to wait, m'dear."

Kate smiled back. "We're looking for a Mrs...." She looked down at her notebook. "Mrs. Saunders."

Sean blinked at her for a moment, thinking. Then he shook his head. "Sorry, love. No Saunders here."

"Are you sure?" asked Kate, her mouth suddenly dry. She could feel the weight of Trepalli's gaze on her.

"I know every owner," said Sean with a shrug. "No Saunders here."

"Perhaps she just moved in," suggested Kate. "She might go by the name Hollister," she added, suddenly inspired.

But Sean was already shaking his head. "No new arrivals since we built three years ago. And no Hollister, either."

And that was that. There was still the phone number, but Kate was willing to bet it would be a dead end, too.

SHE DROPPED TREPALLI off at Grace Hospital and then pulled out her map of Winnipeg from the glove compartment. The dentist lived on Rosewood Street, all the way across town, in Tuxedo. She hoped Trepalli could find enough to occupy himself until she returned.

She hit rush-hour traffic and it took over half an hour to finally reach Rosewood Street.

Tuxedo was an older neighborhood and the homes had a luxurious, well-settled look to them, with mature trees, mostly maples or fir, in the front, and healthy cedar or boxwood hedges lining long drives.

Number 37 was in the middle of the block. No hedges, but a tall, wrought-iron fence surrounded the property. The gates stood open, hooked to fieldstone posts on either side of the driveway. The house itself was well back on the lot, with a driveway curving up to the house, around a small landscaped centerpiece with spiky grasses and flowers, and back to the main gate.

Just how much did dentists make, anyway?

Since the gates were open, Kate drove right up to the door and got out. It was a two-storey affair, with lots of different levels to the roof. She'd lately started watching decorating shows on television and decided that whoever had chosen the color scheme for the window trim—a sage green—and the door—forest green—knew what they were doing.

She went up the five steps to the stoop and rang the door-bell. It chimed somewhere deep in the house. A minute later, the door opened and a small plump woman with a riot of curly red hair smiled at her.

"Hello," said the woman, still wiping her hands on a cloth.

"Ma'am." Kate nodded. "My name is Kate Williams. I'm chief of police in Mendenhall. Is Dr. Yawkichuk here?"

The woman had brown eyes in a face covered in freckles. From the tan on her arms, Kate guessed that she didn't care that redheads weren't supposed to go out in the sun.

The woman smiled. "George isn't home yet. I'm Doreen Yawkichuk, his wife. Is there something I can help you with?"

"I don't think so," said Kate smoothly. "I'd like to ask Dr. Yawkichuk a few questions concerning an investigation. It should only take a few minutes."

Doreen Yawkichuk smiled hesitantly, obviously wanting to ask more questions.

"You're welcome to come in and wait, if you'd like."

Kate made a move to remove her cap, remembered she wasn't wearing one and nodded instead. "Thank you, I will."

The woman turned to lead the way inside and Kate followed, closing the door behind her. A staircase with a white handrail led the way upstairs. To the left of the staircase was a sitting room. Immediately to the right was a set of pocket doors that led into a formal dining room. Past the staircase, the tiles carried on down the hallway. Kate hesitated at the entrance of the kitchen, wondering if she should remove her shoes. The tiles had given way to an ancient wide-plank pine floor that was beautifully kept up. The woman glanced back.

"Oh, don't worry about your shoes," she said. "The kids do a lot more damage every day than your shoes will."

Kids. Great.

"I hope you don't mind waiting in the kitchen," continued Mrs. Yawkichuk. "I was just making supper."

"No problem," said Kate. She followed Mrs. Yawkichuk to the back of the house and into a big room with a fireplace, love seat and a couple of rocking chairs at one end and a modern kitchen with a sit-down counter and a big work table at the other. French doors led to a deck with a patio table and a big umbrella providing shade. On the counter near the double sink sat a cutting board with half-sliced carrots. At the other end of the counter, a pile of brightly colored beach towels were neatly folded.

From the open window above the sink, Kate could hear the shrieks and splashing of children playing in water.

Something smelled wonderful.

"Have a seat," said Mrs. Yawkichuk. "Would you like a glass of wine? Beer?"

"No, thank you," said Kate regretfully. A beer would go down good right about now.

"In that case, I can offer you a variety of juices, water, milk, coffee or tea."

Kate looked at her a second too long and the woman laughed.

"Three kids," she explained. "You wouldn't believe the groceries we go through."

As though called up by her mention of them, a gaggle of kids in wet bathing suits came bursting through the French doors to stand dripping on the linoleum floor.

"Back!" cried Doreen Yawkichuk, waving a plastic spatula in the air. "Back, back!"

Laughing, they all fled back onto the deck while Mrs. Yawkichuk scooped up the pile of towels on the counter and brought them outside. While she handed out the towels and made the kids dry themselves off on the deck, Kate counted them. There were at least six kids out there, varying from about six to ten years old.

And in a minute, they would all be in the kitchen.

At that moment, the front door opened and a man's voice called, "Anybody home?"

Thank God.

A man walked into the kitchen only to stop short when he caught sight of her.

George Yawkichuk, if that's who he was, was not much taller than his wife. Kate judged him to be under forty. His dark hair, what was left of it, was only starting to go gray. He had a soft little potbelly that pushed out his short-sleeved shirt and bulged over his casual slacks. He had the impeccable grooming—including manicured hands—that she always associated with dentists.

"Hello," he said politely, automatically smiling.

Kate got up and offered him her hand. "Dr. Yawkichuk?" At his nod, she continued, "My name is Kate Williams. I'm the chief of police in Mendenhall. Do you know a Judy Hollister?"

At first he looked back at her blankly as if the name meant nothing, then his expression changed to one of alarm and his gaze flew to the chaos outside on the deck. His wife caught sight of him and freed a hand to wave cheerfully. He waved back then turned to Kate.

"Why don't we go into the study?"

He turned and led the way out of the kitchen. Kate followed thoughtfully.

He didn't want his wife to hear what they were about to discuss. Interesting.

He went into the sitting room and through another set of French doors. These were curtained in white gauzy stuff that let the light through while affording a bit of privacy. He made sure to close the doors behind them.

The study was a comfortable room with a window that looked out onto the front lawn, a decent-sized desk with a laptop computer on it, and a grouping of chairs around a small fireplace at the other end of the room. This is where he led her and indicated she should sit down.

"Now," he said, sitting down in front of her. "Why are you asking about Judy? Is she all right?"

Kate allowed an eyebrow to raise. "Does Mrs. Hollister rent a property you own in Mendenhall?"

He nodded.

"How do you know her?" asked Kate.

He swallowed and looked down. "We went to the same high school."

Ah. "Here in Winnipeg?"

He shook his head. "No. I grew up in Vancouver. So did she."

So far, none of this seemed unusual or suspicious. What wasn't he telling her?

"Are you having an affair with her?" she asked bluntly.

"God, no!" said the dentist, his gaze shooting to the door. "Look—has something happened to her?"

You have a crush on her, Kate suddenly realized.

"Dr. Yawkichuk, Mrs. Hollister has disappeared. We have reason to believe she and her son may be in trouble."

"Josh?" He looked genuinely stricken. "What happened?"

"We don't know. That's why we're investigating." She pulled her notepad out of her jacket pocket, along with a pen. "Can you tell me where she works?"

Dr. Yawkichuk still looked shocked. Finally he rubbed his hands over his face as if to scrub it clean and then clasped them together on his lap. He looked at her.

"She works for a colleague of mine. Dr. Janine Horowitz. She's an orthodontist."

Kate jotted down the name. "Where does she practice?"

"She's on Portage," said Dr. Yawkichuk and gave her the cross-street.

"I'm seeing a pattern here, Dr. Yawkichuk." Kate looked up from her notes. "You found her the job, didn't you?"

He hesitated but then nodded jerkily.

"You found her the job. You rented her the house." She studied the pudgy dentist for a moment. He made an unlikely hero.

"What is she running from, Dr. Yawkichuk?"

The man sighed as if all the stress was leaving his body with the breath. "Her ex-husband," he said. "She's terrified he'll find her and Josh."

And the suspicion crystallized into fact. "Hollister's not her real name, is it?"

He shook his head and sat forward on his chair. "Her name is Judy Hollingsworth."

Smart. She kept the assumed name close enough to her real name so her son would respond to it.

"Her husband is a real treat," said Dr. Yawkichuk. "He used to beat her. She got out of the marriage when he started hitting the boy, but he kept harassing her in spite of the restraining order. Finally she left the province and moved here. She's always afraid he'll find her."

Kate nodded and kept writing. Came to Winnipeg where good old George lived.

"Did you witness any of these beatings?"

"Of course not," said Dr. Yawkichuk. "He wouldn't want witnesses."

"What's the husband's name?"

He frowned and looked up at the ceiling. "Let me think. Harrison…Harrison Becker, or Beckman. Something like that."

"You don't know him?"

He shook his head. "I moved to Winnipeg with my family soon after graduating. Judy and I lost touch. I'd heard from mutual friends that she'd gotten married but I never met him."

A door slammed in the kitchen and a child shrieked with laughter. The bathers had passed muster and were now allowed inside.

Dr. Yawkichuk looked at the door with alarm then at Kate.

"There's no need to tell my wife about Judy, is there?" he asked timidly.

He hadn't even slept with the woman and he felt guilty about her. "My business is with you, sir," she said crisply. "What you tell your wife is your business."

Shamed relief flooded the man's face. She could just imagine him in high school. Picked on by the jocks, mooning after Judy Hollingsworth, who probably didn't even notice him. Until she needed him.

She stood up. "I'll need any contact information you have for her, including any cell phone numbers."

He nodded jerkily and went over to the desk.

SEVEN

TREPALLI WAS WAITING outside the main doors of Grace Hospital when she pulled up an hour and a half after leaving him there. Two young women were chatting with him. He had taken off his cap and held it tucked under his arm.

He looked up and saw her. He spoke a few words to the young women, nodded and replaced his cap before running down the stairs to the car. The two young women watched until he got in the car and waved at him.

Brother.

"Constable," said Kate, pulling away from the curb.

"Chief." He placed his cap on the dash and clicked on his seat belt.

"Did you get your statements?"

"Yes, ma'am," he said with satisfaction.

Kate hid a smile. Along with a few phone numbers, no doubt.

"Report."

Trepalli pulled out his notepad and flipped to the right page. "Guy's name is Van der Huyk," he said. "Lives here in Winnipeg. He was on his way back from visiting his girlfriend in Mendenhall when the pedestrian walked out between two cars without looking." He looked up. "He couldn't stop in time and ended up on his side, trying not to hit the pedestrian. Clipped the guy on the leg but he's fine. Meanwhile the motorcycle fell on our guy and broke his leg."

"What does the pedestrian say?"

Trepalli flipped back a few more pages. "Guy was wearing

an iPod and not paying attention to where he was going. Didn't use a crosswalk. He was looking for something on his iPod and didn't see the motorcycle coming." He shook his head. "Guy's forty-five, for crying out loud."

Kate glanced at him. Was the young constable disgusted because the guy should have known better or because he was wearing an iPod at the ripe old age of forty-five? She decided she could live without knowing.

"Charges?"

Trepalli frowned.

"For jaywalking?" He shrugged. "The motorcyclist *could* sue, I suppose."

"Not up to us," said Kate. Then she told him what she'd found out about Mrs. Hollister—Hollingsworth—and her abusive husband.

"Well, that explains the secrecy," he said when she was done. "What I don't understand is where the kid is."

That was the question, wasn't it? Where was Josh Hollister, aka Hollingsworth? Was the kid in trouble or had Judy Hollingsworth stashed him away somewhere safe?

"The phone number she gave us?" said Kate, glancing at the constable. "It was her cell phone."

Trepalli looked offended. "And I bet she has call display," he said bitterly.

Kate would have laughed but she felt the same way.

There was a lot of traffic and she had to pay attention. She hated driving at this time of day—after the sun had gone down but before full night. It was the time of day she'd pulled over Samuel Boynton and seen the boy sleeping in the backseat, the boy she'd thought was his son, the boy he'd stolen.

"Chief?"

She snapped out of the memory and turned her attention back to the present. "What is it, Trepalli?"

"You want me to drive?"

"No." Then, because the answer was too curt, even for her, and because she'd finally made up her mind, she added, "Call Boychuk. Tell him to call the B.C. Motor Vehicles—call, not email. Put in a request for a plate number for a Harrison Becker or Beckman. And a plate number for Judy Hollingsworth, too, for a blue Honda sedan. And find Charlotte. Tell her she can call off her friend in Winnipeg. This is now a formal investigation."

She took a deep breath. "Once the info comes in, put out a BOLO for both of them. Beckman/Becker for possible kidnapping and Hollingsworth for questioning."

Trepalli turned on the overhead light for the passenger seat and began calling on the cell phone.

Less than half an hour later, they drove into Mendenhall. It was six-thirty and already the stores had closed for the day. Only the cinema on Main Street, a couple of restaurants in the downtown core and the bookstore three blocks from Main had any cars parked in front. The firefighters sat on the front stoop of the fire hall, enjoying the warm evening. They waved as she drove by.

Kate pulled into the station parking lot and turned off the engine. Two of the squad cars weren't in their parking spots.

Trepalli held the station door open for her and she led the way inside. McKell looked up from the computer monitor at the duty desk. Shoot. What was he doing there? He was on nine-to-five this week.

She glanced around the duty room, which was conspicuously empty. Were they *all* on patrol? And then she got it.

Boychuk had phoned him.

"Evening, DC McKell," she said calmly. "Did Boychuk call B.C. Motor Vehicles?"

"Why are you interested in a couple of B.C. cars?" asked McKell bluntly.

Trepalli mumbled something and made himself scarce, leaving Kate alone with McKell.

The duty desk was elevated so that whoever sat there had the psychological advantage of height, looking down on people who stood in front of it. Kate didn't like the feeling and suspected most people didn't. But she didn't budge.

She smiled coolly up at her DC. "Did Boychuk phone B.C. Motor Vehicles, as I requested?" *Ordered.*

"No," said McKell. "I told him to hold off until I talked to you."

A familiar tide of anger rose in her but she controlled it.

He was an abrupt man, used to giving the orders. But if he kept countermanding hers, there *would* be repercussions. She could not—*could not*—afford a DC who did not follow orders. Surely he knew that.

As she stood staring up at him, she suddenly realized that this had less to do with resentment over being passed over for a promotion than with trust. Or, more precisely, lack of trust.

He didn't think she knew what she was doing.

Apparently, neither did Boychuk or he wouldn't have called the DC in.

She would have to prove herself to DC McKell before the rest of the crew would fall in behind her. Whatever the hold was he had over the station, she suddenly envied it. A man like that would be an invaluable asset to her, if he was on her side. It was worth an extra effort on her part.

So she began to fill the DC in on what she and Trepalli had learned so far. Before she could finish, McKell held up his hand to stop her.

"Are you talking about that tramp?" he demanded. His face was red. "You've had Trepalli haring off all day on the word of someone who's clearly off his rocker?"

Kate hung on to her self-control with both hands.

"He may not be lucid all the time, but he did see something."

Her voice was a little higher than she would have liked. "And the mother is hiding something." She was suddenly glad she hadn't told him of Boiseman's visit to her home.

McKell took a deep breath. "Why are you assuming she lied?"

She filled him in on what she had learned from the dentist and told him about Mrs. Weissner's assertion that there was no grandmother in Winnipeg, as well as their discovery that the phone number and address Hollingsworth had given them were bogus. Too many little lies added up to a big lie.

McKell didn't agree. "She ran away from an abusive husband—do you blame her for changing her name? She told you her son was fine but you'd rather believe the elderly neighbor, who barely knows her?"

Kate felt herself flushing. Put like that, it did seem ridiculous. But McKell hadn't met Judy Hollingsworth or Mrs. Weissner and bald facts were never enough to convey body language or context. And no one had seen the kid since that morning. But she was damned if she was going to explain herself any further to McKell. She had wasted enough time.

Then McKell leaned forward on the counter. His face was set in hard lines.

"It's because it's a kid, isn't it?" he asked.

Kate's heart stuttered and she felt her face drain of color.

"I beg your pardon?" she asked through stiff lips.

This time, the censure in his eyes was clear. "I know what happened in New Brunswick." He took a breath, obviously ready to add something, and blood rushed back into her face, bringing with it the welcome bite of anger.

"It's now past four-thirty in B.C.," she interrupted coldly. "I suggest you call right away before Motor Vehicles closes."

He stared at her for a long time, his expression unreadable. She held his gaze unflinchingly. Finally, he picked up the phone and started dialing.

"I have the cell phone," she said to his back. "Call me if you learn anything."

She turned on her heel and stalked out.

THE BRAZIER TOOK up half a city block, with the parking lot taking up most of the space. It had been Barney's Tavern for over thirty years. Then the city grew around it and the tavern fell out of favor. When smoking in public places was banned, the new owner turned Barney's into the Brazier, specializing in steak and seafood, which was a little odd, considering they were smack in the middle of the prairies.

As Kate entered, she imagined she could still smell the ghost of hundreds of spilt beers and old cigarette smoke lingering in the rafters. She blinked in the dim lighting, waiting for her eyes to adjust as soft jazz played from speakers.

She hoped the music would calm her, but the familiar frustration was still there. No matter where she worked, Bobby MacAllister followed her. Somehow, word always got out that she was responsible for the capture of Samuel J. Boynton, the notorious child killer. She hated it. Hated being reminded, however unwittingly, that she had let Boynton go free to kill Bobby MacAllister.

But Toronto was the first time anyone had ever openly held her responsible for Bobby's death.

It was politics, she knew. If she'd never applied for the deputy chief's job in Toronto, she would have finished out her career in relative peace. But as soon as she tossed her hat into the ring, the rumors started swirling—about how her ineptitude had killed Bobby, how she couldn't handle cases with children, how she allowed her emotions to make her decisions for her.

How she was unfit to lead.

Until finally, out of desperation, she took the job of chief of police in Mendenhall, believing that when she left the cutthroat competition behind, she would be free to do what she loved best: police work.

But McKell knew about Bobby. No doubt he, like her, had friends in police forces across the country, including Toronto.

God.

"May I help you?"

Kate opened her eyes and took a deep breath. A young woman at a hostess desk was watching her with a smile. To the right of the desk was the restaurant proper. The buzz of dozens of different conversations rose above the faint wailing of a saxophone. To the left was the bar, where people waited for a table to be ready. It, too, was full.

"I have a reservation," said Kate. "Under Williams."

"Ah, Chief Williams." The young woman looked up from her screen. "Your party is already here. Come this way, please."

Kate glanced at her watch to see just how late she was but it was too dark to read the dial. A burst of laughter came from the bar as she turned away to follow the hostess. The woman wore a short-sleeved white shirt and a short black skirt that revealed shapely legs under her black nylons.

Kate had dressed for the occasion in the only dress she owned. It was black and had short sleeves and a hem that grazed her knees. Her pumps were a purple leather that matched the clutch purse she had finally bought, if only to have something in which to carry her keys, her badge and her cell phone. She had left her hair in its accustomed bun but at the last minute, she had grabbed a fine woolen shawl that her friend Jillian had brought back from Mexico for her, with pink and purple flowers and a fringe. She felt ridiculous, as if she were dressed up for a costume party, but Jerry was a formal man, for all that he was only a dozen years older than her. Jeans would not do.

The girl led the way through the crowded restaurant. A few

people looked up as Kate passed by and she got a few startled nods of recognition.

She breathed deeply a couple of times, trying to expel the lingering anger. It wasn't working.

The table was in the far corner, away from the busy kitchen. Jerry Wolsynuk stood up as she approached, unfolding slowly to his full six-foot-two height.

"Hello, Kate. You look lovely." He smiled in genuine pleasure and she accepted a kiss on the cheek. He pulled out her chair and seated her before returning to his seat.

He was a lean man with silver hair and mustache, and the bearing of a drill sergeant. Tonight he wore a dark gray pinstripe suit with the RCMP coat of arms discreetly pinned to his lapel. Just seeing him made her feel better. He liked her. Lots of people liked her. No one she worked with, maybe, but lots of others.

"It's good to see you," she said.

He smiled again and patted her hand. "It's been too long. I wanted to come by sooner, but I knew you'd have your hands full with your new command. Alma expects you to come for dinner soon."

She had known Alma and Jerry for almost twenty years and had even worked with Jerry on a couple of joint investigations when they both worked out of Vancouver. This posting to Winnipeg was his last. He had promised Alma he would retire at sixty-five and he was a man of his word.

The waiter appeared and took their drink orders—soda water with lime for her and a dry red wine for him. It would be perfectly fine for her to have a glass of wine, too, but she knew every eye in the restaurant would be watching what she drank.

"How's your mother?" he asked.

"Stubborn as ever," replied Kate promptly. "She refuses to move in with any of us. I can understand why she wouldn't want to move to Mendenhall or St. John's, but Lily's in the same city. And she'd love to have Mom live with her."

Jerry grinned. "Your mother is an independent woman."

Well, that was certainly true. Ever since Dad died five years ago, Mom had resisted all efforts to convince her to sell the old house and move in with one of them. Fortunately, it wasn't an urgent decision. At seventy-five, Mom was still healthy and active. Kate had to admit that there was no real reason to pressure her to give up the home she loved just to make her children feel better.

The waiter returned with their drinks and took their meal orders.

The conversation meandered pleasantly while they waited and Kate felt the tension of the past few weeks easing from her shoulders. When their meals finally arrived, her stomach grumbled so loudly that Jerry laughed.

The steak—a rare guilty pleasure—melted in her mouth. The baked potato came slathered in butter and she allowed herself a dollop of sour cream. Even the medley of carrots, broccoli and snow peas was perfect, with just enough crunch to complement the tenderness of the steak.

At last she pushed her unfinished dinner away. "If I don't stop now," she informed Jerry, "you'll have to roll me out of here."

"That's right," said Jerry. He'd had a New York cut, rare, with a side salad and no potato. "You have to be able to run a race tomorrow."

Kate barely controlled a wince. Jerry gave her a lopsided smile that didn't hide the concern in his eyes. "I heard that none of your people signed up," he said gently. "I'm sorry."

The steak turned to lead in her stomach as embarrassment flooded through her in a hot wave. "No need to be sorry," she said crisply.

"How many events are you doing?"

"Two," she said. "The 1600-meter race and hand-to-hand."

Jerry sat back in his chair and looked at her. "Well done, Kate," he said with admiration. "If I were a betting man, I'd be betting on you."

"To win?" she asked incredulously. She appreciated his loyalty but there was no way she was going to win either event.

"To win your station over," Jerry corrected gently. "Leading by example is always best."

"Really?" She shrugged uncomfortably. "Right now, leading by decree is looking pretty good."

His lips compressed slightly. Then he sighed. "Quite a few of your people are ex-military, aren't they?"

She nodded. At least five were ex-military.

"I hear McKell served right here, at Shilo," he added.

She looked at him, surprised. She had known that McKell was ex-military—the mayor had briefed her on McKell when she accepted the job—but she hadn't known that he had served at Base Shilo, less than twenty minutes from Brandon.

"But…" She did a quick calculation. "Hasn't he been on force here for at least ten years?"

Jerry nodded. "He left the military when he turned forty. He already had twenty years in as a military policeman, the last five in Shilo. He must like it here."

Kate blinked. He must like it here, indeed. He served in the military here, then became a cop and married here. Something niggled at the back of her mind but the conversation moved on to other topics before she could capture it. She gave up and concentrated on the photos Jerry was showing her of his grandchildren.

Suddenly she realized that the sound she was hearing was her cell phone, muffled by her purse. She grabbed the purse from the table and fumbled with the unfamiliar clasp until it finally opened. Jerry fell silent as the phone rang clearly. She finally managed to flip it open.

"Williams."

"You wanted to be called if we got a hit on anything," said Martins. Kate glanced at her watch. Nine o'clock. Shift change took place two hours ago.

"Prints?" she asked, putting her palm up to her free ear to hear better.

"No. Plates."

"Okay," said Kate. That was fast. "I'll be right there." She flipped the phone closed.

"Time to go?" asked Jerry.

She smiled. "I'm sorry, but yes."

Jerry insisted on buying dinner, then walked her to her car.

The evening had turned cold and Kate had to control a shiver, in spite of the shawl. Jerry waited until she had unlocked the Explorer before asking, "So, how bad is it really?"

She looked up at him. She'd known Jerry and Alma for a long, long time. Seen their kids grow up through pictures and letters, and later, email. Visited with them whenever she got the chance.

He was Old School. A disciplined, by-the-book man who'd come up through the ranks of the RCMP. He'd worked in everything from narcotics to white-collar crime and knew someone in every branch of law enforcement in the country. And while he was proud of her success, he firmly believed that women should be protected and shielded.

As she had for twenty years, she refused to let him. "It'll work out, Jerry. Give Alma my love. Tell her I'll call her soon."

Jerry nodded and patted her awkwardly on the shoulder. Kate thought she heard him sigh as she settled herself behind the wheel, but he was smiling when she looked up at him.

"Good night, Jerry."

"Good night, Katie."

EIGHT

MARTINS LOOKED UP from the duty desk computer when she walked in and his mouth fell open. He took in her dress, legs and lipstick in one astonished glance.

For Pete's sake.

"Report," she said crisply as she walked into the duty room. Except for Martins, it was deserted, as it should be on a Friday night. Nothing prevented trouble like the presence of patrol cars in the bar district. She glanced in McKell's office. Gone.

Martins swiveled in his chair to follow her movements. He was in his late thirties with crinkly auburn hair and light brown eyes. When she'd first met him, she couldn't help staring at the overabundance of freckles on his face. Even now, she had to suppress a smile every time she saw him. From everything she'd seen of him, the man was even-tempered and easygoing. She remembered hearing that he had just celebrated his fifteenth wedding anniversary.

She wished he would stop staring at her.

She placed her clutch purse on the duty desk and looked expectantly at him. "Constable," she prompted gently. "What do you have for me?"

He swallowed and abruptly turned back to the desk to rummage through some papers. He mumbled something and she moved closer.

"Sorry? I didn't catch that."

"Here," he said, turning back to her with pages clutched in his hand. "I printed out the information." His face was red.

"Thank you," said Kate, accepting the pages. She turned to walk into her office.

"Don't forget your purse," said Martins.

Kate turned back and picked up the purse. She nodded her thanks and headed into her office, uncomfortably aware of his gaze following her.

She dropped the purse on her desk and sat down. The search had resulted in no hits for Judy Hollingsworth or Harrison Becker, but there was a hit on a Harrison James Beckman, of 2213 Sallister Road in West Vancouver. According to the report, he drove a 2004 white, four-door TrailBlazer.

Not a white horse, after all.

Relief washed through her in waves and she smiled at the printout. This was a custody battle.

No monsters, Mr. Boiseman, she thought to herself. Just two parents fighting over a kid. Then she remembered what the dentist had said. Mr. Beckman beat his wife, who had taken off with her son when he started beating the boy.

Maybe a monster, after all.

"No HITS ON Hollingsworth?" she asked Martins on her way out.

"Not yet," he said. He glanced at her then turned his attention back to the screen.

It was already ten o'clock. She needed to get some rest before the run tomorrow. She swallowed a sigh and headed for the door.

"I'll be home if you need me."

The duty phone rang and Martins nodded at her. "Good night, then." He picked up the phone. "Mendenhall Police."

Kate shook her head and walked out the door. Annett was just driving in with a man in the backseat. He waved at Kate and kept driving to the back door, which meant he was heading to the booking room. Kate debated returning inside to find out what was going on, then decided against it.

She had enough on her plate.

It was a beautiful night, cloudless, with just a hint of bite in the breeze to remind her that winter was coming. She stood on the stoop and stared up at the sky. There were too many street-lights to see the stars clearly. She'd go home, make herself a cup of chamomile tea and sit on her back deck. Then she'd try to sleep.

She stopped by the Sally Ann on her way home. Clarissa met her at the door. She studied Kate with a grin on her face.

"Well, don't you look like the cat's meow," she said.

Kate laughed and asked if Mr. Boiseman had come back.

"Only one guest tonight," said Clarissa, "and it isn't Mr. Boiseman."

Kate went home. The motion-sensitive light above her front door activated as she pulled into the driveway. Instead of going in through the front door, as was her habit, she walked around to the back. She avoided the gravel path to save her shoes and stuck to the narrow strip of grass next to it. By the time she arrived in the backyard, her eyes had adjusted to the darkness. A glance at the deck showed it was empty. She walked around the small raised garden with its carrots and tomato plants, peered under the lilac bushes and stood at the back of the yard, looking down at the hill, scanning.

Nothing. Mr. Boiseman was well and truly gone.

"You look very nice tonight."

Kate jumped and spun around so fast her left ankle twisted from under her. She would have fallen but for a hard hand grabbing her arm.

"Careful," said Boiseman.

Kate bit her tongue to keep from swearing. Her heart was beating so fast she started worrying about a heart attack.

"Mr. Boiseman," she said after she had calmed down

enough. "What are you doing here?" She tried her weight on her ankle and it supported her easily. She didn't think she'd done a lot of damage but she had to get out of these pumps.

Boiseman slowly removed his hand, as though wanting to make sure she could stand on her own. He'd been standing by the fir tree, which was why she'd missed him.

"Have you found the boy?" His face was lost to shadows and darkness but his voice sounded rational enough.

Kate took a deep breath and noticed a whiff of body odor coming off the man.

"Mr. Boiseman, where are you sleeping?" she asked gently.

He shrugged. "Here and there."

"Why don't you let me take you back to the Salvation Army?" She took a tentative step and winced as a twinge of pain warned her to be careful. At once his hand cupped her elbow, supporting her. Half leaning on him, half hobbling, she made her way back to the side door. "Did they not treat you well there?"

"Captain Bellows and his wife are very kind," said Boiseman gravely. "And Mrs. Bellows makes a mean spaghetti sauce."

Kate grinned in spite of herself. She unlocked the door and opened it. "I believe tonight is stew night. If we hurry, you can have leftovers, a shower and a warm bed."

His hand tightened on her elbow before releasing it. She flicked on the outside light and turned to look at him. His eyes were shadowed and sad.

"I don't deserve a warm bed," he said.

"Why not?" she asked gently. Her ankle was beginning to throb but she stayed still, waiting for his answer.

He looked down at her. She hadn't realized how tall he was.

"Did you find the boy?" he asked again. There was a note of pleading in his voice.

"Not yet," said Kate. Then, when his eyes filled with despair, she added, "but we're getting close." She put a hand on his grubby sleeve. "We'll find him, Mr. Boiseman."

He nodded without looking at her and gently moved his arm away.

"That's good," he said softly. "Poor baby." The last was said in a whisper that barely carried over the sound of the breeze in the leaves.

A shiver of dread crawled up her spine. He was no longer talking about Josh Hollister. Hollingsworth.

"Is there someone I could call for you?" she asked impulsively. She half wanted to invite him inside and feed him, but her pragmatic side forbade it. She would flay any of her officers who took a chance like that.

He looked at her again.

"The monster got them all," he said.

This time, the shiver went all the way to her scalp.

The phone rang in the kitchen, startling her. When she looked back, Boiseman was already heading for the front of the house and the street.

"Mr. Boiseman!"

He raised his hand over his head in a salute but kept going.

She closed and locked the door behind her and hobbled up the stairs, catching the phone on its fifth ring.

"Williams."

"Hi, Kate," said Jerry, sounding very close in her ear. "Just wanted to check you had made it home all right."

Kate couldn't help but grin. "Yes, Dad. I'm fine."

"That's enough lip out of you, young lady," said Jerry gruffly but she could hear the laughter in his voice. "I'll see you tomorrow."

"Tomorrow?" said Kate.

"For the race," said Jerry. "I'll be in your cheering section."

Kate thanked him and hung up. Then she went to find ice for her ankle.

NINE

A FAINT BUT distinct aroma of cow manure lingered at the Mendenhall Fair Grounds, left over from the fall fair and exhibition less than ten days ago. The land, fifteen acres by the highway, had been bequeathed to the city by a childless farmer.

Kate parked in the parking lot and made her way onto the grounds proper. Her ankle was securely strapped and barely hurt. She doubted she'd be able to say the same *after* the race.

Awnings had been set up around the grassy center to provide shade and protection from rain for the timekeepers and other volunteers.

Not that rain was likely to be an issue today. Despite the forecast, which called for scattered showers in the morning, the sky was a cloudless, pearly blue. Of course, it wasn't even nine o'clock yet.

A couple of volunteers looked up as she passed and smiled. In the center, dozens of young men and women stretched in preparation for their event.

She frowned as she tried to remember exactly which events would take place here. The high jump, for sure. Boxing, judging by the boxing ring in the middle of the competition area.

She looked up at the commentator's booth, twenty feet above the grounds. Daisy waved down at her from behind the window.

Kate waved back and headed for the booth.

"Hi," said Daisy as Kate came through the door. She had a pen tucked behind her ear.

The concrete booth was cool and Daisy wore a sweater

against the chill. Kate shivered a little in her short-sleeved uniform shirt. The booth smelled of old coffee.

"Morning," said Kate. Her gaze snagged on the view from the window, so high above the grounds. From here, she could see halfway to Winnipeg. The sky seemed to fill most of the window. When she'd first arrived here, it was the sky that had impressed her the most. She'd found herself breathing deeply, as if she finally had room for her lungs to expand. Every once in a while, the same feeling caught her up again.

Kate pulled up the chair next to Daisy and sat down. Piles of papers sat in neat stacks in front of the woman. Her cell phone sat on top of one of them.

"So?" she asked Daisy. "Everything ready?"

Daisy shrugged. "I hope so."

Kate wasn't worried. Daisy Washburn was the most effective person she'd ever met. After she was through being mayor of Mendenhall, Daisy would no doubt run for premier of the province.

Daisy glanced at her watch and her eyes widened in alarm. "Aren't you running this morning?"

Kate nodded. "Yep. The heats start at ten-thirty."

"But you need time to warm up!" said Daisy, looking her up and down. "Geez, Kate, you're still in uniform!"

Kate got up, favoring her ankle. "Not to worry," she said lightly. "I've got lots of time. I just wanted to check in."

"Everything's fine," said Daisy. "Now, go!"

Kate turned with a grin and headed out the door. Just before her foot hit the top step, however, she turned back.

"Any chance someone else signed up?"

Daisy knew exactly what she was asking. She shook her head and Kate turned away from the sympathy in her eyes.

SHE WENT TO the station to change. O'Hara was filling up his thermos in the lunchroom and looked up, startled, as Kate walked by with her gym bag. He was a taciturn man with few social graces. She'd noticed that most people were uncomfortable in his presence, but she liked him. He was peaceful to be around. She dredged her memory and found that he had a father in a long-term care facility in Winnipeg. O'Hara visited him on his days off.

She nodded at him and walked into the duty room. Charlotte was at her desk and Friesen was filling out the incident log and idly flirting with her. He looked up from the log and nodded a hello.

"Friesen." She glanced at the log and glanced away. She didn't have time to check it out. "Everything all right?" she couldn't resist asking.

"Yes, ma'am," he said, finishing with the log book and closing it. "Fender bender on Main Street. No one hurt."

He was the only other single man at the station. With his dark blond hair and crinkly blue eyes, Kate had thought he would give Trepalli a run for his money. But Charlotte treated him with the same sisterly affection as she treated all the others.

"Charlotte, why are you here?" asked Kate. It was a beautiful Saturday, for Pete's sake. She should be out playing.

"I just had a few things to clear up, Chief." She grinned at Kate, who shook her head in despair. Youth was wasted on the young.

By the time Kate walked out of her office in her running gear and sweats, only Charlotte remained in the duty room.

Charlotte followed her to the door.

"Good luck, Chief," she said with a warm smile.

"Thank you, Charlotte," said Kate, absurdly close to tears. How pathetic. Was she so starved for her staff's approval that she was ready to cry at good wishes?

The high-school running track was close to the Assiniboine River and protected from the wind by a screen of ash trees.

Kate finally found a parking space in the high-school parking lot, at the far end, and walked carefully down the length of the school toward the racing oval.

Spectators lined the oval—mostly cops from other jurisdictions, judging by the number of unfamiliar faces. A few Mendenhall firefighters were sprinkled in there, too. The crowd cheered the runners in the first heat as they ran by. She glanced around and found the warm-up area. A dozen men and women were stretching and preparing for their heat.

The officials' table sat under an awning at the near end of the oval. Several officials clustered there, checking things off on their clipboards and comparing stopwatches.

Kate walked over to the officials' table. Hassim Abouda, the only Middle Easterner in town, was one of the timekeepers. He'd always been friendly to her so she headed for him.

"Hello, Hassim."

He glanced up from the clipboard he was writing on. "Chief. I was beginning to wonder if you were going to show up."

Hassim owned one of the two hardware stores in town. His was the kind of store that had disappeared twenty years ago in most other places. She liked going there. Everyone who worked there knew what they were talking about.

He ticked something off on his clipboard and looked up at her over his glasses. "Nervous?"

"Yes," she admitted cheerfully. And she was. Not only was she twenty years older than most of the other runners, her ankle was beginning to throb and she hadn't even started running yet.

Hassim leaned in to her and whispered, "We're all rooting for you."

She glanced at him and then glanced away. Really? Her face turned hot and she looked down at the ground.

"Thank you," she said and was surprised to find her throat

closing up with emotion. She had to stop this. "I appreciate your support."

He patted her on the shoulder and grinned at her. "Don't. We would all rather Dan Boychuk was running instead of you."

Boychuk? The same Boychuk who couldn't peck out his name on a keyboard or change the toner in the photocopier without spilling half of it on his uniform? The same Boychuk who always looked as if standing up was a chore?

Who called McKell in because he didn't trust her to know what she was doing?

That Boychuk?

"He's a runner?" she asked doubtfully.

Hassim nodded and tucked the clipboard under one arm. "Very good runner. He's not really a sprinter but he has speed and stamina. We had high hopes Mendenhall would win the 1600 this year."

Kate blinked up at the man. Would wonders never cease?

"Kate!"

Kate turned around to see Daisy aiming for her like an arrow let loose.

"What are you doing here?" she asked. "I just left you at the fairgrounds."

"I came to cheer for you, of course," said Daisy. "You should be warming up," she added sternly. "You're in the fourth heat."

Kate nodded. Yes, indeed. She should be warming up. Wouldn't want to lose the race because she hadn't warmed up properly.

She considered peeking at the times of the runners who had already run their heats but decided against it. Why discourage herself before she even got on the oval?

Daisy led her to the warm-up area and stood by while Kate stripped off her sweats and handed them to her.

"What's that?" asked Daisy, pointing at her ankle.

Damn. She'd forgotten about the bandage.

"Nothing," she said. "Just a little support."

Daisy looked unconvinced but walked away with Kate's sweats to stand with Hassim.

The crowd cheered as the runners from the previous heat entered their final lap.

As Kate began stretching, she ignored the curious looks she got from the young men and one other woman warming up around her.

They all looked very fit, very athletic and very young. Where the heck were all the senior runners?

You can never tell, she told herself firmly. Boychuk didn't look as if he could run two steps without tripping over his feet and apparently he was the Wonder Boy of racing.

Well, she was no Wonder Girl and she wasn't going to win this race.

But she didn't plan on losing it, either.

"Five minutes," called a young woman with a stopwatch. "The next heat is with Berg, Eddings, Krentz, Marusek, Webber and Williams."

Nervousness fluttered in her stomach and Kate took a deep breath and let it out slowly. It'll be all right, she told herself firmly. This was *not* the time for nerves. She'd just run the blasted race—hopefully without embarrassing herself or her force—and get back to looking for Mrs. Hollingsworth and her son.

Piece of cake.

She ran long distance all the time. She ran five kilometers every day and ten on Saturday or Sunday.

No, distance wasn't the problem. She just didn't know how much speed she could muster. She hadn't raced in twenty years and even back then, she'd never been very fast.

She sat on the ground and stared at her legs as she leaned over to stretch out her hamstrings. They were good sturdy legs. Not very long, but muscular. They'd taken her wherever she wanted to go for fifty-three years, give or take, and she'd never had any reason to complain about them.

But now, suddenly, she wished she was one of those tall, lanky types with no body fat who seemed to float down the race course.

"Two minutes," called the young woman with the stopwatch. "Take your places, please."

Kate stood up and took a deep breath. She had been assigned lane two. She walked over to the starting blocks and as she continued with her warm-ups, she cast surreptitious glances at her competitors. The man to her left was at least six feet tall with the lean build of a born runner. He ran in place, shaking out his muscles, oblivious to her. The man to her right was shorter but just as lean, with powerful calf and thigh muscles. He glanced at her then glanced away.

They were all taller than her, even the only other female competitor, a Sweet Young Thing who couldn't be more than twenty-one.

Suddenly, Kate felt ridiculous. What was she doing, running against people half her age just to prove a point?

Oh, lord.

"Thirty seconds," said the timekeeper and every runner took position against the starting blocks, including Kate. She crouched in position, aware of the pull on her ankle and the fact that her butt was wider than anyone else's on the line.

"On your marks," said the woman and the line shivered into position. "Get ready." Butts lifted in preparation for the start. Then the starter's pistol went off and they all surged from the blocks as if a powerful gust of wind propelled them.

The spectators roared with approval and shouted out specific names as the runners went past.

Kate forced herself to keep to her regular pace as the others sprang ahead of her. She had four laps of the oval to survive. She wouldn't make it if she tried to keep up to them.

It didn't take long for her ankle to make itself felt, first in a burning sensation then as a steady ache. She was *so* going to pay for this.

After a while, the pain became ignorable as she focused on her breathing. It wasn't about the other runners. It was about her. She concentrated on relaxing her shoulders and on the movement of muscles in her thighs, calves and bum.

One lap.

The other five runners were well ahead of her, some almost an entire lap ahead of her. Now that she was nicely warmed up, she increased her pace a little and was gratified when she closed the gap a little between her and the last runner—a tall, gangly fellow with blond hair.

By the end of the second lap, she had caught up to him. A cheer went up among the spectators and to her surprise, she heard her name shouted out. The crowd's energy fueled her and by the end of the third lap, she had passed the redhead, much to his disgust.

One lap to go. The breeze cooled her sweaty body as she increased her speed yet again. She was closing in on the woman, who was running behind the pack on the inside lane. Her calves burned but she ignored the pain and with a surge, passed the woman and tucked into the inside lane.

She couldn't hear anything past the pounding of her pulse in her ears and the roaring of air in and out of her lungs. Her feet landed on the asphalt of the running oval like pile drivers attacking concrete. She felt the beginning of shin splints.

Then she did hear the roar of the crowd and looked up to see the winner cross the finish line, followed by the next two runners. With the sixth sense she thought she'd lost when she stopped racing, Kate felt the woman closing in on her. Half a lap left to go.

Now, she told herself. Now!

With every last ounce of strength and determination she

had, she surged forward, forcing her legs to move faster than they had in years, and crossed the finish line ahead of the woman.

And then people were on the track and surrounding her, clapping her on her wet back and saying things she couldn't hear past her gasping breath.

Then Charlotte elbowed her way through the people surrounding her and pulled Kate away. Wrapping an arm around Kate's waist, she forced her to walk and cool down slowly.

Finally, Kate's breathing calmed down.

"Keep walking," said Charlotte, tightening her hold on Kate's waist.

That's got to be unpleasant, thought Kate. Her T-shirt was wet with sweat.

"I'm fine," she said, trying to pull away.

"Sure you are," said Charlotte. "That's why you're limping."

And as if Charlotte's words conjured up the pain, Kate's ankle suddenly throbbed. She gasped and stopped, forcing Charlotte to a standstill.

Good lord, that hurt.

Then Trepalli was on her other side, helping support her.

"You did good, Chief," said Trepalli. "You did real good."

THE EMERGENCY MEDICAL tech examined her ankle under the awning of the first-aid tent and gave her a look that told Kate exactly what he thought of her.

"You sprained it yesterday and still ran?"

Kate had already said so and didn't see the need to repeat herself. The ankle hurt enough without having this fellow try to make her feel worse.

The tent was at the far end of the grounds, out of the way of spectators and participants. In the glimpse she'd gotten of the inside, she'd seen two cots and a wheelchair.

Her ankle was nicely swollen. It throbbed with every beat

of her heart—which, she was grateful to note, hadn't conked out on her. The run was the worst of the events, she promised herself. The hand-to-hand would be easy compared to this.

Well, except for the standing up part.

"Ouch!" She yelped when he turned her foot to accommodate the tensor bandage. He raised an eyebrow.

"Stay off it," he ordered. "Put it up. Put cold packs on it—two minutes at a time and don't give yourself frostbite—alternating with heat packs. Stay *off* it," he repeated. He finished wrapping the ankle and clipped the ends of the bandage with tiny metal clips.

"Thank you," she remembered to say as he put his supplies away in his medical kit.

"You're welcome," he said. He left her under the awning, her foot propped up on the folding chair he'd been using. She closed her eyes and leaned her head back.

Thank God that was over.

A sound behind her made her straighten up. She twisted to see Jerry striding over the short grass toward her. The expression on his face was a mixture of concern and glee.

"How are you?" he asked as soon as he saw her looking at him.

"Fine." She smiled up at him. "Why do you look like you just swallowed a canary?"

He grinned. "Because you're the talk of the games, Katie girl. You impressed everyone with your grit, especially when people realized that you ran on a sprained ankle!" He bent down and kissed the top of her head. "You should have seen the look on Stendel's face!"

She must have looked confused, because he went on. "Stendel was with another of his young ladies. When she realized who you were, she asked him why *he* wasn't competing." Jerry laughed outright. "Priceless! You've started a new trend, Katie. Now people are going to expect to see their chiefs competing."

"Jerry, it's not nice to gloat," said Kate, but she couldn't quite hide her smile. She would have liked to have seen Winnipeg's chief of police explain why he wasn't competing.

Charlotte and Trepalli arrived then, walking side by side. Maybe it was the pain clouding her judgment, but Kate couldn't help noticing what a fine-looking couple they made. Charlotte held a bottle of water in her hand while Trepalli carried crutches.

"I don't need those," Kate said firmly.

Trepalli wore well-worn, close-fitting jeans and a white T-shirt that revealed muscled arms and a washboard stomach. He looked down at her, his face set in stubborn lines she was beginning to recognize.

"Chief, the EMT said you needed to stay off the ankle. Unless you want me to carry you, you have to use the crutches."

Charlotte's mouth did a suspicious little twist.

"I thought you were at work, young lady," said Kate crabbily. She allowed Jerry to help her up and stood with her weight on her good foot.

Aw, hell. It *hurt*.

Charlotte placed a hand on her hip. "It *is* Saturday, as you so kindly reminded me," she said. "I wanted to come cheer you on." She looked at Trepalli. "So did Marco."

He grinned shamefacedly at Kate but said nothing.

"Well, thank you," said Kate. Before she could say anything else, Charlotte suddenly jumped and said, "Oh!" as if someone had pinched her bottom. Turning her back to Trepalli, she fished through the collar of her shirt and pulled out a cell phone.

"I had it on vibrate," she explained as she flipped it open. "Yes? Yes, it's over. She's right here." She handed the phone to Kate. "It's Constable Patterson. She called me when she couldn't reach you."

Kate brought the phone to her ear. "Williams," she said.

"Chief," said Patterson, "we just got some info on Mr. Boiseman. I wouldn't have disturbed you but it was flagged as urgent."

Kate forgot all about her aching ankle. "I'll be right there." She closed the phone and looked up at her two frowning subordinates.

"Which one of you is going to drive me to the station?"

BOISEMAN WAS A wanted man.

Kate examined the print-out photograph, trying to convince herself it might be a mistake.

The hair was brown and neatly trimmed. He wore a white shirt and a tie and there was no stubble on the lean cheeks, but the eyes that stared back at her were Boiseman's slate-gray eyes. There were no monsters lurking behind those smiling eyes.

His name wasn't Boiseman, of course. It was James Murray Cusick, from Mississauga, Ontario. And he was wanted for questioning in relation to the death of his daughter, Ellen Cusick, four years old.

My little Ellie...

Kate leaned her cheeks on the heels of her palms and stared down at the write-up. Her eyes kept jumping up to the picture, but it was Boiseman. Cusick.

The girl had been taken by an acquaintance, Derek Allan Jackson, who, it turned out, was a known pedophile. The girl's body was discovered days after the kidnapping in a ditch off the 401 Highway near Toronto.

The paper didn't say why Cusick was wanted for questioning, only that he was a person of interest. Then she glanced at the date of the murder. 1989.

Cusick had been running for over twenty years.

CHARLOTTE BROUGHT HER a steaming cup of coffee and Kate smiled her thanks. She sat up straighter, aware that she hardly looked the picture of a professional police officer in her T-shirt and shorts. She winced as her ankle complained.

"Caroline asked me to give this to you," said Charlotte, handing her a printout.

Caroline? Oh yes, Caroline Patterson, on the duty desk.

In her mid-forties, Patterson had worked in Regina for fifteen years before her husband was offered a position as manager of the local grain board in Winnipeg. She'd stayed behind until a position opened up in Mendenhall, five years ago. She and her husband bought a house in Mendenhall and he commuted to Winnipeg every day. They had two teenagers.

Patterson was Mendenhall's only female police officer. She had been in line to be the next DC if McKell had become chief.

Maybe that's why she doesn't like me, mused Kate.

"BC Motor Vehicles came through with Mrs. Hollingsworth's info," continued Charlotte.

Judy Hollingsworth drove a blue 2006 Honda Accord.

"And before you ask, yes, Caroline put out a BOLO on the car." She leaned against the desk, eyeing Kate critically. "You look like death warmed over."

"No, please," grumped Kate, "tell me what you really think." She took a sip of the coffee before standing up and hobbling over to her door. Trepalli had fetched her gym bag from her car and she wanted to change into her uniform before it got too wrinkled. Daisy still had her sweats, she suddenly remembered. She'd have to get those sometime today.

Behind her, Charlotte sighed. "The first-aid guy dropped by with this," she said. Kate turned to see a small vial of pills in the palm of Charlotte's hand.

"What is it?"

"Extra-strength Tylenol," said Charlotte. "He forgot to give it to you at the high school."

Kate took the vial and shook out two of the pills, which she swallowed with the coffee. No point in suffering more than she had to.

"You should go home," said Charlotte disapprovingly.

"So should you," Kate pointed out. "You shouldn't even be here, this being Saturday and all."

Charlotte ignored her and took the gym bag from her hands to place it on the desk. Then she proceeded to open it and pull out her rumpled uniform.

"Thank you, Charlotte." Kate took the uniform from the girl's hands and then pulled shampoo and a towel from the bag. "I'm going to take a shower now."

"And then you'll go home?"

"No. I have work to do. Stop mother-henning me." She said the last with a smile to soften the words. But honestly…

Charlotte, undaunted, stared back at Kate. There was a gleam in her eye.

"Take care of yourself and I'll stop mother-henning you."

Kate frowned. "You do remember that I'm your boss, right?"

"Occasionally," said Charlotte. "Drink your coffee."

Once Charlotte left, Kate took a quick shower in the empty cell block and changed into her uniform. Her bandage got wet and she grimaced when she pulled her sock over it. The foot barely fit in her regulation black leather boot, so she left the laces undone. When she returned to her office, she found that someone had opened the side drawer of her desk and propped a cushion from the lunchroom on it.

Shaking her head, she carefully pulled the boot off her poor, abused foot and propped her leg over the cushion. Immediately the throbbing eased.

Maybe she would survive, after all.

She sighed. Thank goodness she didn't have to go to the dance tonight. And even if her presence was expected, her ankle gave her the perfect excuse not to go.

There's always a silver lining.

She picked up her cup again but the coffee had grown cold. Instead, she pulled the information sheet toward her and began reading it carefully.

Cusick was thirty when his daughter died. That would make him fifty-one today. Younger than her. She couldn't reconcile the old man she knew as Boiseman with the clean-shaven, handsome Cusick.

But then, she had trouble reconciling the man who had stood in her duty room, ranting about monsters, with the man who had later stood in her backyard, looking at the stars longingly.

Her thinking was all muddled when it came to Boiseman. She didn't think he was a danger to anyone, let alone her. Perhaps he was a danger to himself, but only in that neglect and the road would kill him sooner rather than later.

And yet, the Ontario report listed him as a person of interest in the death of his daughter. Was guilt the reason little Ellie haunted him? Kate shied away from the thought that he might have been involved in his daughter's murder but she'd been on the job long enough to know that monsters came in all guises.

Every instinct told her he was a good man, brought low by a terrible act. But instinct wasn't enough, was it?

She glanced down at the contact information at the bottom of the printout. Detective Laird Macdonald. Was he the primary on the original investigation or was he the poor sap assigned to cold cases?

She pulled the phone toward her. It wasn't even midafternoon in Toronto. Someone would be able to help her, even if it was Saturday.

It took half an hour but eventually she spoke to a Cindy Robertson in the Toronto Police Service's Cold Case unit.

"Chief, it's going to take a while to find the case file," said Constable Robertson, with a note of stress in her voice. "Mississauga amalgamated with Toronto a few years back and we haven't absorbed all the files yet."

"I see," said Kate. She looked up at the ceiling. *God save us from bureaucracy.* "Then maybe you can tell me if Laird Macdonald is still on the force? He may have been the primary investigator."

Cindy Robertson blew out a sigh. "I'll try to find out, Chief. Give me your number."

Kate did and hung up after extracting a promise from the woman that she would call back today.

She hated the waiting that was the biggest part of police work.

Without thinking, she picked up her coffee and drank, then spat the cold coffee back into the cup.

THE AFTERNOON DRAGGED on while she waited for the Be On the Lookout/Observe on Harrison Beckman and Judy Hollingsworth to yield results and for Cindy Robertson to call back from Toronto. She considered putting a BOLO out for Mr. Boiseman—Cusick—but didn't. She wanted to talk to Laird Macdonald first. The last thing that old man needed was cops swooping down on him. That might send him over the edge.

She spent an hour drafting a memo to City Council explaining why she was sending Tourmeline to Ottawa on a forensic fingerprinting course and arranging for first-aid refresher courses for everyone on the force, including Charlotte. Bad enough the city was reluctant to spend money on training, but even her officers groused about the refresher courses. Kate ignored them and signed them up.

Perversely, the phone didn't ring once and nobody came into her office. Every once in a while, she got up to limp through the duty room. Every time she did, people made themselves scarce.

Nobody likes having the boss around on the weekend.

Finally she just stayed in her office.

She took a look at the duty roster, studying McKell's method of assigning shifts. The one stipulation she'd had when he took over personnel was that the teams be staggered so that over a period of six months each officer had worked with every other officer at least twice. She'd worked in some places where some cops only knew each other by the names on the roster and never actually met.

Reluctantly, she decided that McKell had done a good job. He had staggered himself, as well, working one week from nine to five and the following from noon to eight.

She glanced at the file cabinet that contained all the personnel files. She'd read all of them when she first came to Mendenhall, but after last night's conversation with Jerry, she felt the need to refresh her memory of McKell's file.

He'd joined the military at eighteen and served overseas as well as in the east of the country. He'd been a military policeman and had made Warrant Officer before he left, at forty. From what she could remember of military ranks, a warrant officer was one of the highest ranks a non-commissioned member could achieve. His last posting was at Shilo, where he served four years as head of the joint Canadian-German military police detachment.

In spite of herself, she was impressed. Shilo was an international base, where soldiers from many countries—especially Germany—came to train on the wide-open artillery ranges. It would take some finesse to lead a joint detachment and avoid international incidents.

She wondered where all that finesse had gone.

She flipped to the personal information page. He'd been married three times, divorced twice and working on his third. She saw by the dates that he'd been very young when he first married, not even twenty. Divorced two years later. Remarried at thirty-two, divorced four years later. The last marriage was eight years ago, right here in Mendenhall.

Kate glanced at his soon-to-be-ex-wife's name: Elizabeth Dabbs-McKell. It took her a moment but she finally realized where she'd seen the name before. Mayor Leonard Dabbs.

McKell had married the mayor's daughter.

AT ONE-THIRTY she realized that her hands were shaking. She was running on caffeine. She hobbled to the lunchroom and ate alone, listening to the echoes in the station. When she was finished with her soup, she washed her bowl and spoon and returned to her office.

Through the open door, she heard Patterson talking to a woman who had apparently lost her dog. Patterson patiently explained to the woman that she should go to the animal shelter to see if anyone had brought her pet in.

Johnson walked by her open door on his way to the washroom. He nodded when he saw her looking at him.

It was eerily quiet at the station, even for a Saturday afternoon. Normally there would be constables coming in and out, the phone would be ringing and citizens would be coming in to lay complaints about everything from dirt bikes ripping up their lawns to someone stealing their car. But everyone was at the games and too busy to cause trouble.

Instead of sitting here waiting for a call from Toronto, she could be showing her face at some of the events. Public relations and all that.

Patterson stuck her head in the office.

"Mrs. Hollingsworth's car has been found."

Finally.

Kate got to her feet and followed Patterson.

"Where?" she asked, pointing at the four-foot-wide by six-foot-tall map that was nailed to the wall of the duty room.

Patterson walked over to the map and leaned over. The sun

came through the side window and blued her black hair. She had a marker in one hand and she drew a small circle on the plastic sheet over the map.

"Off the highway, in Brandon. She went over the escarpment and into the Assiniboine." Patterson looked at Kate. "They're planning to fish the car out as soon as the tow truck gets there."

Kate nodded slowly. "Anyone in the car?"

"They can't tell," said Patterson grimly. "The car's almost completely submerged."

The cold feeling was back in Kate's gut, like water turning to ice. All right, then. "Who's available?"

Patterson blinked at Kate for a moment before realizing what Kate wanted to know. She headed back to the counter and looked up at her board. She was a tall, lean woman with a swimmer's build. "I'm a little thin on the ground, what with the games." She ran a hand through her short hair. "I've got Johnson, Oppenheimer, Abrams and Parker. I can pull Abrams off patrol. What do you need?"

"Not Abrams," said Kate. He, Johnson and Parker had experience with crowd control—better he should stay in town and help deal with whatever came up because of the games. All she needed was a driver.

"Oppenheimer," she said. Aside from Trepalli, he was the youngest member of the department. He would probably love to skip out on traffic duty. "I want him to come with me to Brandon."

Patterson frowned. Brandon was well out of their jurisdiction. "They're not going to like…" Kate gave her a look and Patterson shut up.

"Call whoever's on the ground in Brandon. Ask them to hold off on pulling the car out until I get there. Say pretty please."

Patterson raised one eyebrow to show her skepticism but

picked up the phone. Kate was skeptical, too. Charlotte had told her about the friendly rivalry between Brandon and Mendenhall. They probably wouldn't wait for her, but it was worth a try.

"I'm going to need one of the patrol cars, too," added Kate as she walked back to her office. Patterson waved a hand over her head to show she had heard but kept talking into the phone.

Kate sank onto her chair and lifted her leg up to the cushion with a groan of relief. She hunted through her Rolodex until she found the number of the chief of police in Brandon. She knew he was out of town—that was the reason he wasn't at the games—but she still had to go through channels. She punched in the chief's direct number and waited while the phone rang once, twice, three times before being picked up.

"Chief Larksen's office," said a female voice.

"Is he in, please? Chief Williams calling from Mendenhall."

"Sorry, Chief Williams. He's out of town right now. His daughter's getting married."

"Who's acting?"

"That would be DC Billings. He should be in Mendenhall for the games. Would you like his cell phone?"

Kate jotted down the number the woman rattled off and called Billings. As expected, he had no problem with her driving to Brandon to inspect the car. He even offered to call the duty desk and have his people hold off on pulling up the car until she got there. Kate didn't hesitate to accept. It might tick off whoever was in charge to have the DC micro-manage from Mendenhall, but she didn't care. She wanted to be there when they pulled the car out.

She hung up, then stared at the phone a moment before picking it up again. McKell's home number was programmed into it, a leftover from the old chief. She hoped that the DC would be out watching the games—it would be some form of support anyway—but he answered on the second ring.

"Hollingsworth's car was found in the Assiniboine in Brandon," she said without preamble. "I'm taking Oppenheimer with me. You're on call in my absence."

There was a silence at the other end. Then he said, "Anybody in the car?"

"Don't know yet," she replied.

Another silence, and she knew exactly what he was thinking.

Judy Hollingsworth's car was in the river and she and her son were missing. No matter how you looked at it, something was wrong here. Even he had to admit it.

Kate took very little satisfaction in being right.

TEN

THE SHADOWS WERE already long by the time Kate and Oppenheimer turned off the Trans-Canada Highway onto First Street and into Brandon proper. She glanced over at her young constable, hoping he would stop talking now.

No such luck.

"The high school is just down that road." He pointed to the east. "There's a community college and a university," he added. "And there's a great Chinese restaurant on Sixth—best wonton soup I've ever had." The lowering sun shone through Kate's window, warming her. The river glittered below, a metal ribbon bisected by the bridge toward which they were heading. The river valley spread in front of her, already golden with autumn.

She cleared her throat. "I take it you're familiar with the city?" Those were the first words she'd had a chance to utter in over thirty minutes.

"Oh, I grew up here," said Oppenheimer cheerfully.

Kate turned to look at him. She'd missed that in skimming his file. "Really? Why did you choose to serve in Mendenhall?" It occurred to her as she said it that this might be a sore point for the constable but he just shrugged his massive shoulders.

"There were no vacancies when I finished at the academy. The *Brandon Sun* newspaper building is down on Rosser. My sister works there," he added with complete disregard to Kate's ability to follow his train of thought. He pointed toward a collection of buildings about a quarter of a mile away. Then he glanced at her, his brown eyes—really, the boy's best feature—

sparkling with mischief. "Don't worry, Chief, I like Mendenhall. Besides, I wouldn't want to live too close to my folks!"

Dizzy, she tried to remember if he was married, but that fact just couldn't surface past all the others he seemed determined to cram into her brain. Maybe she had subconsciously remembered that he came from Brandon and that was why she had picked him to drive her.

He kept talking and she let his words flow over her as she studied the town. They approached the bridge and she saw no evidence of flooding, but the river did seem high to her untutored eye. While there was traffic on First, one of the two main arteries into town, she saw barely any cars on the side streets. Then she noticed the railroad tracks crossing beneath the bridge and realized they were approaching from the industrial side of town.

Oppenheimer took the first exit off the bridge onto Assiniboine Avenue and suddenly the sun was in their eyes. They both automatically brought their visors down and Kate squinted to see past the glare. The river was to their right, about twenty feet below them. Oppenheimer, still pointing out landmarks, turned off again onto a smaller street and then slowed down almost to a stop as he edged past a City of Brandon roadblock that tried to keep traffic off what turned out to be a river access road. It probably led to a boat ramp. Someone had moved the barrier aside already.

Her heart started beating faster.

The smell of dust suddenly filled the car as the wheels raised a plume of the stuff in their wake. The dirt road plunged down to the river. The water lapped perilously close to the edge of the road. In some places, the road had been washed away, only to be temporarily fixed with gravel. Above them, the road they had just left rose while the river road descended. The resulting cliff wall sloped down toward the river, bearing witness to just how high the water had risen—at least four feet above its banks, she calculated as she studied the high water mark. Any business or home right on the river would have been swimming in flood water.

"There we go," said Oppenheimer with satisfaction, and she turned back to the road.

She saw the boat first, an RCMP cruiser anchored off the shore. One officer with rolled up shirtsleeves worked a winch and it was only when she followed the taut line of the cord that she saw the diver at the other end. Her heart slammed into her chest.

Were they recovering a body?

The diver seemed to be standing in the water up to his shoulders but that was impossible. The current was too fast. She peered closer and realized he was clinging to the trunk of a car that was wedged nose-first in the river. The water swirled around it, pushing the diver against the vehicle.

She wiped her palms on her uniform pants. Not a body. A car.

She could just make out the distinctive blue-and-white B.C. license plate against the glare of the car in the silver water.

"It's a miracle someone actually saw it," she murmured.

"It's a miracle it wasn't swept away," countered Oppenheimer.

The diver raised an arm in a signal and Kate finally noticed the tow truck and the police car parked farther down the road. A heavy metal cable led from the tow truck's winch to disappear in a broad curve into the water just below the car's trunk. That was why they had needed a diver, to hook the car up.

Besides the man operating the tow-truck winch, there were two uniforms at the scene, one of whom was standing next to the tow truck. The other one leaned casually against the Brandon Police Service car.

The tow-truck operator fiddled with the controls on the back of the truck and the cable took up the slack, growing taut. Immediately the diver pushed away from the car and was hauled back toward the cruiser.

"Oh crap, it's Carson," muttered Oppenheimer as they pulled up to the other two vehicles. All three men turned to stare at them.

"Say what?" asked Kate.

"Sorry, Chief," said Oppenheimer, but his gaze remained fixed on the uniform leaning against the car. The BPS cars were painted black and white, with a huge stalk of golden wheat slashing diagonally across both doors. Very distinctive, but Kate preferred Mendenhall's sober navy and white.

"Friend of yours?" she asked as he turned the engine off.

Oppenheimer laughed but there was no humor in it. "I knew him in high school," he said shortly.

Kate winced in sympathy. She had her own high-school ghosts, but at least she wasn't likely to meet any of them here.

The cold wind caught her as soon as she stepped out of the car and she tossed her cap onto the seat to keep it from blowing away. Oppenheimer clamped a hand over his to secure it. Kate breathed deeply of the smell of sweet hay and damp earth. Her gaze kept shying away from the car in the river.

The officer who'd been helping the tow-truck driver came to meet them.

"I'm Chief Constable Sanderson." He was a tall, thin man with prominent cheekbones and deep-set brown eyes. He put out a bony hand to shake hers and Kate had to work at not wincing. Skinny but strong.

"Chief Williams from Mendenhall," she said. "This is Constable Oppenheimer."

The two men nodded at each other but made no move to shake hands. Some of that friendly rivalry between the two police forces, or was it personal? Sanderson didn't introduce his constable. What had Oppenheimer called him? Carson.

"I believe DC Billings called ahead to let you know we were coming," said Kate, looking Sanderson in the eye.

He shrugged. "Message didn't get to us." Oppenheimer snorted but when Kate glanced at him, he was pointedly looking away.

"No harm done." She smiled tightly. The tow-truck operator, an older man wearing oil-streaked jeans and a windbreaker with Smitty Towing stenciled on the back, resumed pulling the car in.

"What's the story?" asked Sanderson over the sound of the winch. He, too, had removed his cap and the wind ruffled his dark hair. Silhouetted against the sky and lowering sun, with his wide shoulders and long arms, he put Kate in mind of a scarecrow out of a horror movie.

"We've been looking for this car," she told him. "We're investigating a missing child." At once, his expression changed from almost hostile to somber. He glanced at the car slowly emerging from the water and Kate could read his thoughts as clearly as though they were her own.

Heck, they *were* her own. She didn't want to see what was in the car, either.

Behind her, Oppenheimer's voice rose. "I don't give a damn what you think!"

Carson murmured a reply and even though she couldn't make out the words over the sound of the winch, she could hear the amusement in his voice.

Sanderson glanced over her head at the two men and Kate turned around, but before either one of them could speak, Sanderson's cell phone rang. He fished it out of his pants pocket.

"Sanderson." He moved away from the tow truck and stuck a finger in his other ear.

Kate watched Carson and Oppenheimer. They stood face-to-face, practically toe-to-toe, and their noses were almost touching. They had dropped their voices but clearly were still arguing.

Something told her they hadn't been friends in high school.

Sanderson turned back to the river, drawing Kate's eye to the RCMP cruiser. The diver had removed his flippers and climbed back on board. The captain reeled the anchor back in and talked on a phone at the same time, presumably to Sanderson.

"Yes, thanks, George. I'll let you know what we find." Sanderson flipped the phone shut just as the cruiser sounded its horn in goodbye.

"They have to respond to another call," explained Sanderson. The diver waved his flippers at them and Kate and Sanderson waved back. Then with a full-throated roar, the boat sped away.

Kate glanced over her shoulder. Oppenheimer's round face was getting red.

"Who called it in?" The sound of the motor boat faded, leaving only the grating whine of the tow truck's winch. The vehicle was close to shore now. A four-door blue sedan, streaked with silt. The two front windows were open, which meant the chances of finding any evidence inside the car were practically nil.

"City crew fixing the road," said Sanderson. Then the back wheels of the sedan were on the road and the tow-truck operator cut the power to the winch.

"—me!" said Carson in the sudden silence. "Your entire force is screwed up!" There was no longer any amusement in his voice.

"At least our chief isn't afraid of competing, which is more'n I can say for yours!"

"Oppenheimer!"

"Carson!"

The two men looked around, the anger slowly seeping out of them as they caught sight of Kate's and Sanderson's faces.

Kate glared at Oppenheimer and, with a curt movement of her chin, indicated that he should join her. Heat rose in her cheeks and she refused to look at Sanderson.

"Well?" said Sanderson, looking pointedly at the tow-truck operator.

The man smirked and climbed in behind the wheel and started up the truck. Kate and Sanderson backed out of the way while the driver slowly drove away, pulling the car diagonally onto the road.

Kate tried to recover her poise, but all she could hear were Carson's words echoing in her mind.

Her entire force was screwed up. And everyone knew it.

Finally the driver cut the engine and hopped out of the truck. There was no more time for self-pity.

They all stood staring at the vehicle, reluctant to approach it.

Its blue finish was covered in silt and drowned grasses. Water still sloshed out of the open windows, creating an instant mud puddle around the vehicle. Kate reminded herself to go slow when opening the doors, not to lose any evidence that might still be—miraculously—trapped inside.

She and Sanderson slowly approached the vehicle. Water filled the car to the open window and despite the cloudiness, she could tell that there were no bodies in it. She couldn't help herself. She looked at Sanderson and saw the same relief she was feeling on his face. They walked around the vehicle to see its front end. One of the front wheels was askew and the front grill and hood were crumpled.

She turned to look up at the cliff. She'd been so focused on the car in the river that she hadn't given any thought to how it got there.

Oppenheimer whistled slowly. The path of the car was clearly engraved in the cliff in two clear tracks that split into four tracks as the car had picked up speed and hit bushes and small trees on its way down. She couldn't tell if there was a guardrail where the car had gone off the road. There was a gouge in the dirt road where the nose of the car would have hit on its way down.

"Carson, give me a hand here," said Sanderson.

The constable ambled over to the drowned car, brushing by Oppenheimer as he passed him. Oppenheimer didn't move.

"Slowly," cautioned Kate as Carson put a hand on the driver's side door handle. Sanderson frowned at her and Carson pretended he hadn't heard, but he did lean against the door as it opened, controlling the flow of water out of the car. Despite his best efforts, his boots and the bottom of his pants got wet.

She needn't have worried. There was only silt, twigs and rocks in the water. Once all four doors were open and only a few inches of water remained in the bottom, they each took a door and leaned in to search. By the time they were done, all of them were wet and filthy, and satisfied that there was nothing in the car.

Kate straightened from her stoop at the front passenger door, swallowing a groan. She had been neglecting her back stretches. And her ankle was killing her. She looked at Sanderson.

"Glove box?" she asked. Her hands itched to open it and rummage through it but she didn't want to push her luck.

Sanderson walked around the car, his boots squishing in the mud and she stepped away to allow him access. Her boots were caked in mud, too, and heavy. The smell of pungent river water filled her nostrils and the wind chilled her through her wet pants.

Sanderson opened the glove box and more water spilled out.

She peered over his shoulder as he pulled out a soggy plastic sleeve, the kind insurance companies handed out for insurance and registration papers. He pulled open the folded plastic and peered at the papers.

"Made out to a Judy Hollingsworth. From B.C."

Kate nodded. They had examined everything in the car.

That left the trunk.

This was Brandon, Manitoba. Not Toronto, or Montreal. There wouldn't be a body in the trunk.

There wouldn't be.

Sanderson tucked the plastic sleeve into an evidence bag that he stashed in his breast pocket before turning to the tow-truck operator, who stood by the trunk, waiting. The smirk was gone, replaced by a grim look. He had a crowbar in hand. Sanderson took a deep breath.

"Open her up, Smitty."

Kate held her breath while Smitty slipped the end of the bar between the trunk lid and the car. With a quick jerk, the trunk popped open and they all leaned forward to peer inside.

A spare tire. A plastic container of engine oil floating in a foot of water.

No body.

No suitcases.

Kate didn't know if she was disappointed or relieved.

THE DRIVE BACK to Mendenhall was mercifully quiet. Oppenheimer seemed to have lost his good cheer and drove out of Brandon with his lips pressed into a tight line and his gaze glued to the road. That was just fine by her. She didn't want to discuss that little outburst back in Brandon. It was one thing to have problems at home, but to air them outside the station… that was bad form.

She would deal with that later. Right now, she had thinking to do.

Judy Hollingsworth's body could still be somewhere in the Assiniboine. So could Josh's. She took off two days ago, with suitcases but no son. Instead of heading east toward Winnipeg and the nonexistent grandmother—not to mention her buddy-buddy the dentist—she had gone west toward Brandon. Where had she been going?

She would have reached Brandon in daylight. How long had the car been in the river before someone noticed it? Twelve hours? Two?

And just *how* did the car end up in the river? Kate and Oppenheimer had checked the guardrail on the road above the river, but the car had left the road before the guardrail started. It had rolled down the slope, hit the access road and continued on into the river. No scratches or indents on the back bumper to indicate someone had rammed it. And she was pretty sure the damage to the front end came from hitting the access road, nothing more.

As for the suitcases, they could be floating down the Assiniboine, along with Judy Hollingsworth's body. But according to Mrs. Weissner, the suitcases went into the trunk, not the backseat.

So where were Judy Hollingsworth's suitcases?

And where was Josh? With his father?

She needed to find out who had custody of the boy.

The wind picked up as night fell over the prairies, rocking the patrol car. She felt a hint of moisture, tasted ozone—things she would never have noticed back east. But the climate was so dry here that any hint of moisture got attention.

She rubbed her face tiredly, willing her brain to work better.

Judy Hollingsworth might be dead, but sometime between leaving home and going over the cliff into the river, she had taken the suitcases out of the trunk.

Now all Kate had to do was figure out why.

When they returned to the station, Kate spotted McKell's car parked outside. She let Oppenheimer go inside to report. She didn't have the stomach to deal with McKell tonight.

It took all of fifteen minutes to drive down to Judge Byblow's house outside of town. It took considerably longer to convince him to sign the search warrant.

"You've got nothing," he said, standing in the tiled front entrance. His house was even bigger than Dr. Yawkichuk's in Winnipeg. The judge was a big man with a balding crewcut and stern gray eyes. At sixty-four he still had the wide shoulders of the linebacker he had once been. They had met at the banquet Mayor Dabbs had thrown to introduce her to the town, but this was the first time she had dealt with the judge for work. He did not invite her farther into the house. By the delicious smells emanating from the back of the house, she had interrupted dinner. That was never good.

"Your Honor—"

"Chief Williams, no one's reported the boy missing. His mother's missing, but by the neighbor's account, the boy wasn't with her when she left town. Even if she did go into the river, why do you need to get into her house?"

Kate squeezed the brim of her hat in both hands but kept her voice even.

"Too many discrepancies, Your Honor. The mother claimed the boy was in Winnipeg with his grandmother, but Mrs. Weissner, the neighbor, said the boy doesn't have a grandmother. Now, she may be elderly but she seems sharp to me."

"Damn right, she's sharp," said Judge Byblow. "She's my euchre partner every Tuesday night."

Kate allowed herself a small smile. "I expect you'd *rather* have her as your partner, Your Honor."

The judge grinned. Then he grew serious again. "Is that it?"

"No, sir," said Kate. "We checked the address she gave us for the grandmother. The caretaker never heard of her. The phone number she gave us for the grandmother is Judy Holl-ingsworth's cell phone—which she isn't answering, by the way. The owner of the house she's renting lives in Winnipeg and is a friend of hers. He says there was an abusive husband in the picture and that's why she used the false name."

The judge looked down at his leather slippers. From the back of the house came the sounds of cutlery being rattled. Someone was growing impatient.

The judge finally looked up. "What do you expect to find in that house, Chief?"

It was Kate's turn to look down. The familiar cold feeling was back in her stomach.

"I don't know, sir," she finally said, looking up at him. "All I know is that a little boy is missing and his mother has dis-appeared, too, and may be dead."

"You think you'll find the boy in the house, don't you?" His voice was gruff but low. Before she could say anything, he continued, "All right. You have your warrant."

She handed him the paperwork before he could change his mind.

"Thank you, Your Honor."

SHE MET TREPALLI and Boychuk at the Hollingsworth house. The locksmith was waiting for them in the laneway and they parked behind his van. She didn't want to rouse the entire neighborhood by going to the front door. Boychuk, being taller than any of them, reached over the fence and unlatched it from the inside. The moment they walked into the backyard, a motion-sensitive light clicked on over the deck. Kate glanced back over her shoulder. Sure enough, Mrs. Weissner's back light went on across the lane.

"Take a look around, in case she hid a spare key," she directed the two officers. No point in breaking in if they didn't have to. The locksmith, a small, thin man with a face like wrinkled paper, waited patiently by the back door with his tools.

As she had expected, Trepalli and Boychuk didn't find a hidden key. Judy Hollingsworth was too smart to keep a key in an obvious hiding place. Kate wasn't willing to waste any more time looking. She nodded to the locksmith and he stepped up to the door, his tools in hand.

In less than two minutes, he had the back door open. He stepped back to let Kate go in.

She took a deep breath and stepped over the threshold. She knew at once that the boy wasn't in the house. At least, he wasn't dead in the house. Dead bodies had an unmistakable smell and this house smelled vaguely lemony. As if someone had recently cleaned with a lemon-scented cleanser.

She flicked on the lights to reveal a kitchen painted a cheerful yellow, with a green-and-blue tile backsplash behind the sink and around the stove. A long counter separated the working kitchen from the small table and chairs directly in front of Kate. Green-and-blue linoleum tiles covered the floor. Everything chrome in the kitchen—toaster, kettle, fridge handles—gleamed in the light.

Kate glanced over her shoulder at the locksmith. "We need you to stick around. When we're done here, you'll have to lock up the place."

He nodded. "I'll be in the truck." He went down the stairs and headed for the laneway.

Kate looked at Trepalli and Boychuk. "You've got gloves?"

"Yes, ma'am," said Trepalli, pulling out a pair of latex gloves from his pants pockets. Boychuk nodded.

"Call out anything you find. Trepalli, you do the main floor. Boychuk, basement. I'll do the bedrooms."

Trepalli closed the door behind them and they all split up. Kate left the search warrant on the kitchen counter, where it would be seen as soon as someone walked in.

She took the carpeted stairs sideways, to avoid straining her ankle, but she was still sweating by the time she reached the upstairs. To her surprise, there were three bedrooms upstairs, as opposed to the two she had expected. The rooms were tiny, as was the bathroom.

She started with the bathroom but found nothing but some Lysol, a lemon-scented generic toilet cleaner and a scrub brush under the counter. The sliding mirror doors above the sink opened to reveal narrow shelves, all empty.

The bedroom at the front of the house clearly belonged to Judy Hollingsworth. It held a double bed, a tall dresser, a tiny closet and a straight-back chair by the window. Only one bed-side table, on the left side, with a lamp and a radio alarm clock on it. The alarm clock had those huge numbers that shone like beacons in the dark room before she turned the light on. Judy Hollingsworth wanted to know right away what the time was when she woke up.

Kate searched the bedroom but found nothing. All the dresser drawers were empty. The only thing in the bedside table was a box of tissues. The closet contained a dozen wire hangers and maybe five or six plastic ones. Nothing on the top shelf.

She pulled out her flashlight and examined the corners of the closet floor. Nothing. It had been swept clean.

Nothing under the bed, under the mattress, behind the dresser.

The boy's room was the same. A single bed instead of a double bed. A SpongeBob bedspread and matching sheets. Empty drawers.

When she came to the closet, she found that the space had been converted into shelves.

There was no chair in the boy's bedroom so she went back to the first one and brought the chair back to check on the top shelves. Nothing. Pushing the chair away, she crouched and examined the floor beneath the last shelf.

The kick plate on the right-hand side looked a little loose and when she felt it, it came out in her hand, revealing a gap in the drywall. She shone the light in the hole between the two studs. It was a perfect hiding place, now empty.

He carried his treasures around with him, in his backpack. Was this another hiding place or had some previous tenant created it?

The strain in her ankle forced her to stand up and she stifled a groan as her ankle complained bitterly.

The third bedroom was completely empty—not even a chest of drawers.

Kate returned to the main floor and found Trepalli in the other bathroom. He was squatting in front of the open doors of the vanity and looked up when she walked in.

"Anything?" she asked him.

"Nope." He looked glum. Then he reached inside the vanity and pulled out another bottle of Lysol. "Just this and a toilet brush."

"Did you check the kitchen yet?"

He nodded. "Nothing there, either. The refrigerator is empty except for a box of baking soda. It's been unplugged."

If she needed any more confirmation of the obvious, that was it. Judy Hollingsworth didn't plan to come back here. She left the house empty and clean, either because she was a fastidious woman or because she didn't want to leave a mess for her buddy the dentist.

Or, warned a little voice in the back of her mind, because she didn't want to leave any evidence of having murdered her own child. Kate shied away from the thought—it really didn't bear thinking about—but it was nevertheless a possibility.

Kate shook herself. She didn't like the woman but that didn't make her a killer. And nothing pointed in that direction. The kid played with the neighborhood kids. The bicycle in the backyard and the soccer ball and shoes in the front hall implied an involved mother who cared for her child.

Still, why did she lie about her boy being taken? Did she know who had taken him? Was that where she was heading when her car went into the river?

But if so, why would she waste half a day before taking off after him?

The basement stairs were off the kitchen and before she took them, she checked underneath the sink for garbage, even knowing that Trepalli would have told her if there had been any. Sure enough, the small garbage container was empty.

Boychuk wasn't in the basement and as she stood at the bottom of the stairs, she could see why. The basement was completely empty. Just a concrete floor with a couple of metal poles supporting a ceiling poorly lit by two bare bulbs. They swung a little from their cords, sending shadows back and forth against the walls. A whiff of fresh air made her check out the high windows, but they were all closed. At the back of the basement was another door. It was cracked open.

She was just about to push it open when it pulled away from her hand and Boychuk appeared out of the darkness. He jumped when he saw her, his flashlight almost dropping from his hands.

"Holy…!" He obviously thought twice about what he was going to say. "Geez, Chief—I lost a year off my life there!"

Kate grinned at having surprised him out of his terseness. Then she remembered that Boychuk had called McKell instead of calling B.C. Motor Vehicles, as she had ordered. Her grin faded. "What were you doing out there?"

He studied her face a moment longer than necessary and she held his gaze. Not much got past those sleepy eyes of his. He knew what she was thinking.

Finally he pulled the door open wider and shone the beam

of his flashlight on a set of rough wooden steps leading up to another door.

"I went out to check the yard and the garden shed," he said. "Gardening tools, soil, a kid's bicycle with training wheels, rakes… Nothing out of the ordinary. But." He stepped back and motioned her to follow him into the small space. Then he closed the door and shone his beam on another door that had been hidden while the door to the basement was open.

"I think it's a root cellar," he said.

Kate pulled the rough wooden door open and a waft of cold, dank air greeted her.

"The light's out," said Boychuk, shining his light into the small room. It couldn't be more than four feet by five or six and it was fitted with deep, rough shelves. Except for a couple of cans of peas and a half-empty bag of onions, there was nothing in the root cellar.

What a waste of time.

"All right," she said on a sigh. "Lock it up and meet me upstairs."

In the kitchen, she looked around, trying to figure out what was wrong. Well, besides the obvious.

Trepalli walked in, looking grumpy. He frowned when he saw her. "What's the matter?"

She stared at him. It was right there, at the edge of her awareness. Boychuk came up the stairs and closed the door to the basement.

"What's missing here?" she asked slowly.

Trepalli glanced around the kitchen then looked again, more slowly. He shook his head.

"Nothing."

"No landline," said Boychuk.

"Lots of people only use cell phones," said Trepalli.

True.

"We've got her number," said Kate, patting her notebook. "We can try to locate her using GPS."

Boychuk looked doubtful. "She's smart. She'll have turned it off," he said. "Besides, we'd have to convince the judge that it's important."

Kate shrugged. "He'll agree," she said with confidence.

Somewhere, almost within touch, was the solution to this mystery. It was only a matter of time.

"Are we done here?" asked Boychuk.

"Not quite," replied Kate cheerfully. "We have to check the garbage in the bins outside."

Boychuk and Trepalli exchanged a glance and then turned to look at her. "Oh, no." She waved them off. "I'm pulling rank."

There was nothing in Judy Hollingsworth's trash bins. Literally. They were empty. Kate stood in front of the bins, staring at them in silence. Yesterday she had stood less than a foot from them and hadn't smelled anything.

She glanced over at Mrs. Weissner's garbage bins. She had seen the old woman place a bag of garbage in the bin yesterday morning. The bin hadn't been empty.

Kate could feel the weight of Mrs. Weissner's attention on her. She looked up. The old lady was standing on her back porch, a thick shawl wrapped around her. Taking a deep breath, Kate opened the gate and headed toward her.

"Chief Williams," said Mrs. Weissner when Kate got close enough.

"Ma'am." Kate looked up at the old woman. "When does your garbage get picked up?"

"On Mondays," said Mrs. Weissner, with a hint of asperity in her voice. "Recyclables get picked up on Thursdays."

Today was Saturday. Judy Hollingsworth had cleaned the

house and packed her bags on Thursday. What had she done with the trash?

Kate eyed Mrs. Weissner cautiously, then decided on the direct approach. "I'd like permission to go through your garbage bins."

Mrs. Weissner's right eyebrow rose. "I beg your pardon?"

"I believe Mrs. Hollingsworth may have thrown her garbage in your bins. I have a search warrant to search her property but I don't have one to search yours. Which is why I'm asking for your permission." Although technically, she didn't need a search warrant for garbage left out in the open. Still, no need to point that out unless she had to.

Mrs. Weissner studied Kate's face for long seconds. Kate tried to look trustworthy. She didn't know what she'd do if the old woman refused.

"This is about the boy, isn't it?" asked Mrs. Weissner sharply.

Kate nodded slowly. "Yes, ma'am. And it's about Mrs. Hollingsworth. We need to find her to make sure she and her boy are safe."

The old woman nodded abruptly. "Very well," she said. "You may search my bins, but I want to be present."

Kate nodded her agreement. Without a word, she went up the stairs and offered the woman her elbow. Mrs. Weissner sniffed but allowed Kate to lead her through the dark backyard and out the gate to the garbage bins.

Kate nodded to the two men and they hauled the bins off their platform and removed the lids.

Mrs. Weissner looked inside one of the bins and then turned to Kate. "I only ever need one bin," she said. "I recycle, you know." She pointed at the bin next to Trepalli. "That garbage is not mine."

So they went through the bag, spreading the garbage out in the laneway in front of the platform. There was very little: two newspapers, banana peels, rags.

Nothing that could help Kate find the woman. She leaned back against her car to relieve the pressure on her ankle. A gust of cold wind blew a drop of rain against her cheek and threatened to scatter the garbage down the laneway. While Mrs. Weissner scolded Trepalli and Boychuk, Kate tried to sift through everything she had seen—or not seen—that night, to find a trail. But Judy Hollingsworth had left no bread crumbs that she could see.

"Excuse me."

Kate straightened up and looked around. The locksmith stood on the other side of the squad car.

"Shall I lock up now?"

Kate nodded. "Yes, and thank you for your help."

The locksmith shrugged. "I'll drop my bill off in the morning."

He went through the gate and left Kate staring at the fence surrounding Judy Hollingsworth's house. Why didn't Judy Hollingsworth have any bills? She didn't have a fireplace or a woodstove to burn things in. Most people didn't pack up their bills when they moved. And they weren't in the trash.

Maybe she didn't get her bills by mail. Maybe she paid everything electronically.

In reality, there was only one bill that interested her and it was the cell phone bill. She wanted to know who Judy Hollingsworth had been calling and who had called her.

There was only one problem. Even if she could convince Judge Byblow to issue her a warrant, it would take time.

She glanced at her watch. Eight-thirty. She could crawl under a bush and sleep for twelve hours, easy.

Rob McKell was still on the duty desk. He gruffly ordered Trepalli and Boychuk back on patrol, as if they had been caught slumming on the job.

Kate bit her tongue and went into her office to check for

messages. She was too tired and discouraged to deal with him now.

One voice mail from Jerry inviting her to dinner next week with his wife. One from Daisy reminding her that she had hand-to-hand the next day at two. And a note taped to her computer screen:

Cindy Robertson called from Toronto Police Services. Said Laird Macdonald is retired. Gave this phone number: 705-329-5524 in Orillia.

Finally!

She dialed the number, but hung up quickly before it could ring. It was later in Ontario. She'd have to wait until morning to call Macdonald.

Then she picked up the phone again and dialed Jerry's number in Winnipeg. Alma answered and they spent a few minutes chatting about her kids and grandkids.

"Did Jerry invite you to dinner?" asked Alma finally. She had a soft voice and was as short as Jerry was tall, with short blond hair and a round physique that always caught Kate by surprise, since Alma had more energy than most two people she knew.

"He did," said Kate. "I was calling partly to accept and partly to talk to Jerry. Is he around?"

"Just a sec." Alma set the receiver down and Kate could hear the sound of her feet tapping away on a hardwood floor. "Jerry!"

A moment later, an extension was picked up and Jerry's gruff voice sounded. "Hello?"

"Hi, Jerry. It's Kate."

"Okay," came Alma's voice. "I'll talk to you later, Kate." She hung up her extension, leaving Jerry and Kate alone.

"How's the ankle?" asked Jerry.

"Hurts like hell," said Kate. "But that's not why I'm calling." She proceeded to tell him what she wanted and after a few questions, Jerry promised to get back to her as soon as he learned anything.

Kate hung up and sighed. Now she could go home. In the morning, she'd call John Stendel.

ELEVEN

THERE WAS NO sign of Boiseman—Cusick—at home, but she went through the house out of old habit, making sure the doors were bolted and the windows latched.

She was now certain that Cusick was not involved in the disappearance of Josh Hollingsworth. He couldn't be. But somehow, his story had become woven into Josh's disappearance and Kate couldn't help feeling that unraveling one story would reveal the other.

The man might not be intentionally dangerous, but he was still delusional. Or at least fragile. She would do well to remember that, and not allow her sympathy for him to blind her.

She dreamt of Bobby MacAllister again, the same dream she'd had for years, but this time when he knelt on the backseat of the car to look back at her as it sped away, somehow, he was also Ellen Cusick. And in her dream Cusick came tearing out of the woods, screaming at her to stop the monster.

She woke up abruptly to daylight streaming through her venetian blinds. The bedside clock read 6:03—too early, but there was no going back to sleep now. She got up and put on her robe against the chill of the morning, then went to the kitchen and made coffee.

As she waited for the coffee to finish dripping, she stood in front of the window above her kitchen sink and looked out past her backyard to the town spreading out below.

It had rained overnight and the deck was still wet. The sun was just coming over the horizon. In a few minutes, it would flood her kitchen and breakfast nook with golden light.

Already the drops of rain clinging to the grass and bushes glittered like a field of diamonds.

She debated wiping down one of the deck chairs and having her coffee outside, but finally decided against it. Her muscles still felt weak from yesterday's run and her ankle ached.

She fixed herself a cup of coffee and sat down at the table. She propped her foot up on a chair and absently stirred sugar into her cup. Where was Boiseman this morning? Had he found a dry place to sleep?

Finally she shook herself and got up to get dressed. It was Sunday morning—she'd just drop in to the station for an hour.

ALBERTSON WAS ON the desk. He looked up as Kate walked in.

"Mornin', Chief."

"Good morning, Albertson."

Albertson was always clean-shaven and kept his gray hair neatly trimmed. He had a quiet sense of humor and a perpetual grin that put people at ease. About a month earlier, she'd learned what a good influence he was on the younger members when they were called out to a bad accident on the highway just outside of town. She'd watched him take charge of the scene and assign tasks to the younger patrol officers until the ambulance arrived. His quiet authority had calmed everyone on the scene and ensured the injured were taken care of. She liked him.

O'Hara came out of the lunchroom carrying a cup of steaming coffee in one hand and a file folder in the other. He nodded at Kate in passing and went over to a desk. He hadn't said more than ten words to her in the whole time she'd been on the force. But then he barely spoke to anyone, as far as she could tell. She wondered what he did when he visited his father in the care home. Did they just sit in silence for the entire visit?

"Anything happen overnight?" she asked Albertson as she

pulled the duty log around to scan the overnight entries. She looked up in surprise. "*Three* fights?"

"I guess a few of the locals took exception to the outside cops hitting on our girls." He seemed to be suppressing a grin.

Kate frowned. She didn't see what was so funny. "You mean *my* men were involved…?"

Albertson shook his head. "No, ma'am. Civilians." He nodded toward the cells. "Back there."

Kate's eyebrows rose. "Sleeping it off?" In the two months she had been here, the only "guests" they'd had in the cells were a couple of drunks who were trying to stagger home after a bender. They'd slept it off in the cells and were released in the morning.

"No, ma'am," said Albertson. "Assaulting a peace officer." He glanced at his computer screen. "It was Harriman who charged them. Two local guys got pissed off when a couple of girls wouldn't leave with them and jumped the visiting cops. When Harriman and Boychuk tried to stop them, they swung at them."

"Anyone hurt?"

"Bruises only."

"Anything else?"

"That's pretty much it," said Albertson. "The other two fights were handled on-site. There was one impaired driving charge, but the woman was coming back from a barbecue, not the dance."

Kate nodded and finished going through the log. Albertson was right. Aside from the incidents he'd described, there'd been a fender bender on the corner of Main and Ortona, and a noise complaint at a house party. All in all, fairly quiet. There were some distinct advantages to having a town full of visiting cops.

"Good." She went into the break room where the smell of freshly brewed coffee greeted her. She silently blessed whoever had put on a fresh pot, poured herself a cup and headed for her office. Her ankle definitely felt better, but that could be the extra-strength Tylenol.

On impulse, she checked the cell area. It was rank with the stink of old sweat and vomit. Two men, about twenty years old, were in separate cells, sprawled out over the metal framework of the cots.

She smiled. Piss off a cop in Mendenhall and you slept without a mattress.

She closed the door to her office and dialed the phone number in Orillia. It was about nine o'clock in Ontario. Laird Macdonald should be up.

The phone was picked up after three rings.

"Hello?" said a child's voice.

Oh, great.

"Hello," said Kate. "May I speak with Laird Macdonald?"

"Hello?" said the child again.

Kate closed her eyes and tried again. "Is your mother or father there?"

"Mommy is in the garden."

"Okay," said Kate patiently. "Can you go get her?"

The phone on the other end dropped with a crash that jarred her eardrums. The sound of running feet told her that the kid had taken off.

After a minute of waiting, it became clear the kid had gotten distracted or hadn't understood the request in the first place. Kate was just about to hang up when she heard a heavier tread coming closer to the phone at the other end.

"Hello?" she said when someone picked up the phone.

"Hello?" came a man's voice. He sounded surprised.

Kate held on to her patience with great fortitude. "May I speak to Mr. Laird Macdonald, please?"

"Speaking," said the man. "How long have you been waiting there?"

"Long enough," said Kate crisply. "A child answered the phone and went off to fetch his or her mother, I thought."

"Ah. That would be my granddaughter Lizzy. I'm afraid she forgot all about you. How can I help you?" His voice was a little rough, as if he'd smoked all his life, or enjoyed drinking scotch on a daily basis.

"Toronto gave me your phone number," began Kate. "Are you the Laird Macdonald who was on the Mississauga police force?"

Macdonald considered a moment before answering. "I am, indeed. And who would you be?" There was an edge to his voice.

"Sorry," she apologized. "My name is Kate Williams. I'm the chief of police in Mendenhall, in Manitoba."

"Right," said Macdonald. "What can I do for you, Chief?" His voice was still cautious, but it had lost its wariness.

"Detective Macdonald—"

"It's Mister now," interrupted Macdonald. "I've been retired for nearly ten years."

"Mr. Macdonald," Kate corrected. "I want to know about a case you worked in 1989. About a murdered child."

There was a long silence. "I don't like remembering those cases," he said finally. "Especially now that I have grandchildren."

Kate found herself nodding. "I understand, sir. But the 1989 case has a bearing on another missing child today. Your information may be useful."

He sighed. "All right. Go ahead and ruin my day."

Kate squelched a pang of guilt. "The kid's name was Ellen Cusick. She was four years old. She was taken from her home by a man named Derek Jackson."

"Oh, yes," said Macdonald, his voice low. "I remember that one. She was the sweetest-looking little thing. Big brown eyes." He sighed and there was a world of misery in the sound. "The guy raped and killed her, left her body in a ditch off the 401 near Kingston."

Kate's chest felt tight and she flushed with heat. She stood up, putting her weight on her good foot, and took a deep breath. She tried to force herself to relax.

"I thought the mother was going to die, too, when we told her," continued Macdonald.

The mother. She hadn't been in the report.

"You never caught the guy?"

"No," he said curtly. Then he sighed again. "No, we didn't. I heard that he was murdered in Vancouver a couple of years later."

Kate took note of the information even though it wasn't what she was after. She finally sat down again and swung her throbbing ankle up on top of the cushion over the bottom drawer.

"What about the father?" she asked. "James Cusick? There's an old warrant out on him. He was wanted for questioning in the death of his daughter."

"Cusick?" Macdonald paused as though trying to remember. "Can't be sure without my notes, of course, but I think we wanted to question him about Jackson. I think they played softball together and got friendly."

"Did you think he was involved in his daughter's murder?" Kate's hand clenched around the telephone. *Please say no,* she silently prayed.

"No," said Macdonald. "There was no doubt about it. The kid disappeared when Cusick and his wife went out to dinner and left Jackson to babysit." He shifted at the other end of the line and Kate imagined he had found himself a seat, too. "They came home and found Jackson gone with the girl."

"Then what?"

"The girl's body was found a couple of days later. The mother went crazy, accused Cusick of bringing that monster into their lives. Next thing she knew, Cusick jumped in his car and drove off. That's the last she ever saw of him. Poor woman. She lost her daughter and her husband. What's the case you're working on?"

She was hesitant to discuss a case with a stranger, but he'd helped her out with information. The least she could do was answer his question. So she told him.

Macdonald listened and then grunted.

"I often wondered what'd happened to Cusick," he said. "The man was half off his rocker with grief. And then, when I heard that Jackson had been murdered…"

"Is there any reason to suspect Mr. Cusick?" asked Kate.

"No. At least none that I know of. But whoever killed Jackson knew he was a pedophile. They cut off the offending part, if you know what I mean, and let him bleed to death."

A cold shiver raised goose bumps on Kate's arms.

"Could have been the mother," she suggested.

"No. I checked. She was at home in Ontario when Jackson died."

"Is she still there?" asked Kate.

"Not sure." She could hear the shrug in his voice.

After a few more questions, Kate let the man get back to his grandchild and hung up. She leaned back in her chair and closed her stinging eyes, breathing deeply.

Her breakfast cereal was trying to claw its way back up.

WHEN SHE CAME out of her office two hours later, Albertson was standing in the hallway in front of the duty desk with a stranger dressed in a navy track suit. They were studying one of the lists that plastered the wall, which detailed who was competing when, and where. There was also a huge map of Mendenhall, in color, taken from the visitor guide and blown up to thirty times its normal size, showing all the competition venues.

"Ah, Chief," said Albertson as she joined them. "This is Bert Langdon, the DC in Winnipeg."

Langdon gave her hand a firm shake then released it. His hands were wide and hard. He was a stocky man, only a few inches taller than her five foot three, with red hair going gray and eyes the color of copper. He studied her intently.

"We were just checking the list," continued Albertson. "Turns out you and DC Langdon are both competing in the hand-to-hand this afternoon."

She stared at Albertson blankly for a split second, then almost groaned.

The hand-to-hand combat competition. She had forgotten.

Now she understood why Langdon was looking at her that way.

He appeared hard and fit in his track suit, with not an ounce of fat anywhere on him. He probably practiced hand-to-hand every bloody day of his life.

"Looking forward to it, Chief," said Langdon politely.

Kate raised an eyebrow. "DC Langdon, please don't tell me you came here to check out the competition."

Langdon smiled, and suddenly he looked more like a man and less like a statue.

"No, ma'am," he said. "I'm following up on a call you made to Chief Stendel this morning."

Well. Stendel was efficient.

"What do you have for me?" she asked.

Langdon pulled a notebook out of his track suit jacket pocket and flipped to a page near the end. Out of the corner of her eye, Kate noticed that Albertson had discreetly resumed his post behind the duty desk. Good man, that.

Langdon found the right spot, then looked at her. When he saw he had her attention, he flicked a glance at Albertson then eyed her with a question in those copper-penny eyes.

She nodded imperceptibly and her estimation of the man

went up. She didn't mind if Albertson overheard the discussion, but she appreciated Langdon's discretion.

"Chief Stendel sent an officer to Dr. Horowitz's home. Dr. Horowitz confirms that Mrs. Hollingsworth works for her as a receptionist, but says the woman didn't report for work on Friday and didn't call in. The officer accompanied Dr. Horowitz to the office where she pulled the personnel file for Mrs. Hollingsworth. The only contact information is a cell number." He rattled off the same number Kate already had. "No next of kin listed in her personal information." He looked up at Kate. "The chief wanted you to know that there were no previous employers listed, either."

Kate nodded. Not surprising. Judy Hollingsworth didn't need to list previous employers. Her buddy George Yawkichuk, the dentist, had vouched for her.

"What about at Horowitz's home?" she asked. "Was there a child with her?"

Langdon read through his notes quickly and stopped. "Here it is. No, no children. Dr. Horowitz lives alone in a downtown loft. The officer saw no children and when he asked her about Mrs. Hollingsworth's child, she looked surprised. She allegedly hadn't known Mrs. Hollingsworth had a child."

Kate sighed softly. She had hoped that the boy would be with the orthodontist.

"And the address she gave for the grandmother...?"

Langdon kept reading. "That condo belongs to Dr. Horowitz's mother," he explained. Then he looked up. "The good doctor had Mrs. Hollingsworth send flowers there once a week."

That explained how Judy Hollingsworth was able to jot down the address so quickly.

The screen door opened and Charlotte walked in, followed by Trepalli. It was a warm day for September and Charlotte was wearing a short-sleeved, thin cotton dress and sandals.

Her bare legs were tanned and muscular. Trepalli had changed into a short-sleeved navy T-shirt that featured some band on it, blue jeans and loafers.

They looked perfect together.

Langdon eyed Charlotte appreciatively and smiled. From her ponytail to her coral toenails, Charlotte looked like every man's idea of the girl next door. She smiled back at him. Behind her, Trepalli bristled.

"Hello, Charlotte," said Langdon. "You're looking particularly fine this morning."

Trepalli grunted but Langdon and Charlotte ignored him. She walked over to the DC and kissed his cheek.

"Hello, Bert. It's good to see you, too."

Trepalli looked as if he had swallowed a burr. Before he could explode, Kate stepped forward. "DC Langdon, this is Constable Trepalli, our newest officer."

Langdon shook hands with Trepalli. "Nice to meet you." Then he released his hand and turned to Kate. "If you don't need anything else, Chief Williams, I'd like to go for my run."

"I appreciate your help, DC Langdon."

"My pleasure," he said. Then he grinned. "See you this afternoon." He gave Charlotte a little wave and left.

Kate looked at the young woman. "Can you not get enough of this place, Charlotte?"

She grinned unrepentantly. "We knew we'd find you here," she said. "We wanted to see how you're doing."

At the duty desk, Albertson's eyebrows rose as he glanced from Trepalli to Charlotte and back again.

Kate stifled a sigh. She *really* didn't want to know.

She turned a stern eye on Trepalli. "Shouldn't you be sleeping, Constable?"

"Yes, ma'am, I will in a bit." He took a deep breath. "I wondered if there was any news on Josh?"

Josh. She realized then that she had been avoiding using

Josh Hollingsworth's name, referring to him as the kid, or Judy Hollingsworth's son. It was a defense mechanism, of course. If she didn't name him he wasn't real. And if he wasn't real, he wouldn't haunt her dreams when they eventually found his body.

The coffee turned to acid in her stomach.

The door opened again to let in Voigt and Tattersall.

"Morning, Chief," said Tattersall, removing his cap and scraping his boots on the rug before going into the lunchroom.

You could always tell the married ones.

Voigt walked into the duty room and began to write in the duty book. "Fender bender at the track-and-field parking lot," he explained to the room in general. "Third one since yesterday."

Kate glanced at the clock on the duty room wall. Almost nine-thirty. Pretty soon, the business of the day would pick up and her people would be too busy for a meeting. It was time to fill them in.

"Tattersall!" she called.

He stuck his head out of the lunchroom. "Ma'am?"

"Come out here," she ordered. "I want to talk to everyone at the same time."

Voigt put his pen down, his face alight with curiosity and Charlotte leaned on the duty desk. Albertson swiveled in his chair to face her.

Kate ducked into her office and came back to the duty room with Josh Hollingsworth's red shoes. They had found nothing of any value on them, not even fingerprints on the rubber soles.

"You all know about Mr. Boiseman allegedly witnessing a child's abduction, right?" They should all have read the duty log from the days they were off duty.

"The crazy old guy with the shoe?" asked Voigt, nodding at the shoe in her hand. He took his cap off and scratched his bald head. Kate suspected he shaved it.

"Not so crazy, maybe." She filled them in on what she and Trepalli had found out about the boy, where he went to school, who his mother was.

"The thing is, the mother lied to us about the kid's where-abouts," said Kate.

"And now she's missing, too," added Trepalli.

"Wait a minute," said Albertson, pulling the duty log toward him. He scanned the previous pages. "Wasn't a Judy Hollings-worth's car found…?"

Kate nodded. "In the river at Brandon." She looked around at the group. "Mrs. Hollingsworth was *not* found in the car, nor was the luggage she had placed in the trunk."

"What about the old man?" asked Tattersall, rubbing the back of his neck. "What's his connection to the Hollings-worths?"

"As far as we know, the only connection is that he found the kid's shoe." She looked at Trepalli. "His name is James Cusick. He was wanted for questioning in the abduction and murder of his daughter, back in 1989." She quickly sketched in the details of the girl's murder as she had learned them from Macdonald.

Trepalli looked stunned. "Why is he wanted?"

She shrugged. "It's a closed case. He was never a suspect and no one is looking for him anymore. The pedophile, a—" she searched her memory for a few seconds before pulling out the name "—a Derek Jackson, was murdered in Vancouver a couple of years later."

"So…" Albertson looked confused.

"So now what?" demanded Trepalli. "We don't need to chase after an old man destroyed by grief. Hasn't he been through enough?"

Albertson frowned at Trepalli but Kate waved him off. She understood Trepalli's reaction.

"What we do now is keep an eye open for Mr. Cusick," she said firmly. "He may be grief-stricken but he's also a material witness to the boy's disappearance. He's still in the area, you can be sure of that."

"And when we find him?" asked Trepalli, his jaw clenched in a stubborn line that was becoming all too familiar to her.

"Then we bring him in for questioning," said Kate.

There were a few more questions and then Albertson had to answer a call. Voigt and Tattersall went back to patrol duty.

Kate eyed Trepalli, then decided that what the heck, he was here.

"Come into my office, Trepalli."

Trepalli glanced at Charlotte.

"I'm going to the farmer's market," she said.

He nodded and followed Kate into her office.

"Sit." She indicated one of the visitors' chairs and settled into her chair behind the desk.

"Do you know anybody on the BPS?"

He hesitated. "I know a few people," he said cautiously.

"I want to keep an eye on their investigation of Mrs. Hollingsworth's car. Can one of your connections keep you posted?"

He hesitated again but this time a blush crept up his neck and cheeks. "The chief's secretary might be willing to let me know what's going on."

To hide her grin, Kate pretended to look for something amid the papers on her desk. "Can you call her today?" Just for the hell of it she added, looking up, "If I promise not to tell Charlotte?"

A shamefaced grin split the wall of red.

"I'll see what I can do."

"Thank you, Constable."

TWELVE

THE HIGH-SCHOOL gym bleachers were full to cracking, mostly with out-of-town police officers come to watch the hand-to-hand competition.

And it was loud. There were at least two hundred people in the gym, between spectators, competitors and volunteers. There were shouts from the spectators as their favorites competed, shouts from the referees calling out names, shouts from the competitors as they landed on the mats.

Kate tried not to breathe through her nose until she got used to the smell. Why did gyms always smell like something the cat dragged in and didn't have the heart to eat?

The gym floor itself was broken up into four separate areas. Having seen the list of competitors, Kate could understand why. There were at least fifty competitors registered for this event. At three minutes allotted for each set of two competitors, it would take almost two hours just for the preliminary round. And the gym was needed at four o'clock for the karate finals.

She sat on one of the benches on the sidelines, watching the mixed competition. The wood was cold on the back of her thighs. She had finally decided on shorts, rather than sweat pants, to give her opponents as little cloth as possible to grab on to. Like most of the other competitors, she wore a tank top, although she spotted a few shirtless men sitting on the sidelines.

When she first started competing in the cop games, there were so few women that they'd had to compete against the men. Then, as more and more women became cops and firefighters, the games were divided along gender lines. It was still that way, except in the Senior Division, in which she was competing. Not many women lasted as long as she did.

There now. Wasn't that a comfort?

The timekeeper's harsh whistle brought her back to her situation. It was two-thirty and already half of the competitors had met on the mats. The object of the match was to pin your opponent facedown and handcuff their hands behind their back. Some of the competitors had accomplished this well short of the three-minute time limit, but some were so evenly matched that a referee had to decide the winner.

The only rule was that you were not to physically damage your opponent. Aside from that, you could use any method to pin him or her down. And there were points for style.

In spite of the presence of maybe a dozen female competitors, there was a definite tang of testosterone in the air.

Someone plunked down on the bench next to her and Kate shifted over to give the person more space.

"So," said Bert Langdon over the sound of whistles, shouts and grunts. "How's our competition?"

Kate looked around at the Winnipeg DC and waggled her eyebrows. "Looks like they're just about done with the forty-to-forty-nine age group. We should be coming up soon. Only sixteen of us in the fifty-and-over age category."

Langdon nodded as the whistle blew again. He had changed from sweats to shorts and tank top, like her, only his matched. His red hair looked even grayer under the gym's high fluorescent lights. He glanced sideways at her. "Nervous?"

Kate opened her eyes wide. "Me? Nervous? What's to be nervous about?"

Langdon laughed. He leaned in closer so he wouldn't have to shout. "The chief called again. He sent a patrol car to Dr. Yawkichuk's house but the only children there were two little girls, aged eight and seven. The wife said she knows nothing about Josh Hollingsworth."

Uh-oh. The good dentist was going to have to do some fast talking to explain this one. She hadn't really thought the kid would be with the dentist's family, but it was a loose thread that she'd wanted tied up.

"Thanks again," she said. "I owe you."

"I'm just the messenger," said Langdon cheerfully.

She nodded. If this kept up, she was going to have to revise her opinion of Stendel, Langdon's boss. Apparently, despite his predilection for Sweet Young Things, the Winnipeg chief of police was good at his job.

"Langdon and Seville, Mat Three," came over the loudspeaker and Langdon stood up.

"Wish me luck," he said and took off at a run toward the ref with his hand up.

"Luck," murmured Kate. As if he'd need it.

"Williams and Turner, Mat Four."

Kate walked over to the far mat. No running for her, thank you very much. All she needed was to twist her ankle again. She'd taken off the bandage in the locker room and she made a conscious effort not to limp. No sense alerting your opponent to a potential weakness.

Turner turned out to be a big man with a bald head that gleamed under the fluorescent lights. He was at least six foot one, with shoulders wide enough to look padded and arms long enough to touch either gym wall if he stretched them out. Or so it seemed to her.

Even the referee seemed nonplussed. He glanced down at Kate then at his clipboard. "You're Williams?"

She nodded.

He then looked up at Turner, who grinned down at Kate.

"The match seems a little uneven," said the referee doubtfully.

"I know," said Kate. "But I promise I'll be gentle."

Turner's grin widened. He had a gold eyetooth. The referee

shrugged and handed them each a sash that tied with Velcro. When they were on, he slipped a pair of handcuffs into the back of the sash so that only one cuff hung outside. The metal felt cold through her thin tank top.

Finally the referee stepped off the mat. "Ready?"

At their nods, he blew his whistle and, without giving herself a chance to think, Kate launched herself headfirst at Turner's midriff, catching him by surprise.

He barely had time to put out those freakishly long arms before the breath expelled from his lungs in a loud whoosh and he folded over. Kate kicked his feet out from under him and jumped onto his back when he landed, pulling her handcuffs out of her sash at the same time. Before he could flip over, she slapped the cuffs on him.

Then she stood up and the referee punched the stopwatch.

"Twenty seconds!" he cried. He gave Kate the key to the handcuff and she freed Turner. He took his time standing up and when he finally looked at her, there was a dazed look in his eye.

"Turner, you're eliminated. Williams, back to the bench. Your name will be called for the semifinal round."

Turner stuck his hand out and Kate shook it. Then he turned and walked away, his color high.

The bigger they are, thought Kate smugly. Then she caught herself. *Better watch it, Williams. They're not all going to be that easy.*

At least she hadn't hurt her ankle.

Langdon found her a moment later and she congratulated him on his win.

"Congratulations yourself," he said. "That's quite the cheering section you've got," he said, sitting down next to her.

She looked at him in surprise.

He nodded at the bleacher end of the gym. "Didn't you hear them? They were all calling your name during your round."

Kate peered at the crowd on the bleachers, looking for familiar faces, and finally picked out Charlotte and Trepalli. He was wearing a track suit, not the jeans and T-shirt he'd been in earlier. Trepalli looked up, as if sensing he was being watched, and saw her. He grinned widely and gave her a thumbs-up. Charlotte waved wildly at her.

Kate gave them a small wave and looked away, suddenly embarrassed. Then her gaze caught on a uniform by the door to the gym. Two uniforms.

She squinted and finally realized that it was Tattersall and Olinchuk.

Who was minding the store?

She looked away from her people and stared at the floor. Not one of her people signed up for these damned competitions. Not one. If it was meant as a snub to her, what were they doing here?

She just didn't get it.

Her next competitor was Vikram Kolum, a cop from Brandon. He was a tall, lean man with gray threading through his glossy black hair, brilliant black eyes and a weathered brown face. He bowed gravely at Kate.

Kate acknowledged his courtesy with a nod. He reminded her of Jerry Wolsynuk. She chased the stray thought away— she couldn't afford the distraction.

The referee, a tall woman who Kate vaguely remembered from previous cop games, put the sash on them and slipped the handcuffs in, then stepped back.

As soon as the referee blew the whistle, Kolum moved. For a split second, he was nothing but a blur of arms and legs, and then Kate was falling. She turned and slapped the mat to absorb the impact. She instinctively swept her legs out as she fell and caught Kolum off balance. He fell to his knees.

But he used his fall to throw himself on her, landing with his full weight on her side, trapping her arm beneath his body.

Kate stopped struggling at once. He was as trapped as she was. He couldn't slap the cuffs on her without shifting to reach her hand.

Her cheek pressed against the vinyl mat, she prepared her move. She still had her left arm free but couldn't use it to advantage right now.

"One minute gone," said the referee.

Kate felt Kolum shift and waited until his weight eased off her. Then she twisted beneath him, leveraged her arm up until she could grasp his shoulder and shove him off her. She scrambled to her feet with more speed than dignity, grunting as she put weight on her abused ankle.

Kolum had landed on his back. She feinted and he raised a leg to fend off her anticipated attack. Instead, she stepped in close, placed her foot against his slightly raised hip and shoved.

Off balance, he flipped over. Immediately he tried to raise himself with his arms but she landed on his butt with all her weight, grabbed his right arm and twisted it up his back, a position that hurt like hell and could easily pop his shoulder out of its socket. He stopped moving. Throughout the whole maneuver, he made no sound.

She leaned in on the arm, clamped her hand on his elbow to keep it still and fished her cuffs out with her free hand.

A moment later, she stood up and the referee called out, "Two minutes twenty-three seconds!" Then she handed Kate the keys and she freed Kolum.

"Kolum is eliminated," announced the referee. "Williams moves on to the next round."

Vikram Kolum bowed at Kate and she returned to the bench. She was breathing hard and felt mightily disheveled and her ribs ached from being landed on and her ankle was on fire.

Besides that, she felt great.

However, she was none too sure she'd survive another fight.

The ranks of contestants were thinning out and with each elimination, the sound level in the gym seemed to go up. That and the smell were starting to make her dizzy.

She stole a glance at the bleachers and there was Jerry Wolsynuk, resplendent in his dress uniform. He was standing in front of Trepalli and Charlotte. A couple of people on the seats above craned to see around Jerry but he didn't seem to notice them.

"I'm getting too old for this," said Langdon as he sat down next to her. His cheeks were flushed and there was a mat burn on his chin.

"Tough?"

"She just about whupped me." There was a note of outrage in his voice.

Kate grinned. "Keeps you humble."

He gave her a look that would have curdled milk. "Your bun is undone."

Kate laughed outright and set about tucking her hair back in. After this round, they would be down to four semifinalists. She surreptitiously tested her ankle and winced as sharp pain shot up her leg. Not good.

The last two contestants finished and came to sit on the bench next to theirs. There was one woman and one man. Neither one seemed to be breathing hard.

The woman was a little taller than Kate but walked as if her feet wouldn't leave an imprint in sand. She wore loose white cotton trousers and a tight white tank top that revealed a muscled torso and arms. She had short spiky gray hair and a lean, unsmiling face. As if sensing Kate's attention, she looked around and met Kate's gaze. Kate thought about smiling but nothing in that closed face invited a smile, so she nodded instead. The woman nodded back and looked away.

The man sat a few feet away from her. He was almost six feet tall and had to weigh at least 210 pounds, none of which was fat. He was either completely bald or shaved his head and he wore a loose white muscle shirt and black bicycle shorts that revealed a muscled butt and legs. Sweat glistened on shoulders big enough to be a tailor's nightmare. There didn't seem to be any hair on him anywhere except for his eyebrows.

There was no way she could topple that one.

"Is it too late to back out?" whispered Langdon. She turned to look at him but he was staring at the other two.

The sound level in the gymnasium suddenly died down as two referees stepped away from the officials table and headed for separate mats.

"Williams and Langdon," called one referee.

"Tuchman and Jones," called the other.

Kate and Langdon glanced at each other and stood up at the same time.

Shoot.

They reached the mat and accepted their respective sashes from the referee. As Kate secured hers, she looked up at Langdon.

"How's my bun?"

He gave his sash a final tug and examined her critically. "It'll do."

The referee slipped the cuffs into Kate's sash, then Langdon's and stepped back.

"Good luck," said Kate.

"Same," he replied.

Then the whistle blew.

Kate whipped sideways as Langdon rushed her, pivoting on her good heel, but she couldn't avoid his outstretched arm. Before he could reel her in, she ducked and slipped out of his grasp.

He moved pretty fast for a stocky guy.

They faced each other, five feet apart, while on the mat behind her, the woman shouted something that sounded like,

"Ha-ee!" Then something big landed with a loud thump. The spectators roared with approval.

Langdon edged closer, recapturing her attention. There were several ways she could get him on the mat, if she didn't mind hurting him. But this was a demonstration of skill and strength. Dirty tricks would get her disqualified.

She sensed him tensing for a move and pushed off her good foot to launch herself at him. He aborted whatever movement he'd been about to make and began to turn into her charge.

Too late, she saw his leg sweep out toward her bad ankle just as she grabbed his shirt. Then his foot connected with her ankle and pain stabbed through her entire body.

She instinctively dropped to the mat to avoid his hold. The pain called out for her attention but she ignored it, slapping the mat as she landed. For good measure, she cried out in pain—which wasn't much of an act. Langdon hesitated halfway to a crouch and with a grin, Kate swept his feet out from under him.

He landed hard on one hip but jumped to his feet, beating Kate to the vertical by a second—long enough for him to be in the perfect position to take her down again with a hip check and a foot hooking her bad ankle.

This time, the shout of pain was ripped from her, but Langdon didn't fall for it. As she went down, he landed on her, flipped her onto her stomach and slapped the cuffs on her.

"Two minutes, thirty-six seconds," called the referee.

Kate lay still on the mat, trying not to cry from the pain of her ankle. Langdon unlocked the cuffs then waited for her to get up but she took her time, first rolling over onto her good side and slowly getting up.

"Williams and Tuchman are eliminated," called the official. "Langdon and Jones move on to the final round."

Kate kept her weight on her good ankle but her limp was pronounced as she headed for the change rooms.

Langdon followed her, grinning.

"You can drop the act," he said. "No one's buying it."

Just then, Trepalli and Charlotte came hurrying up and began fussing over her.

Kate shooed them off and turned to Langdon, who was now staring at her in concern.

"Are you really hurt?" he asked.

"She certainly is," said Charlotte stiffly. "And you didn't help any, Bert."

Kate shrugged uncomfortably. "It wasn't you. It happened a few days ago."

Langdon looked at her, then at Trepalli, then back to her, his expression stern. "Then why were you competing?" he asked. "You could have done some serious harm." He frowned at her and she wondered if he had kids.

She shrugged again. "Don't worry about me," she said. "Worry about him." She nodded at the big man waiting patiently on the competitors' bench. Presumably he was Jones. She'd been too busy to follow their match once she and Langdon got started.

Langdon opened his mouth to speak then closed it. Then he nodded and ran back to the bench.

Charlotte came up beside her and wrapped an arm around her waist. Trepalli did the same on the other side. Out of the corner of her eye, she noticed Olinchuk and Tattersall leaving the gym. Where was Jerry?

"Marco competed in the swim competition this afternoon," said Charlotte suddenly.

"What?" said Kate, startled.

"Charlotte," said Trepalli warningly.

"And he came in fourth out of fifteen!" added Charlotte proudly.

Kate looked from Charlotte's grinning face to Trepalli's embarrassed one.

"But the deadline for registration…"

Charlotte shrugged. "Daisy made an exception."

"I asked you not to say anything," said Trepalli stiffly.

Charlotte grinned. "Swimming was the only competition Daisy would allow him to sign up for. She said it fit because he was all wet."

"Thanks, Charlotte," muttered Trepalli, giving her a look that promised retribution.

Charlotte looked unrepentant. "I'm pretty sure you can't come in here," she said.

Trepalli looked up at the sign that read GIRLS above the door and stepped back as if from the brink of a pit. Kate grinned, despite the pain. Trepalli had competed.

She wasn't alone.

Behind Trepalli, she finally spotted Jerry waiting patiently at the end of the bleachers. When he saw he had her attention, he pointed at her, then at himself, then at his mouth. He wanted to talk to her.

She held up her hand and spread her fingers out to indicate five minutes and he nodded. At that moment the Emergency Medical Technician, the same one who had bandaged her up yesterday, bulled his way through the people around her.

"It'll take more than five minutes," he said grimly. "And if you don't start behaving, I'm going to take you to Emergency for X-rays." He scowled at her. "It's just a stupid competition. I don't see what's so important that you'd risk a permanent injury."

He could grump at her all he liked. She didn't care. Trepalli had competed in the games.

Without waiting for an answer, the med tech announced, "Man in the room!" at the door to the girls' changing room and then led her inside.

WHEN SHE CAME back out dressed in her uniform, the med tech was gone, no doubt to share his wisdom with other unfortunates. Her ankle was tightly bandaged and felt much better, even though she couldn't lace up her boot.

The energy in the gymnasium was mounting as the last two competitors got ready to compete. She tried to see over the tops of heads but there were too many people in the way. Was Langdon already fighting?

"How do you feel?" asked Jerry from behind her. She turned to face him.

"I won't be running any races," she admitted.

"Of course not," agreed Jerry blandly. "You did that yesterday."

All right, already. She'd had enough lectures for one day. "Where's my crew?" She was surprised that Charlotte, at least, hadn't stuck around.

"The two uniforms left, suddenly remembering other important duties," said Jerry. "The others only left when I promised to bring you to the station." He raised an eyebrow. "I've got news."

She could tell by the look on his face that it was important news. She glanced at the benches on the sidelines but Bert Langdon and his opponent were still waiting to be called up. The referees were huddled around the officials' table. It might be a while before things got going.

Damn. She didn't want to wait. It might be important.

"All right," she said, raising her voice to be heard above the crowd. "Let's go." She'd find out later how Langdon survived his bout with Jones.

As Jerry drove her to the station, she tried to find a comfortable position but no matter how she stretched out her leg or adjusted her feet, her ankle still hurt. A lot.

Jerry glanced at her in irritation.

"Are you listening?"

"I'm listening," she said contritely. "What did you find out?"

Jerry turned onto Main Street and stopped to let a pedestrian cross.

"Harrison Beckman, better known to his friends and family as Harry, has no criminal record. In fact, except for a few parking tickets—promptly paid—he's never even had a citation. There's certainly never been a complaint laid against him and no restraining order. Whatever problems he and Ms. Hollingsworth had, they kept them private."

He turned into the station parking lot and parked his Volvo in a spot reserved for visitors. "I'm still working on finding out the terms of the divorce. That may shed more light on their relationship."

"I don't suppose you were able to locate him?" Kate asked.

Jerry shook his head and finished parking. "According to my sources, he wasn't at his house. The grass was long and there were a couple of newspapers accumulating at his front door. Neighbors claimed they haven't seen his car in a few days."

"So he didn't arrange for a mowing service or suspend his newspaper delivery," said Kate, staring at the station wall.

"He left in a hurry," concurred Jerry.

"What about his family?"

"He has a sister in Vancouver. She didn't even know her brother was gone. Not close, I take it."

Kate was impressed. "You actually found someone to talk to her?"

Jerry tried to look modest, but he wasn't cut out for it. "Thirty-five years on the force—you accumulate a few favors."

It's nice to have friends in high places, Kate decided.

"Well, thanks, Jerry," she said.

"I'm not finished." He smiled smugly and she rolled her eyes.

"What else, you big baby?"

The smile turned into a self-satisfied grin. "Beckman's

sister mentioned an old flame of Beckman's, the woman he rejected to marry Ms. Hollingsworth when she got pregnant. And guess where she lives?"

Kate's eyebrows rose in expectation and she forgot all about her ankle. "Mendenhall?"

Jerry shook his head. "Next best thing," he said. "Brandon."

DAISY WAS WAITING for her inside the station. Her high heels clicked purposefully on the tile of the lunchroom floor as she came toward Kate. In her straight gray skirt and short-sleeved, fitted white shirt, she looked like she belonged on Bay Street, not Mendenhall. Her ever-present clipboard was tucked under one arm.

"Just the woman I wanted to see," said Kate. "Do you know where I'd find Adam Billings right now?" She knew the Brandon DC was in Mendenhall for the games, but where exactly?

Daisy pulled her clipboard out and began flipping pages. She traced her finger along one list and finally stopped.

"He's got some men competing in karate," she said. "That competition ends in about an hour. Otherwise, I don't know. He's friends with Rob McKell, so maybe he's at Rob's place."

Oh, great. That was all she needed.

"I came to apologize for missing the hand-to-hand," said Daisy, following Kate into the duty room. "I heard you did very well."

Albertson hung up the phone and swiveled in his chair to look at them. "She came in third," he said triumphantly. "Congratulations, Chief. That was the chair of the medals committee. She wanted to make sure you're going to the banquet tonight. They're handing the medals out."

"Tonight?" Kate shook her head. "Can't make it," she said cheerfully. "I have to go to Brandon."

"Well, Brandon is just going to have to wait," said Daisy sharply. "You *have* to be there to accept the medal."

Kate shook her head. "You've got it all wrong, Daisy. First I do cop things. Then I do silly things." She finally had a lead in this not-quite-investigation and she was *not* going to delay pursuing it for the sake of a fancy meal.

"Can't you send someone else to Brandon?" asked Daisy plaintively. "Why do you have to do it?"

Kate opened her mouth to answer, then closed it. The truth made her stomach hurt. She didn't know who to trust in this station. And she was beginning to wonder if McKell was capable of fouling up the investigation just to make her look bad. She wasn't about to risk Josh Hollingsworth to petty-minded politics.

It was an awful thing to think about her people, but there it was.

"Look, why don't you accept the medal on my behalf?" she said to Daisy. "You deserve it as much as I do."

Daisy looked taken aback and, for a moment, didn't seem to know what to say. Kate took advantage of her discomfiture to turn to Albertson.

"Can you try to locate Acting Chief Adam Billings for me? He's not answering his cell phone and I need to talk to him." Then she turned back to Daisy. "By the way, who won the hand-to-hand?"

"Bert Langdon," said Albertson before Daisy could reply. "He beat out that big sucker, Frank Jones."

Kate turned away from the satisfied look on his face. What was it with these people? Clearly, Albertson had been following the competitions, as had most of her constables. Yet no one except Trepalli—who had done it under duress—had participated. Either they were extremely loyal to McKell or they really didn't like her.

Still, she was glad Bert had won.

She closed her office door behind her and made a beeline

for her desk where she sat down and immediately put her foot up on the cushioned drawer.

The throbbing in her ankle eased a little and she sighed. How long was this darned ankle going to be a problem?

A breeze tickled the back of her neck and she smelled rain on the wind. She'd have to close that window before she left. It was already four-thirty in the afternoon on a Sunday. Beckman's girlfriend would likely be home by the time Kate got to Brandon. Heck, Beckman might even be with her. She pulled out her notebook and checked the woman's home address. *Bless you, Jerry.*

Albertson popped his head in the office. He couldn't find Billings. He wasn't at the gym or at McKell's and he wasn't at his Brandon office.

"What about his cell phone?" asked Kate.

"Doesn't seem to be on."

"All right, thanks."

Well, she had done her due diligence.

THIRTEEN

DAISY WAS GONE by the time Kate came out of her office, file folder in hand. Albertson was busy typing at the duty desk.

Kate glanced at the wall clock. Almost 6:00 p.m.

"Who's available?" she asked.

Albertson looked at his board.

"Tattersall is on dinner break and Olinchuk just got off break. What do you need?"

"Who wouldn't mind a little overtime?" She didn't want to risk driving with her ankle so sore.

"Olinchuk," said Albertson promptly. "His wife is expecting and they're renovating their spare bedroom into a nursery."

Kate nodded. "Call him in."

"Yes, ma'am."

She turned to go back to her office, then stopped. "Albertson."

He swiveled in his chair. "Ma'am?"

"I want you to do a little research for me."

"Sure. On what?"

"James Cusick's wife. Her name is Celia. I don't know if she used his name or her maiden name. I don't even know if she's still alive. Cusick disappeared in 1989, so start there." She handed him the file.

SHE DECIDED TO take her car again, partly as a courtesy to the Brandon Police Service and partly so as not to alarm the woman she was going to see.

Kate sent Olinchuk home to change into his civvies and she

changed into hers at the station. She was still waiting for him when Daisy entered the station on a gust of cold wind, struggling with an oversize umbrella. When she finally managed to close it, she propped it in the corner and headed straight for Kate, who was leaning on the end of the duty counter.

"I stopped by your house," said Daisy accusingly. "You're not there."

"That's right," said Kate. "I'm not." She went back to scanning the log book, hoping Olinchuk would show up before McKell came on shift at seven.

Daisy eyed Kate's jeans and white cotton sweater. "And you're not dressed for the banquet."

Kate looked at her and something in her eyes must have telegraphed her thoughts because Daisy put up a hand as if warding off a blow.

"I know, I know," said Daisy glumly. "Cop work before silly work." She had changed, too, and wore a black dress with skinny straps, a pleated, fitted bodice and a wide, filmy skirt that floated around her calves as she walked. Over the dress she wore some kind of cropped, brocade jacket. She'd somehow put her short hair up with a pretty comb to hold it all together.

Kate stared at her for a moment longer than was polite. Daisy raised her hand to her nose self-consciously.

"Is something wrong?" she asked.

Kate blinked. "No. You look very nice. Is your husband going with you?"

Daisy smiled and suddenly Kate remembered that, formidable as she was, Daisy Washburn was still young.

"He's waiting for me in the car," she said. "He looks very good in his tuxedo."

Kate smiled. "I'll bet. Well, you have fun at the banquet." What a dog-and-pony show *that* was going to be. Thank God she was missing it.

The storm door jerked open, letting in a blast of rain-laden air. McKell stood on the carpet, shrugging out of his raincoat and shaking it out. Droplets splashed the walls.

Damn it. He was early.

He looked up at last to find Kate, Daisy and Albertson looking at him. His expression, which had been half smiling as if to say "Phew!", suddenly closed down.

Kate sighed.

He nodded stiffly and headed past them into the duty room.

Kate would never know what possessed Daisy at that moment but she caught a gleam in the young woman's eye just before she spoke up.

"Rob!"

McKell spun around, startled, and even Kate and Albertson were taken aback. But Daisy ignored them as she swept into the duty room after McKell. She glanced over her shoulder at Kate.

"Rob should do it!" Her smile encompassed the entire room. Really, it was a shame to waste it on three puzzled people.

"Do what?" asked McKell suspiciously. He held the raincoat away from his side and it dripped onto the clean floor. He looked at Daisy with dislike, which surprised Kate. You would have to work at disliking Daisy.

Daisy turned to him. "Accept the chief's medal tonight at the banquet. She won't be here. Since you're the second-in-command, you should do it!" She smiled at him, very satisfied with herself.

McKell just stared at her for a second. Then he growled, "Mind your own damn business, Daisy Washburn."

Without another word, he stomped into the back locker room by the lock-up, leaving wet boot prints on the linoleum tiles.

Kate's mouth fell open and for once, the smile disappeared from Albertson's face. He quickly turned back to the computer screen.

Daisy's cheeks were red with mortification.

What was *wrong* with that man?

Without giving herself time to think it through, Kate marched across the duty room and barged into the locker room.

McKell was hanging up his coat in an open locker. He looked around when she entered. His eyes narrowed at her expression but otherwise his face didn't change.

The locker room was a glorified hallway, with only enough room for six lockers on either side and a counter with a sink and mirror at the far end, next to the toilet stall. A narrow bench ran between the two sets of lockers.

Kate walked over and stopped in front of him. Only the bench stood between them.

"You were out of line," she said bluntly. "There was no call to treat her like that."

"I treated her exactly the way she deserves to be treated." McKell's mouth tightened until it was barely a slash and the muscles in his face grew hard and tense.

Kate took a deep breath and tamped down her irritation. She tried again. "Her suggestion is perfectly legitimate—"

He cut her off. "She butts in where she has no place," he said bitterly. He leaned across the bench toward Kate, his blue eyes vivid in his white, angry face. "She meddles and causes problems."

Kate's eyebrows rose in surprise. Okay. This was personal and it was directed at Daisy, not her. She tried to defuse his anger by speaking mildly. "It was just a suggestion, DC. You don't have to do it." *Since you feel so strongly about it.*

He smiled thinly. "I wasn't planning on it."

And suddenly, Kate had had enough. Enough of his resentment, his undermining her, his negative attitude.

But most of all, she'd had enough of tiptoeing around this man.

She leaned closer, into his comfort zone. She could tell he

didn't like it. His nostrils were pinched and white. Only the bench kept them apart. While not exactly a six-footer, McKell was still a good six inches taller than her and she had to look up at him. She could smell his aftershave and caught a whiff of toothpaste on his breath. His hair, as always, was impeccably groomed.

"All right, DC McKell," she said softly. "Let me put this plainly. You hold a grudge against Daisy. Fine. But deal with your personal issues on your own time. Keep them out of my station."

McKell laughed suddenly. "Well, that's rich!" He straightened and crossed his arms, glaring down at her. "Considering how *your* obsession has had the whole department running around on the word of a crazy old man!"

Kate straightened too and wished she was a foot taller so she could look down on him. "My *obsession,* DC McKell? Then how do you explain Josh Hollingsworth's disappearance? His mother's car in the river? How do you explain the fact that his father's car was spotted in town and the fact that that crazy old man, as you call him, saw Josh being abducted?" She stopped when she heard her voice rising.

McKell uncrossed his arms and jabbed a finger in her direction. "Chance. You're so preoccupied with the one kid you let slip through your fingers that you see abductions everywhere. You're bound to be right at least once!" He glared at her. "I heard all about your run for the DC job in Toronto. And I heard how the rumors chased you out." He took a deep breath and visibly calmed himself down.

"Mendenhall is just a pit stop to you," he continued, looking down at her sternly. "A place to lick your wounds and figure out where you'll go next. But it's home to us. And we deserve better than a police chief half-crazed with guilt counting down the days until she can leave."

Kate felt her pulse hammering in her throat. "Have you got it all off your chest?"

"Don't kid yourself," he said bitterly. "You only got the job because the mayor was hoping I'd get mad and leave. But this is *my* town and I'll be here long after you've tucked tail and run!"

She was so mad she was vibrating. "You think you've got me all figured out on the basis of a couple of rumors," she said, enunciating carefully. "Well, that's shoddy police work, McKell. Let me give you a heads-up—you'd better find a way to accept me as chief because I'm not going anywhere, either. And if you undermine my authority even *once* more, I will fire your ass."

FOURTEEN

SUSAN BROWNLEE LIVED in a new condo on the outskirts of Brandon. The grounds were landscaped with bushes and young trees, and flowers now being battered by the rain. Olinchuk found a parking spot near the building and ran to open Kate's door before she could struggle out. He held an umbrella over her head while she climbed clumsily out of the car.

"Thank you," said Kate when she was finally vertical. She closed the door to the Explorer and stayed close to Olinchuk as they walked up to the condo's main door. The buzzers were labeled with random letters of the alphabet followed by an owner's name. Kate approved of the system—it made it harder for a stranger to figure out exactly which unit went with which name.

She pressed on *E,* which had *Brownlee* next to it, and picked up the telephone next to the buzzers. The phone at the other end rang three times before being picked up.

"Yes, who is it?" asked a woman's voice.

"Ms. Brownlee?" asked Kate.

"Yes?"

"My name is Kate Williams. I'm the chief of police in Mendenhall. I'd like to speak with you, please."

There was a long silence at the other end. Finally, the woman said, "Step out from under the awning. I want to see you."

"I have a police constable from Mendenhall with me," said Kate. "We'll both step out."

Letting the phone dangle from its cord, she gestured at

Olinchuk to come with her. He held the umbrella over both their heads as they stepped out from under the protection of the overhang. She stopped a few feet away, still within reach of the door light.

"Get ready to get wet," she muttered to Olinchuk. Then she pulled the umbrella down and looked up at the windows of the condo. Rain immediately washed her face and plastered her hair to her skull, running down the back of her jacket collar. On the third floor, someone stood on the balcony, peering down.

"Try to look inoffensive," she told Olinchuk.

He glanced sideways at her.

"Beg your pardon, ma'am," he said. "But it's not as if I *try* to look offensive."

A joke? Olinchuk had a sense of humor? Kate stared up at him but his face was turned up to the balcony. He was a big guy, well over six feet tall, with massive facial features, including high cheekbones and chocolate-brown eyes. His black hair was cropped short, emphasizing the structure of his face. *He looks Cree,* she suddenly thought. Not that she would know a Cree from an Ojibway, really.

The door buzzer sounded and she started, but Olinchuk got to the door before the buzzer stopped and pulled it open. Kate grabbed the dangling phone.

"Third floor," said Brownlee, then the line went dead.

The floor of the lobby was in faux marble and Kate walked gingerly on it, wary of slipping. Olinchuk finally took her elbow without a word and walked her to the elevator. He'd been a cop for over ten years, she remembered, first in a small town in northern Ontario, then in Mendenhall. He was about thirty-five.

"Thank you, Constable," she murmured as they entered the cage. She pushed the button to the third floor and tried to slick the rain out of her hair. Olinchuk's dark hair was so thick that the raindrops just beaded on the top of his head. His jacket shoulders were damp, as were hers. Not to mention her chest. Like the prow of a ship, she thought, my chest precedes me.

The elevator opened onto a wide hallway that turned at the far end. It was carpeted in a brightly patterned broadloom that swallowed the sound of their footsteps. The walls were painted a blue that matched the carpet. The effect was like walking underwater.

Halfway down the hall, a door opened and a woman stepped out into the hall. She was tall and lean, about thirty, with clear brown eyes, a straight nose and full red lips. Her honey-blond hair was pulled up in a curly ponytail.

She was barefoot and wore some kind of black pants that rode her hips and fitted her butt snugly, but flared out at the ankles. Her white T-shirt left two inches of flat midriff bare and had a drawing of Led Zeppelin on the front.

"Let me see your identification, please."

Kate fished her ID out of her pocket. She held it out to Brownlee at eye level and Olinchuk did the same.

Finally Brownlee nodded. "You can come in," she said. Then she took a good look at them. "Stay on the mat, please."

Brownlee let them in and closed the door behind them. The mat was too small for two people and Olinchuk stood uncomfortably close to Kate. He really was a big guy.

The entrance led to a living room in which the furniture had been shifted to make room for a yoga mat. Beyond the living room was a hallway, which presumably led to a kitchen or bedrooms.

The furniture—the whole room—was done in a modern style, with sharp angles and plastic and bland colors. Even the paintings on the walls were geometric. Except for two piles of carefully placed, neatly stacked fashion magazines on the glass-and-chrome coffee table, there was nothing about the room that would give Kate a clue to the owner's personality. Certainly there was nothing to indicate that someone else might be here.

Brownlee stood in front of them, her arms crossed.

"What can I do for you?"

Olinchuk pulled his notebook and pen out.

Kate smiled. "Do you know a Harrison James Beckman?"

The curse of blondes was that they couldn't hide a blush. Kate watched the tide of red creep up Brownlee's neck. But when she spoke, her voice was calm.

"Harry? I used to date him, back when I lived in Vancouver."

Now there's a careful answer, thought Kate.

"Have you seen him recently?"

Brownlee's response was as emphatic as it was immediate. "I haven't seen him since I moved back home." She looked directly at Kate. "That was five years ago."

The woman had left the balcony door partly open and the rain sounded loud inside the living room. A cool breeze tickled Kate's damp neck and she had to work on controlling a shiver.

There were no suitcases, men's shoes or coats that she could see. She smelled nothing remotely like a man's cologne. Of course, Beckman might not wear cologne, and Brownlee might simply have put away any evidence of his presence, and Beckman could be hiding in a back bedroom. But she didn't think so.

No, Brownlee had agreed too easily to see them, had even allowed them inside. A canny woman would have done the same, of course, and brazened it out, but Brownlee wore her emotions on her face. No way could she have hidden the fact that someone else was in the condo.

Olinchuk kept writing in his notebook and Brownlee's gaze flickered to him before returning to Kate. "Why are you looking for him?"

"His wife and son have disappeared," said Kate. "We suspect he may be involved."

Brownlee shook her head and her ponytail swung heavily from side to side. "No way," she said firmly. "No way. Harry is the most honorable man I've ever met. He would never hurt his son or that conniving little witch who tricked him into marrying her." The color rose in her cheeks again and she clamped her mouth shut.

Don't be shy, thought Kate. *Tell us what you really think.*

She glanced at Olinchuk but his head was bowed over his notebook.

"You don't like Ms. Hollingsworth?" she asked mildly.

Susan Brownlee took a deep breath and the color once again receded from her cheeks, leaving behind two bright splotches.

"No. I don't like her. She seduced Harry, got pregnant and forced him to marry her."

Right. Poor old Harry is the victim in all this.

"Have you seen Ms. Hollingsworth in the past five years?"

Brownlee opened her mouth to speak then hesitated.

And then Kate got it. "You did see her, didn't you?" she said softly. "After all, she only lives forty-five minutes away. You could easily have spotted her here in Brandon or even in Winnipeg." In the two months since she'd moved to Mendenhall, Kate had discovered that everyone went to Winnipeg, either to shop or go to the theater or the movies or some other form of entertainment. Even Brandon got its share of Mendenhall shoppers.

Susan Brownlee remained silent, her brown eyes revealing nothing.

"You saw her and you called Harry, didn't you?" said Kate softly.

The woman was apparently done blushing. She crossed her arms and stared at Kate.

Kate had about enough of this woman. "Judy Hollingsworth's car was found in the Assiniboine yesterday morning. She and her son are missing. And we've had a report that a boy matching Josh Hollingsworth's description was abducted by someone driving a white vehicle." She gave Susan Brownlee a hard look. "Harry drives a white TrailBlazer."

She stepped closer to Brownlee. "If you're involved in any way, Ms. Brownlee, at the very least you will be charged with being an accomplice to a felony kidnapping. At the worst, you'll be charged with attempted murder."

Brownlee's face was so white Kate thought she was going to faint. But it was anger, not fear, that drained the color from her.

"I want you to get out now," she said, her mouth so tight it was a wonder the words slipped out. "And Josh's last name is Beckman. Not Hollingsworth."

Kate shrugged. She'd warned her.

FIFTEEN

SHE AND OLINCHUK sat in her car for fifteen minutes before the underground garage doors to the condo opened and a dark green Tercel emerged.

Olinchuk waited until the Tercel was well ahead before pulling out behind it. They drove slowly down the rain-slick street and sure enough, the Tercel drove into the Mac's Convenience Store parking lot and pulled up next to the MTS phone booth. A figure in a bright yellow raincoat emerged from the Tercel and ran the few feet to the booth. Once inside, Susan Brownlee pulled back the hood to reveal her blond hair.

Olinchuk turned to Kate. "How'd you know?"

She shrugged. "She's afraid we'll be able to access her phone records or that we tapped her phone. She thinks she's safer calling from a pay phone."

Olinchuk grinned. "She would be wrong."

Finally, a break. All they had to do now was follow Susan Brownlee when she left the pay phone. She would lead them straight to Beckman.

But Brownlee finished her call, got into her car and drove back to the underground garage of her condo.

"Damn it," she muttered.

"Why take the car if she was just going to the pay phone?" asked Olinchuk.

"Because she was planning to drive out to him and he talked her out of it." Clever boy, that Harry.

Brownlee had him stashed far enough away that she needed

a car to get to him. Wherever it was, it had phone service. Or maybe only cell phone service.

Why couldn't it ever be easy?

"All right, then," she finally said. "We'll do this the hard way."

She pulled out her cell phone and called the station. To her surprise, Trepalli answered. She glanced at her watch. It was eight o'clock.

"Hello, Constable," said Kate. "Everything quiet?"

"So far," he replied cheerfully. "Shift just started. Last shift there was a fender bender on Main and Third and two kids were caught spray painting the high school. It's Sunday."

Kate nodded. Sunday shift was notoriously quiet.

"We do have a guest in cells," said Trepalli cautiously.

Kate's eyebrows rose. On a Sunday? Two nights in a row?

"Who is it?"

"Mr. Boiseman."

Kate tensed. "Why?"

There was a pause. "He took a swing at DC McKell."

"Excuse me?" No way. Boiseman—Cusick—might be delusional, but the man wasn't violent. At least, she didn't think he was.

"Mr. Boiseman came in looking for you, just after you left. He became agitated when we told him you weren't around. DC McKell attempted to calm him down but Mr. Boiseman tried to slug him."

"So McKell *arrested* him?" she asked incredulously.

Trepalli cleared his throat. "I'm sure the DC will do so once he returns. Mr. Boiseman is not locked in. Of course, if he happens to be sleeping when DC McKell returns, the DC may wait until morning. And if it's stopped raining by then…"

McKell was letting Boiseman sleep in the cells, out of the cold rain.

The guy actually had a heart. Who knew?

"Thank you, Constable," she said quietly.

"How was the interview?" asked Trepalli.

She filled him in, then said, "I need you to find Judge Byblow and get a court order from him. I want to know what number she called from the pay phone." She supplied the exact location of the phone booth—MTS could find the phone number from the location—and then she thought for a moment. "Actually, I want records from her home number, as well, and any cell phone numbers she has."

"Yes, ma'am," said Trepalli. "Anything else?"

"What's happening with the Brandon investigation?"

"Ms. Hollingsworth's car?" She could almost see him shaking his head. "Nothing. They plan to drag the river tomorrow but if Hollingsworth died in the crash, she'll wash up somewhere downstream."

"Okay," said Kate. "I'll be in touch."

"Before you hang up," said Trepalli quickly.

"Yes?"

"Albertson left some information for you."

For a moment she didn't know what he was talking about. Then it clicked and she pulled out her notebook and a pen.

"All right," she said. "Go ahead."

"Celia Cusick remarried in 1994, to a Gary Carlisle. She lives in Calgary. She and her husband have two children, ten and thirteen. Albertson found a phone number for her." Trepalli hesitated. "Do you want it?"

It was her turn to hesitate. Did she want it? Did she want to phone up a woman who had gone on with her life to tell her that her ex-husband was a homeless man still trapped in the past?

She silently blew out a sigh. "Give it to me."

OLINCHUK SAT IN silence, tapping the wheel to a rhythm only he could hear, watching the condo.

Even if the judge were willing to issue the court order, it would take time. Time to serve the court order to the nearest MTS representative in Mendenhall. Time for that rep to contact his or her boss in Winnipeg. Time for the Winnipeg boss to contact a lawyer. Time for the lawyer to tell them they had to produce the records.

The clock was running out on this case. She could feel it in her bones.

She flipped open the cell phone again. While Olinchuk looked on curiously, she punched in Sally Thompson's number, praying to anyone listening that Sally would answer, and not Tom.

Sally answered on the fifth ring, just as Kate was about to hang up.

"Hello?"

"Sally, it's me Kate."

"Hey, Kate—twice in one week? What's up?"

"I need a favor."

"Sure."

"Hear me out, first," cautioned Kate. "It's a big one."

"Hang on." There was a pause and Kate heard a door close. Then Sally came back on the line. "Okay, what is it?"

"I need to know what property a certain person owns. Can you dig that out?"

"If it's in Manitoba, probably," said Sally cheerfully. "Outside Manitoba may take longer. Is this for an investigation?"

"Yes, it is," said Kate quickly.

"Good, because you know there *is* such a thing as privacy protection."

Kate grinned. "Yes, Tom."

Sally laughed. "He may resent authority, but he is right about protecting people's privacy."

"I know, but—"

"Relax," said Sally. "This is all information that you could find yourself if you went digging. And since you're telling me it's for an investigation…?"

"It is," Kate hurried to assure her. "A boy has gone missing, along with his mother. The information you provide could help us find them." Or at least, help them find the boy.

"Okay," said Sally. "Give me an hour."

Kate took a deep breath. "Thank you, Sally. Sooner is better. We may not have much time."

She gave Sally Ms. Brownlee's particulars then closed the cell phone and tucked it back into her jacket pocket. Then she sat back and listened to the sound of the car heater for a few seconds.

She glanced at Olinchuk, who stared back at her silently, his eyes hooded in the dark interior of the car. His silence was comfortable. It gave her room to think.

"I don't know about you, Constable Olinchuk," said Kate, "but I'm starving."

"Yes, ma'am!"

"Unfortunately," she continued, "we have to keep an eye on Brownlee's condo."

Olinchuk looked at her, then at the Mac's across the wet road.

"I have a raincoat and I can run fast," he said firmly.

Kate laughed. She glanced at the Mac's parking lot and then back at Brownlee's condo. "I think we'd still have a good line of sight, even if we parked in front of the door."

Olinchuk pulled out into the road and drove to the Mac's parking lot, making sure to park so that Kate had a clear view of Brownlee's condo.

She fished through her pocket and came up with a twenty dollar bill. "Grab us some sandwiches and coffee. But first, get the phone number from the pay phone." Might as well make it easier for MTS.

Olinchuk put on his cap and got out of the car. The sound of the rain drumming on the car and the pavement got louder then dulled when he slammed the door shut. He ran to the pay phone and jotted the number down in his notebook. Then he ran to the store.

Her ankle throbbed. She wished she'd thought to ask Olinchuk to pick up some Tylenol while was he was in the store.

She leaned her head back against the headrest. How the hell had she gotten here? Based on a rookie's gut instinct, she'd ferreted out the identity of the supposedly missing kid, found his mother, *lost* his mother and now she was staking out the father's ex-girlfriend.

And as far as she knew, Harry Beckman had done nothing illegal. All she had was the dentist's say-so that Beckman used to beat his wife. And all *he* had was Judy Hollingsworth's say-so. Judy Hollingsworth, proven liar. There were no Vancouver police records or even complaints to back up that allegation. For all she knew, Hollingsworth had made up the story to get the dentist to help her.

There was no crime here. She was asking Sally Thompson to go against her principles and provide private information on a woman who hadn't done anything wrong. Even if Brownlee had hidden Beckman—so what? She could offer him hospitality if she wanted. The man wasn't a criminal.

But…

But.

Trepalli was right. Too many things didn't add up. Hollingsworth's lies and their inability to find the boy, especially. She wished she knew who had custody of the kid, but that information wouldn't be available until office hours tomorrow.

If Beckman had taken the kid, why hadn't Hollingsworth

reported it to the police? If Beckman had custody, why hadn't *he* contacted the police when Hollingsworth took off with the boy? And if he had custody, and the kid, why wasn't he getting in touch with police now?

None of this made sense, but she just couldn't make herself ignore Trepalli's instinct. She had ignored her instincts twenty-five years ago when she stopped Boynton and found Bobby MacAllister sleeping in the backseat. The boy might be alive today if she had listened to the little voice telling her something was off.

And then there was Boiseman. Cusick. A poor sick man who needed help. Who needed peace of mind more than anything else.

She was still clutching her cell phone. Now she looked down at it as if it could answer the Celia Cusick/Carlisle question. Finally, she flipped it open and punched in the Calgary number Trepalli had given her. If it was eight o'clock here then it was seven o'clock in Calgary.

The phone was picked up after two rings.

"Hello?" said a deep male voice.

"May I speak with Celia Carlisle, please?"

"One moment."

A minute later, a woman's voice said, "Celia here."

Kate took a deep breath. She should have rehearsed what she would say to the woman.

"My name is Kate Williams. I'm the chief of police in Mendenhall, Manitoba. I apologize for disturbing your evening." She watched Olinchuk talking to the girl behind the sandwich counter inside the Mac's.

"What can I do for you, Chief Williams?" A note of puzzlement crept into the woman's voice.

"Ma'am, were you once married to a James Cusick?"

There was a long silence at the other end. Finally, there

came a sound like a chair being pulled out and the woman said, "Yes."

Kate could see her in her mind's eye—a matronly figure suddenly sitting down at the telephone table before her legs gave way.

A girl's voice in the background said, "Mom, are you all right?"

Kate didn't bother hiding her sigh. "I *am* sorry, ma'am, but I have a few questions about Mr. Cusick."

"Why?" said Celia Carlisle, her voice wobbly. "Did you find Jimmy?"

Kate's eyebrows rose. She would never have imagined Boiseman as a Jimmy.

"Yes, ma'am, we have."

"Is he all right?" Her voice was almost a whisper, as if her throat was too tight to let much out.

There was no help for it. She couldn't sugarcoat this.

"Not really," she said gently. "He's here in Mendenhall. As near as we can tell, he's been on the road since—" She stopped suddenly, realizing that she was about to rip open some old wounds.

But Celia Carlisle was made of sterner stuff than that.

"Since my daughter was murdered. Yes." She took a deep breath. "I tried finding him for years. I even hired a private investigator. But it was as if he'd fallen off the earth." There was a world of regret in her voice.

Kate let the silence linger, then asked, "You never heard from him?"

Celia Carlisle was silent for so long that Kate looked at her cell phone to make sure she hadn't lost the signal. Finally, Celia went on.

"I got a postcard from him once, a couple of years after he left."

Kate waited but the woman seemed to have run out of words. "What did the postcard say?"

Celia started to speak, then stopped. Finally she said, "Why is Jimmy in…Mendenhall, did you say? Is he in trouble?"

Kate hesitated. She didn't want to lie to the woman, but at the same time, she didn't want to worry her needlessly.

"I don't think so," she said. "He's not always lucid. He reported what may be a child abduction. I think that's why he's still here. To make sure the boy is safe."

"Oh, my poor Jimmy," whispered the woman.

Sympathy tears pricked Kate's eyes and she cleared her throat.

"That's why I'm calling, Mrs. Carlisle," she said. "Does Mr. Cusick have any family? Any parents or brothers and sisters that I could call?"

"No. He was an only child. His parents passed away years ago." She took a deep shaky breath and even over the phone, Kate could hear how the tears had thickened her voice. "I was the only family he had, until Ellen was born."

Oh, God. Now what? This woman had moved on with her life. Her husband certainly wouldn't appreciate a half-addled ex-husband suddenly appearing at their doorstep. He might even scare the kids.

"I'll come for him," said Celia Carlisle softly into the silence. "I'll look after him if he needs it. I owe him that much."

Kate suddenly remembered Laird Macdonald telling her how Cusick had taken off after his wife accused him of bringing the monster into their home.

"I'll tell him I've talked to you," she said finally.

"Let me know…" Celia Carlisle hesitated. "Let me know what he decides to do."

"I will," promised Kate. Then, just before the other woman was about to hang up, she said, "Mrs. Carlisle?"

"Yes?"

"What did the postcard say?"

Celia Carlisle remained silent for ten long seconds. Then, "It said, 'He's dead.'"

"That's it?" asked Kate. "Was it signed?"

"No, it wasn't, but I recognized his handwriting."

"Where was the postcard from?"

"Vancouver."

"Thank you, ma'am." Kate closed the connection and sat staring at Brownlee's condo.

Vancouver was where Derek Jackson's body, minus genitals, had been found. Had Boiseman tracked down and killed the pedophile who murdered his daughter? Had the postcard been his way of bringing a kind of closure to his wife?

Olinchuk came out of the store with a bag in one hand and a cardboard tray in the other. Kate leaned across and opened the driver's door. A wave of cold air chased the heat away until Olinchuk slid in and handed her the tray. Then he closed the door.

"Wet," he said as he removed his cap and placed it on the dashboard. His coat glistened with beading raindrops and he wiped the worst of the wetness from his face with his hands.

He pulled out his cell phone and called Trepalli with the pay phone's number while Kate fished through the plastic bag and came out with a turkey-and-tomato sandwich. She was about to unwrap it when her own phone rang.

"Williams," she answered.

"I've got something for you," said Sally. "The tax rolls show that Ms. Brownlee owns a condo in Brandon—that much you knew. She also owns a cabin near Riding Mountain Park."

After nearly thirty years as a cop, Kate recognized the spike of adrenaline for what it was—her body's reaction to the clue that could unravel the mystery.

"Where?" She fished through her pockets for her notebook. Olinchuk stuck his under her nose and then handed her a pen.

She nodded her thanks and quickly found a blank page to jot down Sally's information.

"Okay, got it," she said when Sally had finished. "Thanks."

"No problem. Go catch some bad guys," said Sally. "Just be careful."

Kate closed the cell phone and turned to Olinchuk. "Who on the force knows the Riding Mountain area?"

SIXTEEN

FOR ALL OF three minutes, she seriously considered telling Jerry what she planned to do. But he'd have reservations…might want to check on cross-jurisdictional protocols…would send a couple of members to meet her…

He might even take over.

Better to ask forgiveness than beg for permission.

Besides, she was just going to ask a few questions, that was all. No crime was committed, that she knew of. For all she knew, Judy Hollingsworth could be in Winnipeg, haggling with her insurance company over a replacement for her car, while her boy played by her side.

Fortunately, Susan Brownlee's cabin was just outside Riding Mountain Park, otherwise she would have had to involve the park wardens. And while she didn't mind taking liberties with the RCMP and jurisdiction, she had learned never to cross Parks Canada.

It was almost ten o'clock by the time she and Olinchuk drove into the station's parking lot. She wanted to change into her uniform and switch to a patrol car before heading out again. She struggled out of the passenger seat and hobbled to the door.

"Chief?"

She stopped on the stoop, her hand on the screen door, protected from the rain by the overhang.

"What is it, Olinchuk?"

He looked up at her, his wide face gleaming wet in the light above the door.

"Request permission to come along."

"You're supposed to be off duty," she pointed out.

"Yes, ma'am," he agreed, watching her expectantly.

Just when she had begun to think that Trepalli was the only one with any kind of gumption in her station. Who was she to blunt an officer's enthusiasm?

"I'm leaving in twenty minutes," she warned. "If you're not back by then, in uniform, I'm leaving without you."

"Yes, ma'am!" He turned and took off at a run for his car.

"And don't break the speed limit!" she called after him.

She grinned and went into the station. The warmth of the lobby wrapped itself around her and she gave a massive shiver before shrugging out of her raincoat and shaking the rain off it.

"Chief?"

She looked up to see Trepalli sticking his head through the opening of the duty counter.

"Are you ready?" she asked, walking toward the duty room.

"Yes, ma'am. DC McKell is on his way in. Harriman is in the weapons locker, checking out our weapons. Abrams will hold down the fort. Tremblay is still on patrol and Fallon is on call."

She nodded. She would rather have had McKell coordinating at the station, but he was the best shot among all her officers. God forbid she should need him, but if she did, she wanted him with her.

Trepalli looked bulkier than normal, thanks to the armor vest he was wearing. This was likely the first time he'd ever had to wear it, outside training. He looked older, somehow, as if the implications of wearing the vest had aged him.

"I pulled out your gear, Chief." He pointed toward the back. "It's laid out in your office."

She nodded her thanks. "Pull up the squad cars to the back door," she instructed. "We'll store a rifle in each trunk. We won't need them," she added hastily as his eyes lit up. "It's just a precaution."

"Yes, ma'am," he said. "I put some coffee in two thermoses."

"Good man!" He'd make some woman a fine husband one day.

She hurried toward her office but as she passed the door to the lock-up, she saw the light spilling out of it and remembered Cusick. She stifled the sudden urge to tell him about his ex-wife's offer. There would be time enough after they returned from Susan Brownlee's cabin.

Ten minutes later she was ready. She had rewrapped the tensor bandage around her ankle. It still hurt. And the vest pinched in a variety of places. The vest was probably overkill, but she wasn't taking chances with her men. And she couldn't expect them to wear theirs if she didn't wear hers.

When she came out, McKell stood at the duty desk, rifle in hand, giving instructions to Abrams who nodded solemnly.

She was suddenly aware of the weight of the 9 mm in her holster. She wore it every day, as part of her uniform, so that she usually never even noticed it anymore. She'd had to draw her weapon exactly five times in her career and only shot it once, and that was over a suspect's head. She'd never liked the damned thing but appreciated that it would make itself felt most by its absence.

McKell looked around and saw her. He gave a noncommittal nod.

"Everyone's suited up and ready," he reported.

"Good. Is Olinchuk here?"

McKell nodded. "He's with me. I've been to Riding Mountain Park. I'll lead."

"All right," said Kate equably. "Rifles in the trunk?"

"Except for mine," he said, raising the hand with the rifle. "This one rides in the front seat holster."

Kate nodded. It was a good precaution. If something happened unexpectedly, they didn't want to be scrambling for the trunk.

"Let's go."

Trepalli was already behind the wheel and she slid into the passenger side without a word. The soft flesh of her belly caught between the bottom edge of the vest and her utility belt, pinching her.

The radio crackled to life as Olinchuk did a radio check to make sure they were on the same frequency. Then Trepalli drove out of his stall and followed the other patrol car toward the highway.

Kate pulled out the map from the side door compartment and fished the tiny flashlight out of her coat pocket. According to McKell, it would take at least an hour to reach Brownlee's cabin.

THEY REACHED THE fork to Neepawa and headed north on Highway 16. On the way, the rain slacked off. It finally stopped just before they reached the village of Riding Mountain. On a Sunday night in late fall, there wasn't much open in the hamlet. They drove past cottages with signs that read Closed for the Season—See You Next Year! and a few gas stations and one grocery store tucked away behind a parking lot.

When McKell finally pulled over after they'd passed through the village, Trepalli followed suit. As they had driven north, the farmland had gradually given way to forests and wild fields. But Trepalli's headlights picked out the ragged stalks that were all that was left of some farmer's crop. The stalks bent slightly as the wind picked up from the north. A forest loomed just beyond the field. The tops of coniferous trees spiked against the lighter sky.

The rising wind shredded the dark clouds, allowing the almost-full moon to peek out. Trepalli turned the heater up.

Kate grabbed the map, placed her cap on her head and stepped outside.

"So where's this cabin?" asked Olinchuk, joining her.

Kate unfolded the map on the hood of the patrol car, which had dried. McKell came to stand next to her and Trepalli and Olinchuk leaned over her shoulder.

"We're here." Kate pointed on the map. It was a mineral map and it showed elevations and logging roads as well as identified mineral deposits. "The cabin is here." She pointed to another spot about half a mile away. "There's a more direct access, a front way, but we'll take this logging road." She pointed to the thread of ink on the map. "It should take us to within a few hundred feet. We'll stop well before that and scout out the place."

She looked around at the officers gathered around her. "We suspect that Beckman kidnapped his son and is hiding with him here. However, we may be wrong and he may be a perfectly innocent man. I don't want anyone pulling a weapon unless I say so. Is that clear?"

McKell's eyebrow went up and she met his annoyance with a stony face. He finally nodded.

They all piled back into the cars. Now that they were so close, Kate and Trepalli took the lead. Still, even with both of them looking for it, they would have missed the logging road if not for the deer they startled. It leapt out of the woods and across a gap before disappearing like a ghost into the forest on the other side.

"I guess that's the road," said Trepalli dubiously.

Kate shared Trepalli's doubts. It looked more like an overgrown trail than a road. It had been raining for hours—if their car bogged down, they'd have a heck of a time getting out.

"We'll walk from here," she finally decided. Trepalli nodded and pulled over.

It was a good thing they left the vehicles behind, because

there probably hadn't been a wheeled vehicle on the logging road in years. The almost-full moon gave enough light to keep them from breaking their necks, but it was slow going along the weedy and brush-overgrown track. If not for the moon, Kate would have had trouble finding the indents in the brush.

The ankle was a problem until Olinchuk found her a sturdy branch to use as a walking stick. After that, she was able to move much faster.

Still, it took them much longer to cover the two hundred or so yards than she would have expected. Either that or the map was wrong and the cabin was much farther than she thought. It was close to twenty minutes before she caught sight of a light among the trees and halted.

"Radio silence," she ordered. Everyone turned their radio off. "Cell phones, too," she added. A flurry of muted bell tones told her everyone had turned off their cell phone ringers.

"McKell," she said softly. The DC moved up close to her. "You and Olinchuk take the south approach. Cover both sides of the cottage. Trepalli?"

"Chief," said the constable.

Kate looked at him. "You take the back, in case he tries to run. McKell and Olinchuk, cover me. I'm going to knock on his front door."

Trepalli hesitated. "Chief…"

"You heard her, Trepalli," said McKell roughly. The DC turned away and took a few steps, then stopped to look at her. He held up the rifle he had pulled from the front seat scabbard.

"I know this guy's got no criminal record," he said. "But we both know that means squat." With a nod to Olinchuk, McKell and the tall constable disappeared into the woods. Kate and Trepalli listened to the cracking of twigs breaking and the rustling of underbrush. She hoped Beckman was inside and couldn't hear their clumsy approach.

Trepalli looked down at her with a grin, his teeth gleaming white in the moonlight.

"I think that's his way of telling you to be careful," he said.

"He makes a good point," she said crisply. "Watch yourself. Yell if you get in trouble."

"Will do."

Without another word, he set off through the trees, too. He disappeared into the woods without a sound, as silent and graceful as a deer.

She gave them a good five minutes to get into position.

The wind shifted and the smell of wood smoke overlaid the smell of wet soil and decomposing plants. Whoever was in the cottage was using wood to heat it.

"All right," she whispered at last. She set out for the light, ignoring the ache in her ankle and the shooting pains in the other leg from her unnatural gait. If not for the improvised walking stick, she would have fallen half a dozen times. Within fifty feet, she stumbled onto a driveway.

There were no power poles along the driveway. No electricity, no landlines for a telephone. The light had to be kerosene or maybe propane. As she got closer to the dark bulk of the cottage, she saw that a porch ran around the front and both sides. A couple of wicker chairs waited invitingly on either side of the front door. She thought she caught a whiff of gasoline. So there was a car here somewhere, probably parked on the side of the building she couldn't see, or maybe in back. More than likely, it was a white TrailBlazer.

The low growl was all the warning she got.

She spun around and something heavy slammed into her chest, knocking her to the ground.

Dog, she realized, as it snapped its teeth, barely missing her ear.

She instinctively slipped her walking stick under the animal's lower jaw and pushed up, keeping the sharp teeth away from her neck. Its back claws scrabbled on her thighs, ripping her uniform pants and soaking her with blood. Medium-sized dog.

The dog twisted its head and clamped its jaws on her walking stick, wrestling it out of her hands. She let go and immediately the dog released the branch. Before it could lunge at her again, she threw a handful of soil into the animal's eyes and was rewarded with a strangled yelp of distress. She heaved the whining animal off her and scrambled to her feet, yelping herself when she stepped wrong on her injured ankle.

The branch was at her feet. She reached down and grabbed it. As she straightened up, the dog also rose, growling. She swung down just as it sprang at her. The branch connected with a sound like an axe splitting wet wood and broke. The dog fell to ground, unmoving.

Dear God. Had she killed it?

Hobbling over to the downed dog, she tried to decide the best way to determine if it was alive or dead without actually touching it. In the moonlight, she couldn't tell if its ribs were moving. But within a few feet, she heard its breathing.

Not dead, then. Good.

When the blood finally stopped pounding in her ears she heard the sound of twigs snapping in the underbrush to the side of the driveway.

Jesus! Was that Beckman? Why was he going *toward* the cottage?

"Mr. Beckman!" she called loudly but the crackling in the underbrush didn't stop.

She followed as quickly as her ankle would allow, grateful for the relatively smooth driveway. The heavy bulk of the cottage loomed straight ahead.

Then the door of the cottage burst open, spilling light out and ruining her night vision. A tall silhouette ran out of the house.

Son of a bitch! He was making a run for it!

"McKell, he's heading for you!"

Kate hobbled as quickly as she could toward the far side of the cottage where, presumably, the car was parked. She was almost there when a voice cried out, "No!"

Trepalli! She put on a burst of speed and came around the corner of the cottage. In the light spilling from a side window, she saw five figures frozen in a tableau. She blinked, trying to understand. McKell and Olinchuk had been on either side of the cottage. That made two. Trepalli at the back made three. Beckman made four. Who was the fifth?

"Mr. Boiseman," said Trepalli in the sudden silence, "please don't do this."

Boiseman?

"It's the monster!" cried Boiseman.

Kate finally picked him out. He was standing no more than ten feet from a tall figure that was presumably Beckman. The man had his back to the wall of the cottage and his hands up.

And then she saw the boy. He was huddled behind Beckman, one arm wrapped around his father's leg. He wore pajamas and his feet were bare.

The scene froze Kate in place for a split second as all her assumptions shifted. The boy was looking to his father for protection. He was afraid, but not of his father. And Beckman had placed himself between Boiseman and his son.

"Please," said Beckman, "don't shoot."

Shoot?

"Monster!" cried Boiseman. She heard the same ragged edge in his voice that had been there the first time she met him. How the hell had he gotten here? "I won't let you get her!"

Kate caught the gleam of a rifle held low in Boiseman's hands.

Oh, please no.

"Mr. Boiseman," she said softly.

He swung the rifle on her, and Trepalli and Olinchuk stepped forward. Kate raised her hand to stop them. Now that her vision had adjusted to the light, she saw McKell out of the corner of her eye, slowly circling behind Boiseman. He still held a rifle, too.

"Mr. Boiseman, it's me," she said. "Kate Williams."

"I know who you are," he said roughly. He sounded like he'd been crying. "I found the monster."

"Please," said Beckman. The rifle swung back to him. "Please don't hurt my son. Let him go." His voice held trembling supplication.

"No, Daddy!" cried the boy for the first time. "I want to stay with you!" The boy's voice was high and tight with fear.

"You deserve to die!" screamed Boiseman. "You baby killer!"

"What?" cried Beckman, forgetting to keep his hands up. "What are you talking about?"

"I won't listen to your words!" screamed Boiseman. "You fooled me once, but never again!"

A movement beyond Boiseman caught her eye and she focused on Trepalli, who held his handgun down by his side. Until McKell got into position, Trepalli was in the best position to stop the old man, but if he missed, his shot would hit her. She edged her way closer to Beckman, out of the line of fire.

If all else failed, she might be able to throw herself in front of Beckman and his son. At least she had a vest.

But only as a last resort. She could talk the old man down. He was confused.

"Mr. Cusick," she said, still moving toward Beckman. "James. This man is not your monster."

He didn't budge, didn't acknowledge hearing her. In the sudden stillness, she heard the distinct sound of the rifle's safety being disengaged, followed immediately by the sound of another handgun sliding out of a holster.

Think! There had to be a way to reach him.

"James," she said softly. "James, look at me."

As if drawn against his will, his eyes turned toward her. It was too dark to see the feverish cast to his eyes, but she remembered it clearly from the first time they met.

"This is Harrison Beckman. His little boy's name is Josh. Mr. Beckman is not the man who hurt Ellen. That man is dead, James. Remember?"

"Dead?"

"Yes. Do you remember now? He died in Vancouver." She took a quick breath, trying to keep calm. "Please, James. You're scaring the boy."

She pushed away a stab of guilt—how frightened had Bobby MacAllister been when Samuel Boynton abused him? How abandoned had he felt as Boynton's hands squeezed the life out of him?

Boiseman's rifle dropped an inch. She couldn't tell for sure but it seemed to be wavering, as if the hand that held it was none too steady.

The soft light from the window caught the glint of tears in Boiseman's eyes. "He killed my little girl."

"I know," she said and refused to acknowledge her own answering tears. "But this man isn't your monster, James. Please. Give me the rifle."

She took a tentative step forward.

He was going to hand her the rifle, she realized with relief. But at that moment, something came hurtling out of the darkness past Kate toward the old man.

She had time only for impressions—screams and snarls, shouts of warning, a flurry of movement, the rifle swinging up.

Then a train slammed into her, knocking her to the ground. The last thing she heard before the stars swept down on her was the sound of a child sobbing.

SEVENTEEN

KATE STRUGGLED OUT of the darkness and emerged into bedlam. Unintelligible shouts filled the night air as twigs snapped and branches rattled against each other. A stink of musk reeked all around her, mixed with the smell of blood.

"Let! Go!" grunted a man. She recognized McKell's voice. Another man cried out in pain.

Dear God, what was happening? She heard grunts of effort nearby and tried to move her legs out of the way.

"Daddy!" shrieked a child.

"Drop it!" shouted someone, she couldn't tell who. Something flew by, twisting and growling, and landed with a thud ten feet from her. She blinked in confusion, trying to make sense of the bundle of fur.

The bundle shook itself out and rose to its feet, growling and baring its teeth.

Her memory snapped back into place. The dog! Where was Boiseman?

"Drop your weapon!" shouted a man—Olinchuk—just as someone else screamed, "Down, Rupert!"

Kate struggled to sit up and cried out as pain speared through her shoulder.

"Stay down!" shouted Trepalli, suddenly appearing at her side. He fell to his knees and pushed her down onto the cold ground, his hand flat against her chest. Something metallic clinked against a rock. She fought against his restraining hand, gasping at the pain stabbing through her.

"Don't shoot him!" she called out. "McKell, don't shoot!"

"It's all right," said Trepalli, keeping her down. He leaned down until he was only a few inches away from her face, forcing her to focus on him. "They got the rifle away from him."

"Don't shoot him!" Not his fault, she wanted to say. The dog had jumped him. It was an accident.

She must have spoken out loud because Trepalli said, "I know. It's all good. You have to stay still now."

The pressure disappeared from her chest and she heard the sound of a metal clasp being opened. She began to shiver with the cold.

"He's got some nasty bites," Olinchuk said.

Trepalli shoved something under her shoulder and she cursed at the surge of pain.

"I'm sorry," he muttered, then did the same thing to the front of her shoulder.

She must have passed out again for a minute because when she came to, Trepalli was gone and McKell was leaning over her, shining a flashlight in her face. He moved it away as soon as she opened her eyes.

"Can you hear me?" he asked. The flashlight lit his face from below, giving him a demonic cast.

Waves of pain rolled through her, cold and nauseating. The shivering got worse. *I'm shot,* she wanted to say, *not deaf.* Instead, she nodded.

"We've called EMS," he said. "But we're not waiting. We're going to transport you in the back of the squad car and meet them on the highway."

The copper smell of blood was making her gorge rise. She breathed through her mouth, trying to control the nausea. McKell made to rise, but she clamped her good hand on his arm and he stopped.

"Boiseman." She couldn't manage any more.

"Defensive bite wounds on his forearms," he said. "Nothing fatal. We've applied first-aid. Olinchuk will take him back in the other squad car."

Kate nodded. She desperately wanted to get up and take a look for herself.

"The boy?" she whispered.

"Safe. He's in his father's TrailBlazer. Beckman put the dog in the cabin. Everything's under control."

Under control? She'd never been in a situation *less* under control.

She had to see what was going on. "Help me up." She turned onto her good side and pushed herself up on her elbow.

McKell hesitated, then wrapped both arms around her to support her while she got to her knees. She could smell his sweat and his aftershave, mixed in with a hint of wood smoke and the overpowering stink of blood. Her whole body shook with cold.

Deep breaths.

"Ready," she whispered.

She gasped when he lifted her to her feet. She had time to note Trepalli hurrying toward them, and then the whirling sky came crashing down on her head, taking her out.

PAIN SLOWLY SEEPED into her awareness. Something was hurting her shoulder. She came to cursing and opened her eyes to see a red-faced Trepalli looking down at her.

He stepped back, his eyes wide with relief, and said over his shoulder, "She's conscious."

Immediately the curtain behind him swished open and a woman in a white coat came in. She had crow's feet and a few strands of gray mixed in with her upswept chestnut hair. She had dark circles under her eyes.

"Are you back with us, Chief?" asked the woman. She shone a pencil light into Kate's eyes.

Kate blinked at the light and glared at the woman. What

the hell? Oh, God—what was wrong—? And then it all came crashing back.

She sat up abruptly only to cry out when agony stabbed through her shoulder. The woman pressed her back with a firm hand on her chest.

The woman was a doctor. For the first time, Kate took in her surroundings: curtains on a track hanging from the ceiling, the muted noise of wheels rolling down a hallway, voices moaning in pain and crepe-soled shoes squeaking on linoleum.

She was in a hospital emergency room.

"Take it easy," said the doctor. "You've been shot in the shoulder."

Oh, man. Boiseman had shot her.

She closed her eyes. Just how badly had she messed things up?

When the dizziness abated, she opened her eyes again and found Trepalli, standing just behind the doctor. "The boy?"

"He's fine," Trepalli assured her. "Being checked out now."

"How long have I been here?" And what happened while she was out?

"You were brought in about an hour ago," said the doctor. "Your officers provided first aid at the site and met the ambulance. You've lost blood but not enough for a transfusion."

Trepalli grinned at her. "The bullet went clear through," he said. "Just missed the vest. It nicked the bone but didn't break it."

"Thank you, Officer," said the doctor sternly. She glanced back at Kate and rolled her eyes.

"He's young," explained Kate.

"Indeed," said the doctor, a small smile on her lips. Then she turned serious again. "We've packed the wound and dressed it, but you need to keep still or it'll start bleeding again. Your arm is strapped to minimize movement." She sighed. "You're going to need a lot of therapy to regain the full use of that shoulder."

For the first time, Kate glanced down at herself.

Someone had removed her Kevlar vest and her uniform shirt. Replacing them was a washed-out blue hospital gown with a big lump at her right shoulder where the dressing bulged. Her right arm was strapped down by some kind of white, stretchy fabric that wrapped around her and fastened with flat clips.

There was an intravenous needle stuck in her left hand.

"Standard procedure," explained the doctor, nodding at the bag of clear fluid hanging off the spindly stand. "You were going into shock. It can probably come out now."

Kate pulled the collar of the gown away and peered underneath. The skin around the bandage was an ugly shade of orange from the disinfectant, underlaid by an unhealthy blue from incipient bruising.

She swallowed hard and shifted in the bed, trying not to move her shoulder. Then she became aware that her thighs were on fire.

"What's wrong with my legs?" she asked and was moderately proud that her voice didn't shake.

"We dressed the scratches," said the doctor.

"Scratches?"

"You were attacked by a dog," explained the doctor. "Do you remember?"

She remembered. The dog had scrabbled all over her legs as she fought him off. Then it had hurtled through the air at Boiseman.

Her heart sank. Boiseman.

She took a deep breath filled with the astringent smell of antiseptic, plus a few more unpleasant ones.

"Trepalli?"

He stepped around the doctor to the other side of the bed. "Yes, ma'am?"

"Report."

For the next ten minutes, Trepalli told her what had happened after she was shot.

She remembered bits and pieces. She knew it was an accident. The dog jumped Boiseman—Cusick; she had to start calling him by his real name—and the rifle went off. Unfortunately, Kate was in the path of the bullet. Or fortunately, perhaps, as she was standing between Cusick and Harry Beckman.

McKell finally calmed everyone down, organized first aid for Kate and Cusick and got everyone back to Mendenhall.

"It's now almost 4:00 a.m.," concluded Trepalli, glancing at his watch. "Mr. Cusick's been stitched up and given a shot of some kind." He looked a question at the doctor.

"Against rabies," she explained. "Just in case. And a tranquilizer. He was very upset." She looked to Trepalli expectantly and Kate almost smiled. Either the boy's charm worked on tired doctors in the middle of the night, or she hadn't heard the whole story, either.

"That's right." Trepalli nodded, turning back to Kate. He sighed. "He was really upset about hurting you."

Kate nodded. She'd been worried that someone had shot the old man. But it sounded like McKell had held everything together.

"Help me up," she said to Trepalli. "I need to see the boy first, then Cusick." She held out her left hand, but Trepalli looked to the doctor, who was shaking her head.

"You need to stay put and rest," she said firmly. "You were going into shock when they brought you in and you've received a trauma. I want you to stay here for observation."

Kate considered. She felt as though she'd been hit by a freight train and suspected she would feel worse once the painkillers wore off. She wasn't in terrible shape, but she might be in worse shape tomorrow.

She *had* to see the boy tonight.

"Where's Beckman?" she asked Trepalli.

"DC McKell took him to the station," said Trepalli. "But he called his girlfriend and won't talk until she shows up with a lawyer."

All right. Beckman was out of the way, at least for now. "And the boy?"

The doctor spoke up. "A social worker from Family Services is on her way."

Alarm spiked through Kate. If Family Services got their hands on him, she might never get a chance to question him.

"Sorry, Doctor," she said. "I need to talk to that little boy." Without giving the doctor a chance to object, she pushed herself up to a sitting position with her good hand, biting back a curse as her shoulder filled with shards of pain. *God damn!*

Trepalli put a steadying hand on her back. Her head spun and she clutched the edge of the bed to keep from falling back.

The doctor swore under her breath. Kate thought she heard the word "pigheaded" before the doctor said, "Stay there!" and swept out of the cubicle.

"Chief," began Trepalli uncertainly.

"Don't start," she said grumpily. "I feel bad enough."

The curtain was pushed aside and a nurse dressed in pink scrubs pushed a wheelchair into the small space. The doctor followed.

"I don't need a wheelchair," said Kate. What a great way to reinforce her authority—rolling in like an invalid.

"The only way I'm letting you out of bed is if you use the wheelchair," said the doctor. She looked down at Kate and crossed her arms over her chest. A few strands of hair had come undone from her bun but she didn't seem to notice.

Kate stared back at the doctor, wondering just how the woman planned to stop her.

"What'll it be?" asked the doctor as the nurse looked on

disapprovingly. She was a small, older woman with cropped gray hair and gold-rimmed bifocals.

Kate decided that this wasn't the hill to die on.

"I'll take the wheelchair, but only if you take this needle out."

"Fine," said the doctor. "Gisele, please help me."

The nurse removed the intravenous needle and stuck a cotton ball over the puncture, then taped it down. Already the top of Kate's hand was black-and-blue.

It was only when she pulled the sheet off that Kate realized that her legs were bare under the skimpy hospital gown. Her upper thighs were covered in gauze bandages.

Trepalli blushed and looked away. Kate sighed. She couldn't go to the kid looking like death in a hospital gown. Her uniform was nowhere in sight. No doubt it was irreparably bloodstained.

"Constable," she said crisply.

"Chief?" He kept his gaze averted.

"Get somebody to bring me my spare uniform. It's hanging behind my door."

"Yes, ma'am!" He left with more zeal than was entirely necessary.

By the time she was dressed in pants and a clean shirt, thirty minutes later, she was soaked in sweat. Her arm had been freed so that she could slip into the shirt and the pain of moving had made her see stars. The nurse pressed her lips together in a tight line of disapproval as she wound the elastic bandage around Kate, binding her arm securely to her midriff once again.

Kate swallowed a sigh when it was over. It sure didn't look this hard in the movies.

Finally, she was seated in the wheelchair, dressed and ready to face one little boy.

The nurse pulled open the curtains to reveal the dimly lit

emergency room. It was close to four-thirty and it seemed that there were no emergencies left on this Sunday night. Monday morning.

"Where's Boi—Cusick?" she asked Trepalli, who rose from a chair in the waiting area.

"Upstairs." He nodded toward the ceiling with his chin. "Sleeping. Olinchuk is on guard."

She nodded. She wasn't ready to think about the old man yet, or what to do with him. First she had to find out if the boy was all right.

"The father?" she asked.

"Still at the station. I guess it's hard to scare up a lawyer at this hour." He grinned.

"Family Services?"

"No sign of 'em yet," said Trepalli.

"All right." She took a deep breath. "Let's go see the boy."

They had put him in a tiny waiting room inside the emergency area. It had a door that now stood ajar. The lights were out but a television flickered silent cartoons in the corner near the ceiling. Trepalli pushed open the door and light from the emergency room spilled into the waiting room.

The boy was curled into an uncomfortable position in one of the padded armchairs, his head leaning on the armrest. Someone had pulled a blanket over him.

She and Trepalli watched him for a long moment.

Poor kid. It felt cruel to wake him up, but she had to speak to him before the social worker arrived or she might not get another chance to talk to him alone.

What was his name again?

"His name is Josh," said Trepalli, guessing her question. "He's six."

"All right," she said finally. "Help me up." The nurse had gone back to the nursing station desk, behind Plexiglas. She occasionally glanced up at them suspiciously. An orderly entered from the hallway pulling an empty gurney. He nodded at them curiously and headed for one of the far curtained-off areas, presumably to drop off the gurney.

"Chief?" said Trepalli. "You need to—"

"Constable," she said firmly. "I need you to help me up." She couldn't be an authority figure if she was being pushed around in a wheelchair. She briefly considered having him remove the bandage trapping her arm against her belly but decided not to. It would be even harder to be an authority figure if she fainted.

"Yes, ma'am," said Trepalli dubiously.

She placed her feet on the floor between the footrests and looked up at him. He leaned into her and she leaned forward. With both arms wrapped around her, and being careful not to apply pressure on her wounded side, he hauled her to her feet.

He kept his hands on her good shoulder and her waist while she waited to see if she would collapse. But her legs held and the light-headedness passed quickly. Finally she nodded, and he led her inside the tiny waiting room.

"Close the door," she ordered. He did. "Turn on the light."

The light came on like a floodlight, but the kid didn't even twitch. She stared at him, envying him that ability. His knees and elbows looked too big for his skinny arms and legs. His cheeks—at least the one she could see—were flushed. He had long, curly eyelashes that were much darker than his thick blond hair, which was growing out of a buzz cut.

"Hello, Josh," she whispered. *I'm so glad you're still alive.*

"Doc says there's no evidence of abuse," whispered Trepalli.

She couldn't take her eyes off the boy. Such a small boy, to have caused so much trouble. He hadn't been abused or killed. How close had he come? Was it just a question of time before his father beat him, or worse?

Or was he never in real danger?

"Wake him up," she said. Trepalli hesitated then stepped toward the boy. She swayed, missing his supportive hand, but braced herself and held firm.

The constable crouched next to the sleeping boy. "Hey Josh," he whispered. "Can you wake up for me, buddy?"

It took a few more whispered entreaties and a gentle nudge on his shoulder before the boy finally opened his eyes. He blinked at Trepalli in confusion for a few seconds then sat up.

"Where's my dad?" he asked at last. His eyes were brown and they looked huge.

"He's at the police station," said Kate, taking a tentative step toward the boy.

He recoiled and she stopped. What? Did she still have blood on her? She glanced at Trepalli but he was shaking his head at her.

What? What did she say?

"Is he in jail?" asked the boy and to her horror, his bottom lip quivered. Dear God…he was going to cry.

Trepalli's eyes narrowed in warning and he turned back to the boy. "Nope. He's not in jail. We needed to talk to him and there was no place here," he explained. "This is a hospital."

The little boy's eyes filled with tears and he sat up straight. "Why didn't he wait for me?" he asked. "Is he coming back?"

This wasn't going well at all.

Kate calculated the distance between herself and the empty chair next to the boy. Only four feet. She could do it.

She managed to sink down into the chair without jarring her shoulder, but sweat broke out on her forehead and scalp, and her whole body trembled with exhaustion.

Talk fast, she told herself grimly. *Before you collapse.*

"My name is Kate Williams," she told the boy. "I'm the chief of police in Mendenhall. Do you remember me from earlier tonight?"

He nodded uncertainly, glancing up at Trepalli, who smiled reassuringly.

"Kinda," he said. "It was dark. And noisy."

Kate took a deep breath to try and slow her heartbeat. "Josh, we've been looking all over for you."

"Am I in trouble?" he asked.

"No." She tried a smile but he only blinked up owlishly. "Someone thought you'd been stolen by a man in a white car."

"I'm not stolen," said the boy, frowning. He pulled the blanket off his chest and let it pool on his lap. "My dad has a white car," he said, "but he didn't steal me."

Kate started to speak then paused to choose the right words. "Did you want to go with your dad?"

"Sure."

Kate waited but he didn't say anything more. He looked puzzled, curious, and maybe even a little angry. He did *not* look like a kid who'd been taken against his will. She studied his face and started rearranging the pieces of the puzzle.

"You were at school on Friday, weren't you?" she asked.

He nodded. "It was dinosaur day. We were going to build a Tyrannosaurus Rex out of paper and glue."

"Did you?"

He shook his head. "No. Daddy came for me before the bell even rang."

Trepalli looked over the boy's head at her. She nodded. He couldn't possibly be any worse at this than she was.

"Were you surprised to see your dad?" he asked the boy.

Josh shook his head. "He promised he'd come for me," he said simply. "I just didn't know when."

"He came to the playground fence," said Trepalli.

"I crawled under the fence," said Josh, looking quickly up at Kate. "I know we're not supposed to, but Daddy said we were in a hurry. We ran to his car. It was parked on the road."

Yes, thought Kate. I know the place.

"How did you lose your shoes?" asked Trepalli.

She had completely forgotten about the shoes.

"I don't know." His face clouded over. "They were tied to

my backpack. I think one came off when I went under the fence." He glanced at Kate warily, as if worried she would punish him. She did her best to look nonthreatening.

"And the other one?" she prompted.

Josh shook his head. "I don't know. Daddy and I ran through the field to the highway. Maybe it fell off there."

"Did you go through the ditch?" asked Trepalli.

Josh nodded. "My good shoes got wet," he said solemnly. Trepalli ruffled his hair.

That explained what Cusick had seen: Josh and his father running out of the field and into the waiting TrailBlazer. To the old man, it would have looked as if Beckman was kidnapping the boy. Then, when they left, he found the shoe where it had finally tumbled off the backpack and into the ditch.

Still, none of this explained where Judy Hollingsworth was.

Careful, she told herself. Trepalli was looking at her expectantly. She needed to ask the question in such a way that the information she got for it wouldn't get thrown out of court.

"Josh," she said gently, "where's your mother?"

His small face closed as suddenly as a door slamming shut. He shrugged and looked down at the floor. "I dunno."

Trepalli's expression was troubled. "Have you talked to her since your dad came to get you?"

The boy shook his head without looking up.

"Did she go to your grandma's?" asked Kate.

That got the boy to raise his head. "Grandma doesn't like Mommy," he said, cocking his head to look at her.

"What about your other grandma?" asked Kate.

He crossed his legs under the blanket like a tailor and leaned his elbows on his knees. "Only got one."

"I only have one, too," said Trepalli, finally rising from his crouch to sit down next to the boy. "Mine lives in Toronto. Where does yours live?"

"Vancouver," said the boy promptly.

The Vancouver grandmother was Harry Beckman's mother. And according to the boy, she didn't like Judy Hollingsworth.

Kate leaned forward then drew in a sharp breath when her shoulder warned her against sudden movements. Josh looked at her curiously. His gaze dropped to her shoulder.

"The man shot you with his rifle," he said matter-of-factly.

"Yes, he did," said Kate. "But it was an accident."

He blinked at her. "He was going to shoot Daddy."

Kate took a deep breath, then let it out. Why had she thought interviewing the kid was a good idea?

"Josh, the man's name is Mr. Cusick. He thought your dad was a bad man who was going to hurt you."

The boy's eyes widened in surprise. "Daddy wouldn't hurt me," he said confidently.

No, Kate thought. He wouldn't.

She'd gotten this all wrong. What a royal mess.

The door to the waiting room suddenly opened and a slim young woman in tight jeans, a purple sweatshirt and a navy down vest walked in. Her hair was a fiery red and cropped close to her head with a few extra-long spikes sticking out around her face. She had a silver post through one eyebrow and a delicate ring through one nostril. Her green eyes flashed a glance around the room and settled on Kate.

"I'm Sandy Murphy," she said. "I'm the duty social worker with Family Services." She stuck her hand out and Kate automatically reached for it only to stop short with a gasp of pain.

Sandy Murphy's eyebrows rose and she glanced at Kate's padded shoulder.

Trepalli had jumped to his feet at her entrance. Now he stepped forward and held his hand out. "Constable Trepalli, Ms. Murphy. And this is Chief Williams."

Sandy Murphy nodded then turned to the boy.

"You're Josh Beckman?" she asked in a no-nonsense tone that still managed to be friendly.

"Yes." He looked up at her, his eyes sparkling with interest. He looked completely awake now.

"Good," she said. Then she grinned at him. "I'm going to take you to a comfy bed for the rest of the night until we figure out what's going on." She held out her hand.

Without hesitation, Josh pushed the blanket aside and slid off the chair to take her hand.

"Will Daddy be there, too?"

Sandy Murphy shook her head. "No." She squatted down to face him. Her green eyes were level with his. "I know it's scary right now," she said softly. "But I promise you I'll take good care of you until we figure everything out, okay?"

He stared at her for a long moment, then nodded.

Sandy Murphy stood up and, still holding the boy's hand, fished through her vest pockets until she found a business card, which she handed to Kate.

"I'll be in touch in the morning," she said, "but if you need to reach me, the service will know how to find me."

"Wait." Kate slowly got to her feet. Out of the corner of her eye, she saw Trepalli hovering, ready to catch her if she fell.

Sandy Murphy waited patiently. When Kate was sure she wasn't going to fall, she continued. "I need to know where he'll be."

Trepalli's eyebrows rose in surprise, but the young woman nodded. She let go of Josh's hand and fished through her pockets until she found a pen. Then she took the business card back from Kate and scribbled something on the back.

"We'll both be staying at this address," she said, handing the card back to Kate.

Kate finally relaxed. All right. For the first time since she learned of the boy's existence, she finally knew where he was, where he was going to be and that he was safe.

EIGHTEEN

By the time Kate called the station, from a phone in a common office shared by on-call doctors, it was almost six in the morning and she felt punch-drunk with exhaustion. Trepalli left her there, still sitting in the wheelchair, to look for coffee. She gazed longingly at the cot tucked against the back wall while the phone rang, but she had to know what was happening with Beckman before she gave in to her body's demands.

"Mendenhall Police Department," came Abrams's voice over the phone.

"It's Chief Williams. Is DC McKell still there?"

"It's good to hear your voice, ma'am." Then, before she could say anything, he said, "Hang on, I'll transfer you."

"McKell here," came his voice a moment later.

"It's me," she said, too tired for the niceties. "Report."

"The lawyer got here half an hour ago," said McKell without missing a beat. "We had to let him go."

Crap. She had wanted to talk to the man. Still, they didn't really have any evidence to hold him.

"Did you get anything out of him?"

"Oh, Mr. Beckman had *a lot* to say," drawled McKell. "According to him, he has custody of his son. He says his ex-wife crossed provincial borders with the boy."

Huh. They would know soon enough who had custody, once offices opened in Victoria.

"Why the hell didn't he report it?" Then every police station across the country would have been on the lookout for the boy.

McKell was silent for a long moment. When he finally

spoke again, all trace of humor was gone from his voice. "He says she threatened to kill the boy if Beckman reported it."

"Holy…" Kate took a moment to absorb that. "Sounds like a load of horse doo-doo to me," she finally decided. "He must have known it was an idle threat." Most women would rather cut off their hands than hurt their children.

"That's what I said, too," said McKell. Kate heard him swallow over the phone line. "Then he pulled his shirt up. He had a knife scar that ran up his ribs from his waist to his armpit." He cleared his throat. "I called Vancouver General Hospital. They confirmed that Harry Beckman came in on July sixteenth this year with a knife wound. He claimed it was from a mugger."

So. If Beckman's story was true, Hollingsworth knifed him—bad enough to prove she was serious but not badly enough to kill him—then grabbed her kid and ran for Manitoba where her friend the dentist lived.

Trepalli arrived carrying two cups of coffee. He set one down in front of her and sat down on the edge of the cot.

"How did Beckman know where she was?" Although she was pretty sure she knew how.

"Susan Brownlee," said McKell, confirming her guess. "He'd been looking for the boy for months when Brownlee called him out of the blue. She saw Hollingsworth in Brandon last week and called Beckman to find out if he was free. So Beckman hired himself a private investigator who found out where Hollingsworth lives and where the kid goes to school. Then Beckman got in his car and drove east. He got here on Thursday and found his son." He sighed. "I think he's telling the truth."

Yeah, she thought so, too. "We still need to check."

"First thing," agreed McKell.

"What about Judy Hollingsworth? Does he know where she is or what happened to her?" If his story was true, the woman was unstable. Maybe he got rid of her to make sure she never hurt Josh.

"He denies even seeing her," said McKell. "He says he got the school's location from the private investigator, drove there directly and once he had the boy, went straight to Brownlee's cabin. I got the P.I.'s name, so I can check out that part of his story soon enough."

Kate's eyes closed involuntarily and she jerked herself awake. "Good work, McKell," she managed to mumble. "I'll check in later." Then, just before he hung up, she said, "Wait!"

"What?" said McKell, startled.

"Why did Beckman stick around? He's had the kid for a few days—why didn't he leave? Better yet, why didn't he call the police at that point?"

McKell sighed. "At first, he was waiting to see if Hollingsworth reported the kid missing. She didn't, of course, but once you started nosing around, he and Brownlee decided to lay low."

Kate blinked. Was it her imagination, or was there a conciliatory tone in his voice?

McKell kept going. "And once he realized Hollingsworth had disappeared, why report anything at all? She was finally gone from his life. He could just wait for Brownlee to give him the all clear, then drive back to Vancouver with his son, possibly with his old girlfriend along."

Her thinking was getting fuzzy, but she couldn't see any way of holding Beckman. Just because his ex-wife's disappearance was awfully convenient didn't mean he had arranged it. There wasn't a shred of evidence linking him to her disappearance.

Damn. She wished she could have interviewed the man.

"Do you believe him, DC?" she asked.

There was a long silence at the other end of the line. She could hear him breathe. It was uncomfortably intimate.

"Yes," he said finally. "The guy's an idiot, but I don't think he killed his ex-wife."

Kate sighed. "I don't want him leaving until we check out his story."

She could almost hear the nod in McKell's voice. "I made it clear to him and his lawyer that it would be in his best interest to stick around. He's agreed to stay at Brownlee's for the time being."

"Good." She hung up and, without a word, Trepalli got up and swung her chair away from the desk.

"Wait," she said. He stopped and came around to face her.

"How did Cusick get all the way to Riding Mountain?" she asked. She was so exhausted she could barely keep her eyes open, but she needed to know. "How did he know where to find Beckman?"

Trepalli looked down at his boots. "He overheard us," he said. "We'd kept the door to the cell area open to hear if he called out. He slipped out while we were busy and hid in the trunk of one of the patrol cars." He looked up at her and shrugged. "We hadn't locked him in."

"But the cars were locked, weren't they?" None of this was making sense.

Trepalli didn't look up. "I had started the cars to warm them up," he said in a low voice. "Then I went back inside and put on my vest. All he had to do was hit the trunk release and get in. The rifles were already in, we didn't open the trunks again."

What a resourceful man, that Mr. Cusick. Resourceful enough to hunt Derek Jackson down in Vancouver and kill him? He had certainly been prepared to shoot Beckman.

Kate sighed and nodded at Trepalli. "I'm ready to go."

"About time," muttered the nurse at the desk as he wheeled Kate out.

"Which floor?" he asked the nurse.

"Third. Check in at the nursing station."

If they said anything more, Kate didn't hear. Her chin bumped her chest and she slept.

SHE STARTLED AWAKE from a dream in which McKell was trying to shoot Mr. Cusick. Then she tried to roll over onto her injured side and pain stabbed through her shoulder, arm and hand. She groaned.

"Easy," said a woman's voice as a hand pushed her gently back. Kate opened her eyes to find Charlotte looking down at her. At once, it all came rushing back to her. She groaned again.

"Good afternoon," said Charlotte. Her green eyes sparkled with youth and health and her hair was pulled back into a neat ponytail. In her jeans and a yellow cotton shirt, she looked like sunshine personified.

Kate closed her eyes against the sight while she catalogued how she felt. Shoulder: hurt like hell. Thighs: still burning but bearable. Head: surprisingly clear.

"What time is it?" she asked, opening her eyes.

Charlotte smiled and sat down in the visitor's chair by the bed. "It's a little past two in the afternoon."

"Which day?"

"Same day," Charlotte assured her. "Monday."

Oh, good. She hadn't lost too much time, then. She glanced around the hospital room and blinked in astonishment. Someone had robbed a flower shop. She counted at least a dozen bouquets strewn around the room, on the window sill, the side table, the lap table—even on top of the television set.

If there was a telephone hidden among the flowers, she couldn't see it.

"How do you feel?" asked Charlotte, bringing Kate's attention back.

"Like I've been run over by a truck," she answered truthfully. "Aside from that, not bad." She looked around again.

A breeze blew the curtain out. She could see blue sky out the window and nothing else. "Do you know where my cell phone is?" The room smelled like a funeral parlor.

Charlotte shook her head. "Sorry, no."

Kate flipped the covers off, pushed herself up with her good hand, swung her legs over the side…and would have fallen right on her face if Charlotte hadn't leapt forward to hold her back.

"Where do you think you're going?"

"I've got an investigation to finish," said Kate grimly. The cell phone was probably in her uniform and her uniform was probably in the closet. *Was* there a closet? She glanced around but couldn't see one.

And who had taken her uniform off?

Charlotte grinned down at her. "I think Constable Olinchuk wins the pool."

Kate frowned. "What pool?"

"The one with everyone taking bets about how long it would take for you to try to leave." She glanced at her watch. "Under a minute. Maybe Marco wins it. I can't remember now."

Kate scowled at her, not amused. "Why are you here, Charlotte?" She knew she sounded petulant, but she'd just been shot. She figured that would cut her some slack.

Charlotte shrugged. "It was either me, guarding the door, or you would have had to put up with a different constable here every hour."

"What are you talking about?"

Charlotte nodded. "They were fighting for the honor of keeping watch over you." She gave Kate a sly look. "I guess guilt is a good motivator. I refused to let them in and DC McKell backed me."

What a disturbing thought. Constables wanting to sit by her while she slept and McKell actually defending her right to privacy. This was all too confusing. "Can you get me my clothes?"

"Of course," said Charlotte pleasantly as she reached for the call button clipped to the bedsheet. "As soon as the doctor says you're well enough to go."

No amount of arguing would sway Charlotte. Nor did it sway the nurse who arrived moments later. Or the doctor who trundled in half an hour later.

Somewhere in the confusion of bandages, prying fingers and exposed flesh, Charlotte left the room, but not before Kate got her to promise to bring back a phone and a directory.

At last the nurse, the doctor and even the student nurse who arrived late agreed that Kate could go home, but only as long as she promised to go straight to bed.

Kate solemnly promised and then asked for her clothes.

To her immense relief, the student nurse not only found her clothes—in a metal basket that slid out from under the bed, she helped Kate get dressed once the other nurse and doctor had left. By the time they were finished, they were both sweating but at least Kate had her cell phone again.

The student nurse went to fetch a wheelchair, leaving Kate sitting on the chair Charlotte had vacated. She leaned back, acutely aware that she was trembling.

In twenty-five years as a cop she'd had guns pulled on her, but she'd never been shot at, let alone hit. She could have died.

A rap on the door stopped the incipient shakes. She straightened just as the door opened and McKell stuck his head through the opening.

"You receiving visitors?" he asked gruffly.

The room suddenly felt too hot, in spite of the cool air flowing through the open window. She hated being weak.

She raised an eyebrow. "Do you have a spy on the nursing staff?"

He smiled a tight little smile and came in, closing the door behind him. "A friend on staff owed me a favor."

She found herself smiling, too. She didn't know any cop, anywhere, who could do the job without a network of "friends."

McKell stopped at the foot of the bed, holding his cap awkwardly in front of him.

"Sit down," said Kate. "You look like a priest about to administer last rites."

This time the smile reached his eyes. He turned away to haul the second chair closer to the bed. His aftershave smelled faintly musky. Not bad.

"You look like you're ready to leave," said McKell, nodding at her clothes.

"Apparently I have to wait for a wheelchair," said Kate.

His short bark of a laugh startled her. "You can always race it down to the elevator," he said.

She smiled at the thought, then sobered. Was McKell offering her an olive branch? Or was this pity for the wounded?

"DC McKell, thank you for your quick actions after the shooting."

He looked away. "Don't thank me," he said softly. "We botched the whole operation."

Kate studied him silently for a moment. She couldn't argue with him. "Nevertheless, I'm glad you were there. Now," she said brusquely, "report."

"Trepalli is working on finding out who has custody of the Hollingsworth boy," he started. "The dad insists the boy's name is Beckman, by the way."

Should have asked the boy last night, Kate realized.

"Is the boy still with Social Services?"

"Yes, ma'am," said McKell. He suddenly looked bemused. "That social worker? The one who took him last night?"

"Yes?"

"She's not from here, is she?"

Kate started laughing but stopped when pain lanced through

her shoulder. With her flaming red hair and piercings, Sandy Murphy definitely didn't fit the Mendenhall profile.

"Where's Beckman now?"

"He decided to stay in Mendenhall. He's at the Talbot Arms, on Princess."

Kate's eyebrows rose. The Talbot Arms wasn't exactly five stars. Or any stars.

"They take pets," explained McKell.

Kate's opinion of Beckman rose slightly.

"He didn't want to stay with Ms. Brownlee then."

McKell sat back. "She's staying with him at the hotel."

Kate nodded. "He wants to be close by."

"That's my read of it," agreed McKell. "He's accused his ex-wife of assault and kidnapping. I'm sure the lawyer will help him come up with a few more charges."

"What about Cusick?"

"Still here," said McKell. "In a secure room. They want to do a psych evaluation on the old man."

Old man. He was her age, for Pete's sake. And McKell wasn't that far behind.

"Good." Kate nodded. "He might finally get some help."

"We still need to charge him," said McKell. "He *did* shoot you."

"We'll see," said Kate. "If he doesn't get treatment, then maybe we will charge him. At least in prison he'll have access to treatment."

He looked down at the floor. "I should have charged him when he took a swing at me," he said softly. "Then he would have been locked in."

Kate stared at the top of his head until he looked up at her. She held his gaze while she said, "I would have done exactly the same, Rob."

He nodded. Something flashed through his eyes, an expression gone so quickly that she couldn't identify it. But it left her feeling hopeful.

Then a yawn surprised him and he barely had time to cover his mouth. "Sorry!" His face flushed.

"It's been a long shift," she said. "I appreciate you staying on."

"You'll be back in no time."

Damn right. How hard could it be to sit behind her desk and order people around?

"All right," she said finally. "The only loose thread now is Hollingsworth. Did the Brandon cops find anything in the river?"

McKell shook his head. "I don't know," he admitted. "I haven't followed up. But I can do that right now."

"Get someone else to do it. Go home. Sleep."

McKell hesitated, then nodded. It was a small detail. Anyone could call Brandon and find out. They both knew that if something had turned up, Brandon would have called.

"I'll give you a ride home."

Kate shook her head. "Thank you, but Charlotte is around here somewhere. She'll give me a ride." Whatever fragile *détente* they had achieved might not survive them being trapped in a car alone for any length of time.

"All right, then." He stood up and moved the chair back to where it had been. Then he pulled a small flat box covered in black velvet out of his jacket pocket and handed it to her.

"Thought you might like to have it," he said gruffly.

She flipped it open one-handed. Inside was a bronze medal depicting two figures bowing to each other.

A medal. A bronze medal, at that. Was that all she had to show for the months of organizing those stupid games? For being snubbed by her men? For being humiliated in front of her peers?

She looked up at McKell, her chest tight with resentment. Then she let it go.

"Thank you," she said gravely.

McKell looked away. He started to say something, then hesitated. Finally he shrugged and looked at her. "No problem."

He left and Kate sat staring at the closed door for a long time, wondering what he'd been about to say. Then the door opened again, startling her, and she jumped and bit off a curse. But it wasn't the student nurse with the wheelchair.

"You're dressed," said Charlotte. She carried a cordless phone and a directory for southern Manitoba.

"I'm ready to leave," said Kate. "I found my cell phone." She patted her left pants pocket with her left hand. "Will you give me a ride home?"

"Of course," said Charlotte, dropping the phone book and cordless phone on the bed. "By the way, Marco called and it's confirmed. Mr. Beckman has custody of Josh."

Another loose thread snipped off. "Thanks, Charlotte."

Charlotte's glance fell on the case McKell had left behind. "I saw DC McKell leave." She looked up at Kate. "I heard about the argument."

Kate winced. By now, everyone in the station would know.

"I guess I can understand how he feels," continued Charlotte.

Kate's stomach dropped. Not Charlotte. "You think I'm obsessed, too?" Her voice wobbled a little.

Charlotte frowned and looked confused. "What?"

Kate took a deep breath. "What are you talking about?"

"Daisy," said Charlotte. "I can understand why the DC is so mad at her."

Oh. "Why?"

Now Charlotte looked uncomfortable. She sat down in the chair next to Kate. The breeze ruffled her ponytail. A cloying scent wafted over. Lilies, maybe.

"I thought you knew," said Charlotte. When Kate looked at her expectantly, she took a deep breath. "Daisy and Lizzy Dabbs have been friends since grade school. You know that DC McKell was married to Lizzy, right?"

Kate nodded. She'd only known for a day or so, but no matter.

"And you know that Lizzy is the mayor's daughter, right?"

Again, Kate nodded.

"Well, it's no secret that Lizzy and the DC were trying to have children. They tried for a few years. Daisy suggested they should get tested and they found out the DC can't make babies." She shrugged. "Lizzy went a little nuts. She accused him of knowing all along that he was infertile, because he'd been married twice before. She accused him of stringing her along."

"Adoption?" asked Kate, sucked into the story in spite of herself. Infertile. That would be a bitter pill for a man like McKell.

"Neither one wanted to adopt."

"So what's Daisy got to do with any of this?"

"Daisy encouraged Lizzy to get a divorce. Said she was still young enough to start over with someone who could give her babies."

Kate's lips pursed as if she had just sucked on a lemon. That was cold. Pragmatic, but cold. This was a side of Daisy Washburn she hadn't seen.

"And then the old chief died and instead of making Rob McKell the chief, like everyone expected, the mayor insisted on advertising. Then you got the job."

"Oh." She'd known that the mayor and council had snubbed the DC. She just hadn't realized that the snub was personal. This was what McKell had meant yesterday when he said the mayor had hoped he would leave once Kate got the job.

Charlotte smiled briefly. "Yes. Rob's been going through hell these past few months."

No wonder the man had resented her. No wonder the entire station had resented her. They were trying to support McKell.

All because of the absence of a child.

Kate smiled mirthlessly. Who would have thought she'd have something in common with the good DC?

She was suddenly impatient to get the hell out of this place.

"Can you find out what's taking so long with the wheel-chair?" she asked Charlotte.

"They said you can go?" asked Charlotte.

"Even helped me dress."

"Okay." She stood up. "I'll be right back."

The moment the door closed behind her, Kate flipped open her cell phone and reached for the telephone book.

A moment later, she was dialing Doreen Yawkichuk's number in Winnipeg.

NINETEEN

KATE DEBATED A long time before finally calling Trepalli at home. He was off shift after a brutal night and had earned his downtime. On the other hand, it was his instinct as a cop that had started this whole thing. He deserved a chance to see it through.

Trepalli jumped at the chance and showed up at her house fifteen minutes later. She had considered changing into her civilian clothes, but none of her pants were loose enough around the thigh to accommodate the bandages. And frankly, she didn't think it was worth the exhaustion that was sure to follow.

Trepalli roared up her driveway in a pickup truck, a small, neat thing, navy with white detailing. It looked as if it had just come out of the car wash. "Chief!" He jumped out and came toward her, stopping on the walk just below the stoop.

He looked her up and down. "Are you sure you're up to this?" Eagerness fought with concern on his handsome face and she almost laughed. He was going to have to learn to hide his emotions better. He had shaved recently and showered, too, judging by the clean, shampoo smell of him. His blue, blue eyes were clear and bright and his uniform looked as though it had just returned from the dry cleaner's.

Next to him, Kate felt like the Frump Queen of Mendenhall.

"Yes," she said. "Let's go. She's waiting for us at her house." The truck, while not particularly tall, had a built-in step to help passengers climb up into the cab. She gingerly stepped up onto it and grabbed onto the sissy bar just above the door.

Awkwardly, she swung herself in, managing not to jostle her strapped-in arm or hurt her ankle. Unfortunately, there was no way she could manage the seat belt and she had to suffer the embarrassment of Trepalli buckling her in like a child.

They drove in silence. Kate used the time to rest. It was getting on to dinnertime, and the sun was low, chasing long shadows toward the east. The air coming through the vents was cool and scented of sweet clover—a farmer's bane, but she enjoyed its perfume.

She had only taken half of the painkiller prescribed, since she didn't want to be fuzzy for the confrontation she expected. It was just enough to take the edge off, but not enough to let her sleep. There would be plenty of time to rest when this was all over.

They reached Winnipeg just as rush hour began, but as they were driving into town, rather than out, they had no problem reaching Mrs. Yawkichuk's house. They pulled up to the house and Kate made Trepalli wait in the pickup while she struggled out of the cab and rang the doorbell.

Doreen Yawkichuk had been waiting and the door opened immediately. She flashed a tight smile at Kate.

"Ready?" she asked. Then her gaze landed on the sling and bandage keeping Kate's arm strapped to her body. Her eyebrows rose in concern. "What happened?"

Kate suppressed a shrug just in time. "An accident." She glanced beyond Mrs. Yawkichuk into the empty hall. "Kids away?"

"They're at the neighbor's." Mrs. Yawkichuk closed the door behind her and tested the handle to make sure it was locked. She was dressed in denim clamdiggers, a light green V-necked sweater and flat, no-nonsense sandals. She seemed even more freckled than the last time Kate had seen her.

"This has something to do with an investigation?" she

asked, staring at Trepalli's truck. Trepalli nodded at her, although he couldn't have overheard the comment.

"Yes," said Kate. "Someone we've been looking for in relation to a child kidnapping."

"Oh, no!" said Mrs. Yawkichuk. "That's terrible!"

"The child is safe and sound," Kate assured her.

"I wish George was here," said Mrs. Yawkichuk. "He'll be very upset when he finds out someone's broken into our cottage."

Kate hadn't been surprised to learn that the good dentist was out of town, on a business trip. She watched the dentist's wife climb into the backseat of Trepalli's truck. She hoped for Doreen Yawkichuk's sake that she was wrong.

THE YAWKICHUK COTTAGE was two hours north of Winnipeg on a glorified pond called Boulder Lake. The cottage apparently sat at the end of a very long, narrow dirt road that cut through a forest of fir, poplar and spruce. The road hadn't been graded in years. Trepalli's headlights picked out most of the potholes but he couldn't avoid them all. He slowed to a crawl to avoid jarring Kate's shoulder any more than necessary but after a few minutes of navigating the country road, her teeth were clenched so tightly against the pain that her jaw ached. It was a welcome distraction from the shoulder.

Except for Mrs. Yawkichuk's voice occasionally guiding them through the gloom, the drive was made in silence. Kate was sure Trepalli was thinking of last night's foray to Brownlee's cottage.

She was beginning to second-guess herself. How likely was it that two suspects would be hiding out in two different cottages? But once Doreen Yawkichuk had confirmed that yes, they owned a cottage, Kate couldn't let go of the idea that Judy Hollingsworth could be hiding out there.

There were more cottages around the lake than Kate would

have thought—at least twenty, according to Mrs. Yawkichuk. Many of them were closed down for the season.

Mrs. Yawkichuk spoke suddenly, startling Kate.

"Why do you suppose this person picked our cottage?"

Kate felt the weight of the woman's stare on the back of her head. She could sense the courage it had taken Doreen Yawkichuk to come even this close to asking the real question she wanted to ask.

She took a deep breath. She didn't want to get George Yawkichuk in trouble, especially if this was a wild-goose chase, but at the same time, she couldn't lie to his wife.

"We think this person might be a friend of your husband's."

The truck bumped along the road as Doreen Yawkichuk lapsed into silence, her sudden burst of courage having failed her. Dust filtered into the cab and Kate opened the window a crack. At once, the damp night air dispelled the cozy warmth of the cab, filling it with the smell of water and rotting leaves.

The sky above the trees was slowly losing the last of the light when Doreen Yawkichuk next spoke up.

"Turn right up here."

"Is that your driveway?" asked Kate.

"Not quite," she said. "The driveway is about a hundred yards up."

Kate and Trepalli glanced at each other. Without a word, Trepalli pulled over and stopped the truck. He turned the engine off and in the sudden silence, they could all hear the clicks of the engine as it cooled down.

Kate turned in the seat and looked at Doreen Yawkichuk. "You need to stay here, Mrs. Yawkichuk," she said. "I don't think there's any danger, but I don't want to take any chances."

Mrs. Yawkichuk didn't answer and Kate spoke more sharply. "Do you understand me?"

The woman nodded, a movement visible only as a jerk in the darkness.

"Now, where exactly is the cottage?"

Mrs. Yawkichuk gave them directions and they left her in the truck. Kate and Trepalli turned up the little side road and walked side by side, looking for the driveway. As promised, it was about a hundred yards up, to the right.

It was that strange time of day when most of the light had left but night hadn't quite fallen yet. An in-between time. It always made Kate think of ghosts, in particular of Bobby MacAllister, a boy forever trapped in her soul. She felt very vulnerable suddenly, and was glad of Trepalli's solid presence by her side.

"I see a light," whispered Trepalli.

Kate peered through the thick trees. Sure enough, a light flickered through the branches of a fir tree. She stopped to consider their next move and her shoulder throbbed a warning. "I don't think there's going to be a problem," she said in a low voice, "but I want you to be ready to draw your weapon if needed."

He nodded in the growing darkness. "I don't think we should split up."

Kate didn't think so, either. For one thing, nothing in this investigation led her to believe that Judy Hollingsworth would be armed. Besides, Hollingsworth would not be expecting them.

And Doreen Yawkichuk had assured her there would be no dog.

So they turned up the driveway and made their cautious way to the cottage. A hundred feet later, they finally saw it. It was two storeys high, with a balcony on the second floor and what appeared to be a wraparound veranda on the ground floor. Light streamed faintly through the tiny window on the door.

As Trepalli set foot on the first of three steps leading to the veranda, Kate put her good hand on his arm. They listened and once again, Kate thought she could make out the sound of voices.

"Around the back of the house," whispered Trepalli.

Kate hesitated. She didn't want to take a chance on startling Judy Hollingsworth—if that's who it was—into taking to the woods. She sighed and told Trepalli to go around the house on the other side. She could see he didn't like the idea, either, but neither one of them had a better one.

Without a word, they parted to work their way around the house. Kate passed a series of paddles in various lengths and shapes clipped to the house's board and batten siding. She was careful where she placed her feet, but needn't have worried. Grass surrounded the house and muffled her steps. Grasshoppers sang their last goodbye to summer and somewhere off to the right, a frog serenaded the night. A cool breeze blew the smell of lake water and tar and pine to her.

The veranda continued around the side and to the front. A soft light spilled from the front of the house, illuminating the swaying trees. As she drew closer, the trees thinned out until she could make out the glimmer of water through ghostly birch trunks. Water lapped gently at the shore. She was willing to bet there would be a dock at the shore, and a rowboat tied up.

Then she was around the corner of the house and could hear the voices clearly.

A woman's laugh. "I've always wanted to go to Buenos Aires." Her voice was low and throaty. Kate couldn't be sure it was Judy Hollingsworth's voice.

Dr. Yawkichuk's voice, however, was clear. "Buenos Aires? What about my kids?"

"They can come visit us," said the woman reassuringly.

Kate crept closer. Dr. Yawkichuk and Judy Hollingsworth were sitting on wicker chairs, facing each other, not the lake. The breeze ruffled the long white skirt Hollingsworth wore.

"What about Josh?" asked Dr. Yawkichuk. "Don't you want

to fight for him?" His voice was full of pleading and Kate couldn't help but feel sorry for him. He hadn't even run away with her yet and already he was begging her to be a better person.

Praying that Trepalli was in position, Kate walked up to the veranda, expecting an outcry at any moment, but it wasn't until she spoke up that they both jumped out of their chairs.

"Actually, Dr. Yawkichuk," she said conversationally, "Ms. Hollingsworth wants to get out of the country so she won't get arrested for assault with a deadly weapon and kidnapping."

"What?" cried the dentist but before Kate could step up to the veranda, Judy Hollingsworth broke for cover. She ran toward the far side of the house only to jerk to a halt when Trepalli's flashlight beam speared her in place.

Kate hurried up the wide stairs and was ready when Judy Hollingsworth spun on her heel and headed in the opposite direction. What she wasn't ready for was Judy Hollingsworth barreling straight for her. When she saw that the woman wasn't going to stop, she raised her good arm to fend the woman off. But Judy had seen the sling gleaming palely in the night and with the instinct of a born fighter, she shoved Kate into the wall, injured shoulder first.

A cry that was half pain, half rage ripped out of Kate as she fell to the floor of the veranda. With more instinct than forethought, she shot her legs out and tripped the other woman. With all that momentum behind her, Judy Hollingsworth fell with a sound like a tree falling on soft loam. Dr. Yawkichuk squawked in alarm, adding to the confusion.

Cursing, Kate fought to regain her feet, but the other woman scrambled up more quickly.

"Trepalli!" shouted Kate just as he leapt over her struggling body and reached for Judy's hair.

Then, to Kate's amazement, he skidded to a stop just before he reached the corner.

Beyond him, Judy Hollingsworth had come to a stop, too. In fact, she stood stock-still, her arms away from her sides, her head tilted up and a little to the right, as if she were listening to a voice from above.

In the stillness of that moment, Kate held her breath. She was vaguely aware of Dr. Yawkichuk standing next to her, of Trepalli poised midstep, of the sudden silence of the night.

Then Judy's knees began to buckle, as if in slow motion, and she began to twist downward.

Trepalli snapped out of his paralysis first. His arms automatically shot forward to break the woman's fall. An owl screeched in the distance.

Trepalli lay Judy down on the veranda and stepped back. Only then did Kate see Doreen Yawkichuk. She stood over Judy, the paddle she had used to knock her out braced in both hands.

"George," she said ever so dangerously, "who is this woman and what is she doing here?"

THE WOUND HAD opened up again and Kate landed back in Emergency. She endured the doctor's scowl—a different doctor from last night—and promised she would be more careful from now on.

In spite of the pain, she felt euphoric. They had figured it out, she and Trepalli. Josh was safe and would be returned to his father. Judy Hollingsworth was in custody and would likely go to jail for a while. And Mr. Cusick…

Her euphoria leaked away. What was she going to do about Mr. Cusick?

"I would like you to stay overnight," said the doctor. Another Sweet Young Thing who had probably just left medical school.

Kate had had enough of hospitals, however. "I'm going

home to sleep," she said. "I promise I'll be good and if anything happens, anything at all, I'll come right back."

The doctor's eyes narrowed in suspicion at her tone, but finally he nodded.

"Come back tomorrow morning," he said. "I'll want to check it again."

"Sure." Kate slid off the side of the emergency room bed and stood up, being very careful not to sway.

"And eat something," said the doctor. "You look like you need red meat."

At the thought of food, Kate's stomach rumbled loudly and she laughed. "Sounds like a plan, Doc."

Finally she was free, with another bottle of painkillers rattling around in her pocket. She walked out of the emergency room and into the waiting room and there, to her surprise, was DC McKell. He was slouched in one of the waiting room chairs, alone in his row, scowling at half a dozen patients facing him. He wore jeans and a heavy gray sweater. Kate glanced at the clock on the wall.

Ten-thirty.

"DC McKell?"

He jumped up at the sound of her voice and turned to face her. What he saw must have reassured him because the scowl left his face.

"How're you doing?" he asked, walking up to her.

She half smiled, half frowned at him. "Another orderly who owed you a favor?"

He laughed and fell into step with her. "Trepalli, actually. He figured I'd want to know and I figured you'd want a ride."

Kate had been planning to take a cab, but maybe this was better.

Maybe.

"Do you think Mr. Cusick is asleep?" she asked as they passed the elevators.

McKell's lips pursed and he studied her face. Finally he shrugged.

"We could always go see."

JAMES CUSICK STOOD up when she entered his room. He had been seated in a chair in front of a barred window, staring out at the night. Gone were his grubby clothes. Instead, he wore hospital greens that did nothing to disguise how gaunt he was. Clearly he had showered and shaved in the past twenty-four hours.

There were bandages on both his forearms where the dog had bitten him.

Kate blinked at him for a few moments before finding her voice.

"Mr. Cusick, you remember DC McKell, don't you?" She had wanted McKell to wait outside but he refused point-blank and she was too tired to argue.

McKell nodded and Mr. Cusick followed suit. Kate couldn't tell if he actually remembered the DC or not.

To be honest, Kate had no idea what she was doing here. She had wanted to see for herself that he was all right. But beyond that?

She could always ask him if he'd killed Derek Jackson, but she really didn't want to know.

Cusick's gaze fixed on her shoulder, where the new dressing bulged under her uniform. There were new bloodstains on the shirt. Then he looked her in the eye.

"I shot you."

Kate's stomach did a slow flip, but she didn't show him she was upset. She nodded. "Yes, you did. It was an accident."

He slowly shook his head. "No. I meant to shoot the monster. The man." He took a deep breath and his gray eyes filled with misery. "I thought he was the monster."

"I know," she said softly. "But he isn't. He's just a dad, like you. He just wanted to protect his little boy."

Cusick looked away. Kate couldn't begin to imagine what he was thinking about, what he might be imagining. "Mr. Cusick?"

He looked up. He seemed clearheaded today, seemed to understand what he had done. "Mr. Cusick, is there someone I could call for you?"

He smiled sadly. "The monster took everyone."

She hesitated for a moment, but he deserved to know. "Mr. Cusick, I spoke to your wi—to Celia yesterday." She felt McKell start with surprise behind her but kept her attention on Cusick. "She wants to help if you'll let her."

He looked uncomprehendingly at her, then stumbled back to the chair, sinking into it when the back of his legs found it. "Celia?"

His voice sounded hopeful and Kate's heart squeezed. Twenty years the man had been running. Running from the horror of his daughter's death, his wife's rejection. Maybe he was ready to stop running now. And maybe Celia Carlisle needed to see him, too, to lay her own ghosts to rest.

"Yes, Celia," said Kate gently. "Would you like me to call her?"

Cusick stared at her for a long time before finally nodding. "Yes. I would like to see her again."

"All right, then," said Kate. "I'll come back and tell you what she said."

"Thank you," he said formally.

Kate and McKell headed for the door. Then Cusick spoke again.

"Chief Williams?"

"Yes, Mr. Cusick?"

"I'm sorry I hurt you."

"I know."

TWENTY

"CHIEF!" CHARLOTTE JUMPED up from her chair at the duty desk and ran to Kate.

Kate smiled. It was almost lunchtime. She had slept for twelve hours and felt much better. The shoulder still hurt like hell, but at least the sprained ankle was better. Or maybe it was only in comparison.

"Hello, Charlotte."

DC McKell and Trepalli came around the dividing wall more slowly, although their grins were no less sincere. Kate was surprised to see Trepalli, but then, she had completely lost track of who was on shift.

"You're looking much better," said Trepalli approvingly.

"Why, thank you," said Kate with a wry smile. "Now…" She turned to McKell. "Report."

McKell looked at her quizzically. "As soon as you sit down."

"Fine," she said. "Let's sit down."

"She tends to get cranky when she's been shot," explained Trepalli in a stage whisper.

Kate rolled her eyes but couldn't hide her smile. Trepalli took her good elbow and led her to the one club chair in the lunchroom. Once she was sitting, he went to fetch her a glass of water.

"Josh?" she asked McKell.

"Custody is cleared up. The boy's with his father at the hotel. They're getting ready to go back home in a couple of days."

Kate wondered if the delay had anything to do with Susan Brownlee, but frankly, she didn't care.

"Hollingsworth?"

"In Winnipeg. The Mounties will fly her back to Vancouver to face court. Attempted murder, kidnapping and crossing provincial lines without permission of the custodial parent, for starters. I doubt she'll get bail." He looked down at Kate, his blue eyes serious. "She won't be a danger to the boy anymore."

Kate swallowed and looked away. She took a sip of water.

"The good dentist?"

"Charged with obstructing justice. He'll probably get a slap on the wrist. I expect he'll have a harder time from his wife."

No kidding. The last time Kate saw Doreen Yawkichuk, she looked more like an avenging Valkyrie than an earth mother.

"Ma'am?" asked McKell.

"Yes, DC?"

"Things are under control here." His gaze swept the station. "We can handle things until you get back."

"In other words, stop checking up on you?" She grinned at him and he blushed. But he was smiling at the same time.

Kate looked down at her jeans. The bandages on her legs made them look even bulkier than they were. She was still tired and in pain, and had some serious thinking to do about her role here in Mendenhall—and whether or not she was going to stay.

But right now, there was only one thing she really wanted to do.

"Constable Trepalli."

"Yes, ma'am?"

"I was wondering if you felt like taking me shopping."

He looked at her uncertainly, then glanced at Charlotte, who shrugged slightly.

"Sure," he said finally. "Do you have a prescription to fill?"

"Nope," she said with satisfaction. "I want to go shopping for a pair of red high-tops, a kid's size four."

She looked around at her staff, at their answering grins. They were good people. They were worth fighting for.

* * * * *

About the Author

MARCELLE DUBÉ grew up near Montreal. After trying out a number of different provinces—not to mention Belgium—she settled in the Yukon, where the carnivores almost outnumber the people. Undaunted, she started her family and now has two beautiful daughters. Along the way, she spent a few years in Manitoba, where she fell in love with its people and endless skies. Her short fiction has appeared in a number of magazines and anthologies, including the award-winning *Polaris: A Celebration of Polar Science.* Her previous novel, *On Her Trail,* was published by Carina Press in 2010. Learn more about her at www.marcelledube.com.

REQUEST YOUR FREE BOOKS!

2 FREE NOVELS
PLUS 2 FREE GIFTS!

MYSTERY

W RLDWIDE LIBRARY®
Your Partner in Crime

YES! Please send me 2 FREE novels from the Worldwide Library® series and my 2 FREE gifts (gifts are worth about $10). After receiving them, if I don't wish to receive any more books, I can return the shipping statement marked "cancel." If I don't cancel, I will receive 4 brand-new novels every month and be billed just $5.24 per book in the U.S. or $6.24 per book in Canada. That's a saving of at least 34% off the cover price. It's quite a bargain! Shipping and handling is just 50¢ per book in the U.S. and 75¢ per book in Canada.* I understand that accepting the 2 free books and gifts places me under no obligation to buy anything. I can always return a shipment and cancel at any time. Even if I never buy another book, the two free books and gifts are mine to keep forever.

414/424 WDN FEJ3

Name   (PLEASE PRINT)

Address   Apt. #

City   State/Prov.   Zip/Postal Code

Signature (if under 18, a parent or guardian must sign)

Mail to the **Reader Service:**
IN U.S.A.: P.O. Box 1867, Buffalo, NY 14240-1867
IN CANADA: P.O. Box 609, Fort Erie, Ontario L2A 5X3

Not valid for current subscribers to the Worldwide Library series.

Want to try two free books from another line?
Call 1-800-873-8635 or visit www.ReaderService.com.

* Terms and prices subject to change without notice. Prices do not include applicable taxes. Sales tax applicable in N.Y. Canadian residents will be charged applicable taxes. Offer not valid in Quebec. This offer is limited to one order per household. All orders subject to credit approval. Credit or debit balances in a customer's account(s) may be offset by any other outstanding balance owed by or to the customer. Please allow 4 to 6 weeks for delivery. Offer available while quantities last.

> **Your Privacy**—The Reader Service is committed to protecting your privacy. Our Privacy Policy is available online at www.ReaderService.com or upon request from the Reader Service.
>
> We make a portion of our mailing list available to reputable third parties that offer products we believe may interest you. If you prefer that we not exchange your name with third parties, or if you wish to clarify or modify your communication preferences, please visit us at www.ReaderService.com/consumerschoice or write to us at Reader Service Preference Service, P.O. Box 9062, Buffalo, NY 14269. Include your complete name and address.